It's one thing to *wish* your boss would die. . . .

"We've got a white male, approximately fifty years of age, brown pin-striped suit, balding. No ID on him. My team is in there now, going through the place. The victim was shot twice. Looks like a small-caliber weapon. Dead . . . maybe twenty-four hours or so."

"What makes you think it's Mr. Janowski?" If I was going to look at the body, I thought I deserved the particulars.

"At about eight-thirty this morning, when alternate side parking went into effect, a black 1985 Lincoln with Connecticut plates was towed from down the block. A run through the computer identified it as a car you reported missing earlier today, registered in Janowski's name. Highway Patrol's been looking for it all over New England." He looked kind of severe, like all that wasted manpower was my doing. "We need a positive ID."

As Detective LaMarca opened the door, he turned to me and said, in the best 1950s B-movie style, "He's not a pretty sight right now."

I had to clench my teeth to stop myself from saying the obvious: Albert Janowski was never a pretty sight.

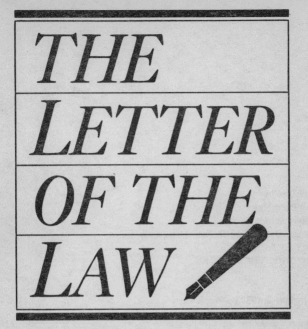

THE LETTER OF THE LAW

BY CAROLE BERRY

A DELL BOOK

Published by
Dell Publishing
a division of
Bantam Doubleday Dell Publishing Group, Inc.
666 Fifth Avenue
New York, New York 10103

ISBN: 0-440-20524-7

Reprinted by arrangement with St. Martin's Press

Printed in the United States of America
Published simultaneously in Canada

February 1990

10 9 8 7 6 5 4 3 2 1

KRI

In memory of Robert E. Berry

PREFACE

I am sitting in a canvas deck chair, bathed in the afternoon sun, watching a red and yellow spinnaker fill with the rising breeze and race across Long Island Sound. What a delight these leisure-class pleasures are for me. At this time of day six months ago I might have been struggling to clear a paper jam in an obsolete duplicating machine, or delivering a pep talk on phone manners to a burnt-out receptionist. All this—my tan, morning swims, long naps on the terrace—stems from those three weeks early last spring when I was a bewildered participant in Ely Sneed's second scandal.

None of the papers got the story right. The *Post* chose to plow the fertile fields of naked attorneys and over-the-hill strippers and, for reasons unknown to me, saw fit to include my photograph twice. The *Times* caught the facts, but the essence escaped them. Now that the dust has settled on Ely Sneed, et al., I would like to put the record straight. What follows is simply the truth—no more and no less.

As for my prose, I apologize. It suffers from too many years on the lunatic fringe of law firms like Ely Sneed. I was able to curb a regrettable tendency to begin paragraphs with NOW, THEREFORE, and TO WIT. My editor's blue pencil took care of the "notwithstandings" and "albeits." An "inasmuch as" may have slipped through, though. You can only do so much.

Bonnie Indermill

THE LETTER OF THE LAW

It was the morning of my thirty-sixth birthday, and rain fell in cold gray sheets. This being New York City, the transit system had collapsed. Forced to abandon a drowning A train a dozen blocks from my office, I was sloshing through dirty puddles, reflecting on the sad state of my affairs—personal, financial, you name it—when I witnessed a mugging.

Half a block ahead, walking toward me, was a bent old man, wrestling a big black umbrella in one hand and a bulging, tattered briefcase in the other. I heard, or felt, the two kids' presence before I saw them. They came from behind me, swift hooded figures, and walked by, one on either side. Reacting with a New Yorker's sixth sense, I clutched my handbag. An almost imperceptible signal—"This old hen's not quite ready for plucking yet"—passed between them. They walked on to the old man and quickly shoved him into the wall of a building, snatched the briefcase, and disappeared up the street.

By the time I reached him, he had pulled himself to his feet. He was an ancient, shrunken gutter-fighter, and he was mad.

Fightin' mad. I collected his umbrella from the gutter while he, lacking a better object for his anger, gave me a piece of his mind.

"Lousy kids. Usta' be I could walk anywhere in this city any time, day or night. Nobody messed with me back den. Lousy punks. No respect for nothin'. You see how dey run? If I could get my hands on 'em, I'd slam 'em up against the wall so fast dey wouldn't know what hit 'em! You think the cops gonna' do anything? Nothin'."

As he ranted a trio of businessmen, trench-coated, grim and inaccessible, splashed past us. They cast a supercilious look our way: a damp woman with a torn umbrella and no boots getting a sidewalk lecture from a crazy old coot. Two candidates for Bellevue, no doubt.

I helped the old man get on his way and continued my walk to work, something I approached with less than enthusiasm even on good days. By neighborhood standards the incident didn't amount to much. No blood, no pain. Just a little injured pride. That's what struck me as so sad, though. The old man's impotent fight. Hope may spring eternal, but flesh does not. Old people live too long in New York City. They should have the good sense not to allow their spirit to outlast their ability to sprint.

That episode had nothing whatever to do with what followed, except that for me it set a standard for the futile thrashing that dominated the next three weeks.

Ely Sneed, Kellogg & Petit, Attorneys-at-Law, had their offices on the twenty-fifth floor of the Hayworth Building at 23rd Street and Park Avenue South. The firm, under several names, had been in the neighborhood for almost a hundred years, and in the Hayworth Building since the mid-1930s.

Park Avenue South is not Park Avenue proper. It is separated from that bastion of corporate prestige by 34th Street and about fifteen dollars a square foot. Ely Sneed's offices were ten blocks south of the border, on the wrong side of the tracks.

The Hayworth Building itself, along with its neighborhood,

had fallen on hard times since Kellogg & Petit nailed their shingle to the wall. The larger part of the ground floor was given over to two commercial enterprises: the Rose of Killarney Bar, and a newsstand where you could pick up your weekly lottery ticket. Separating these was a central lobby, its marble yellow with age and stained with abuse. Obscenities had been carved into the walls of once-ornate oak elevators long before my time, and Ely Sneed's fellow tenants were a multitude of ne'er-do-well employment agencies, any number of people calling themselves promoters, of what is anyone's guess, and something called "Hollywood Enterprises," the staff of which appeared to consist of young women in tight satin pants and young men in mustaches.

Five days a week, for over three years, I stepped out of that scarred elevator and walked into a reception room most generously described as nostalgic. The carpeting, eons ago, had probably been described by an enthusiastic decorator to one of my poor predecessors as café au lait or crème de cocoa or some such nonsense. By 1987 its color and texture was that of a large beached sea mammal, decomposing in the sun. The furniture was an unhappy, unstylish assemblage of hard cracked green leather and much-varnished mahogany. Over the sofa, adding a final somber note to the mausoleum effect, hung a portrait of Thurston Kellogg and Lawrence G. Petit, flanking the dapper Ely Sneed, the three of them captured in blacks, browns, and grays by an artist I only hope achieved the recognition he deserved.

I was Ely Sneed's office manager, dealing in tears, tempers, and malfunctioning telephones. At best, the job was comfortably dull and paid the rent. At worst—and, toward the end worst was more often the case—I felt I was being buried in a mountain of trivia. Broken duplicating machines, broken radiators, broken typewriters, bruised egos, petty cold wars and brief hot ones. And yet, with all this I wonder sometimes how much longer I would have lasted if Albert Janowski hadn't delivered his unintentional coup de grâce. Would I have trudged on, propelled by my inertia, and one day found myself a pinch-faced hag, scrawling reluctant okays on vacation request forms and begrudging initials on secretarial overtime slips? Possibly; but I like to think that something—perhaps a typical Ely Sneed Friday—would have sent me scurrying for the help-wanted section.

Fridays at Ely Sneed were pure hell for me. My job included an impossible function our Management Committee called, in appropriately warlike terms, "non-legal personnel deployment." What they meant was that I had to make sure there was a secretary for every one or two attorneys. By ignoring any personality conflicts that stopped short of violence, I was able to cope most of the time. Fridays, though, were impossible. That was the day Ely Sneed's secretaries called in sick with such regularity I could almost imagine an angry god, intent on decimating the secretarial population, skulking unseen through New York the night before. "Must be something I ate," they moaned. "Throwing up all night." "Fell down on the ice," worked until April. After that it was heatstroke and sunburn. A veritable panorama of flus and mysteriously swollen parts—fingers, feet, gums, what-nots—went on year-round.

Unfortunately, there are never too few lawyers. They breed like rabbits, and their approach to their work can be described as lunatic frenzy. From the youngest, newest associate to the silver-haired senior partner, any one of them will happily drag his disease-racked carcass through a blizzard to get to the office.

So there you have it. Too many lawyers, their work ethics run amok, too few secretaries, and me, a trifle-ridden mess by the end of the week responsible for doing something about it, and most Fridays we could count on chaos within fifteen minutes of opening our doors.

The Friday Albert Janowski disappeared was nothing if not typical. I remember fighting my way off the elevator—balancing coffee and Danish—past a large, belligerent couple loaded down with plastic shopping bags who were equally intent on fighting their way in. As I stumbled over their paraphernalia, the man shouted across my back: ". . . and you can tell Janowski to call us. Some nerve. He's not the only lawyer in town, you know." The woman was a shrill echo: "Some nerve. Almost an hour. Who does he think. . . ?" They disappeared behind the sliding doors and I found myself facing Miss Harriet Peterson, all knit suit, tight yellow curls, and high excitement in front of the elevator bank.

Miss Peterson, secretary to Mr. Janowski and Mr. Petit, Jr., was in her mid-fifties. She had once been "on the stage," or had been on the stage once. Whether burlesque, a high school play, or the Royal Shakespeare Company was never made quite clear, but she infused her days at Ely Sneed with a level of drama unrelated to anything that was going on there. Miss Peterson's tears flowed at the merest provocation, her giggles ranged the halls at the stalest old jokes and knock-knocks. Deafening "ooohs" greeted the arrival of new steno pads, new lawyers, and any of the many cockroaches that shared our offices.

Generally, I enjoyed her company. The superlatives were a lot more pleasant than the jaded boredom common to the rest of the long-time staff. But that morning, when I saw the tear welling in her eye and the enraged thrust of her chin, I just didn't think I could take it. I tried slipping by, eyes glued to my feet, muttering a brief "Morning." As I might have expected, she answered with a sob, and:

"Did you hear the way they spoke to me? Bonnie, some of these clients—I simply can't believe. . . ." With arms waving in operatic flourish, a tremor in her voice, and no encouragement on my part, she proceeded to tell me her problem. In short, it amounted to this: Albert Janowski had asked her to set up an early appointment which he then hadn't shown up for.

"Maybe he got the dates confused," I said in passing, trying to hang on to my uninvolved status. I paused at the desk to collect my messages. Two secretaries had called in sick. The words I said under my breath had nothing to do with Miss Peterson, but that didn't stop her.

"No, Bonnie. Mr. Janowski mentioned it to me when he left yesterday. And"—here a look of alarm crossed her face—"he said I should keep them here if he was late."

"Well, I'm sure he didn't expect you to chain them to the furniture. Now, if I can get my coat off. . . ." All I wanted on earth was my hot black coffee. I started toward the waiting room. Miss Peterson stopped me, a hand on my arm.

"And, as if that isn't enough"—her voice fell to a whisper as she nodded toward the waiting area—"one of Mr. Petit's criminals was there when I got here this morning. Don't look," she said as I stuck my head through the door. "I had the receptionist tell him that Mr. Petit would call him later, but the man refuses to leave. He's the one Mr. Janowski fired for stealing. Tate. Andrew Tate."

Ignoring Miss Peterson's warning, I peeked through the door. A young black man was sitting on one of the armchairs, elbows on his knees, staring into space. He looked like he was there to stay.

Gary Petit's "criminals" were, in fact, part of a city-wide parolee rehabilitation program. Under Gary's administration, we employed one or two of them at a time as messengers until they were able to get on their feet. That way, the firm had its messengers subsidized by the city, while at the same time doing something about its liberal guilt.

"What does he want with Gary Petit?" I asked her.

"I didn't speak to him. I'm sure he's violent."

"Where is Gary?"

"He's gone to open his summer house. He won't be in today."

"Maybe you should try to reach him."

"When he's at the shore he always calls in at two, right on the dot. I have strict instructions he shouldn't be disturbed except for emergencies."

"Well, we can't just leave him sitting there until two."

Leaving her by the door, I walked up to the man. "Mr. Tate, I know you're waiting to see Gary Petit. I understand that Mr. Petit won't be in today. Perhaps I can help you?"

6

Tate straightened in his seat and glared up at me. "This place owes me my last paycheck, and I'm not leaving here without it."

"Oh." He looked like he meant it, but there was no way I could have Tate sitting in Ely Sneed's lobby looking mad at the world. I made a quick call to the bookkeeping department, explained the situation to them, then turned back to Tate.

"All right, Mr. Tate. Someone from Accounting should be down here with your check in a minute."

Without so much as a grunt of thanks, he sank back into his chair.

I had started toward my office when Miss Peterson appeared by my side. Her face was full of admiration.

"What did you do?"

"I arranged for him to get his check."

"Oh." She was disappointed. In a place where bad tempers were common, she probably thought I should have given the man a tongue-lashing.

"Well, then, Bonnie, getting back to Mr. Janowski," she went on.

So we were back to that! She couldn't have missed my disgusted look, but she continued.

"It's not like Mr. Janowski to be this late. That man prides himself on his punctuality. Where do you suppose he is?"

My Styrofoam cup was leaking its hot contents onto my Danish, turning a bad morning into an utter disaster. "Probably sitting on a stalled train, Miss Peterson. Just look at the weather."

"But I called his wife." Scooting nearer, she looked around to see if we could be overheard. I could smell her sweet gardenia scent. "Mrs. Janowski said he wasn't at home last night. At all! She thought he might have gone with Mr. Petit to the shore for a long weekend, but she wasn't sure."

"All right, when Mr. Petit calls in at two, you can check with him."

By that time I was several feet ahead of Miss Peterson. Her next words, or rather, the way she said them, stopped me.

"Mrs. Janowski was on her way to the airport. Aruba." It was said with a little coo: "A-rooo-ba." I turned and looked at her. It was one of the wonders of Miss Peterson's temperament that she could go from near hysteria to a little harmless gossip with complete equanimity, and of mine that I could go from absolute disinterest to total attention with no embarrassment. On her face I saw the familiar glow—the cocked eyebrow, the pursed lips. Albert Janowski's whereabouts were suddenly wildly important.

"Last month it was Aspen, and now," she said with enough pause to frame her next words, "Club Med, I'll bet. And not by herself, either."

"No kidding?"

She answered with a knowing nod, and we giggled like schoolgirls. Stephanie Janowski's antics had brightened many dull moments at Ely Sneed.

"Do you have any idea who he is?"

"No, but he's not someone from the firm, or I would have heard. If you ask me, Bonnie, it's some state of affairs when a wife isn't sure where her husband spent the night, and doesn't care enough. . . ."

Yes, I thought, but then again, better a weekend in Aruba than one with Albert Janowski any time. Sun-soaked beaches, tall pineapple drinks with those tiny umbrellas in them. I was on my way to a tropical oblivion when my nemesis, Wilbur Decker, rounded the corner and headed straight for me. Miss Peterson, a veteran herself, faded into the background.

As far as office administration went, Ely Sneed was a do-it-yourself operation. Each of our partners had his own bailiwick, chosen, from what I could see, with perverse disregard for ability. During my time with the firm, Wilbur Decker had had a dozen permanent secretaries and enough temporary ones to crowd Yankee Stadium. He was head of non-legal personnel administration, and my immediate supervisor.

"The first order of the day is"—he spoke in a kind of puffed-up management lingo—"that temp you assigned to me yesterday called in sick this morning. I'd like her replaced. She's terrible anyway."

I've heard it said that when you reach forty, you have the face you deserve. Decker was close to fifty. He more than deserved his. To begin at his highest point, a cheap dry toupee sat on his head, offering sharp contrast to the oily ring of natural hair under it. He had wire-rimmed glasses, a short upper lip, and no chin to speak of, and reminded me of those small animals, occasional subjects of television specials, which eat their young. That, coupled with his disposition, produced a vile human being.

". . . considering finding another employment agency to supply these women. As you know, Miss Indermill, the secretarial situation around here is one thing that really gets my blood boiling. As a group of professionals, we should strive . . ."

The list of things that got Decker's blood boiling was staggering. I'm sure my work attitude was among them. I have no illusions about having been the ideal employee. The fact is, I was raised for housewifery and not office management. It's unfortunate that I found the former pursuit even more disagreeable than the latter, but I care very little about dressing for success, and the notion of hacking a career path out of the *Sunday Times* want-ads leaves me comatose.

". . . and what, if I may ask, is the matter with her?" He nodded toward Miss Peterson, skulking not quite out of sight by my office door.

"Oh, apparently Mr. Janowski missed an appointment. The client was quite . . ."

"Really? Not very professional of Albert, was that?"

The only time Decker ever waited for my answer was when a response was impossible. After three years in the trenches I'd developed an impressive repertoire of noncommittal noises and gestures. I twitched my shoulders and, unfortunately, smiled. It wasn't intended as a friendly signal, but that's how he chose to interpret it. He returned it with a beauty of his

9

own and then, without warning, launched into his favorite subject.

"And by the way. I'd almost forgotten. How are we doing with *The First Hundred Years?* I've been meaning to interface with you on that."

He hadn't forgotten; it was something he never forgot.

"Oh—about as well as you'd expect, Mr. Decker."

"Glad to hear it. That's our little pet, eh, Miss Indermill?"

I nodded. From the corner of my eye I saw our bookkeeper walk up to Andrew Tate and hand him an envelope. A moment later Tate rose and headed for the elevator. At least I'd accomplished something that morning.

"I read recently that General Motors has commissioned a writer to do something similar. What do you think?" Decker spun me around by my coat sleeve. "A bound copy right there on the coffee table, under the portrait. A little pocket of legal history. Hmm?"

Damned little, I thought. "Good idea, Mr. Decker," I said.

"Perhaps leather binding. We'll have to prepare some cost studies." He rubbed his nonexistent chin with a bony forefinger and looked at me like I owed him an answer.

"Yes, sir," I said, trying to convey an impression of rapt interest.

"And in the meantime, Miss Indermill, full speed ahead, as they say. We have some very prestigious clients here. I'm sure they will enjoy something like that."

Prestigious clients? Like our cabbie from the Bronx who, having lived through two gunpoint robberies and a near-fatal stabbing, was patenting a bullet-proof louvered blind, in pastels, for cabs? Or our Ukranian immigrant who had come up with Flush and Brush? What Ely Sneed's lobby really needed was a rack of comic books.

I had inherited *The First Hundred Years* from a pale young man, a graduate student in English literature hired by the firm, at Decker's urging, to put Ely Sneed's glorious past into written form. Eager and bewildered at first, he was, within three weeks, as lethargic and even surlier than the rest of the staff. Since he came out of my paltry budget, I had asked him for an informal status report. His response was a few pages of jumbled notes and dates and this simple statement: "Man, I just can't get into this shit."

I thought it would end with his departure, but when Decker caught me with my nose in a crossword puzzle he suggested I might want to "attempt it," like it was Everest or something. It might as well have been Everest, for all the progress I'd made. The pale young man's nicely lettered folder, covered with his doodles and containing three pages of notes, had lain, untouched, in my bottom drawer since.

There was a noise across the corridor, and I looked up at the unsuspecting solution to one of my problems. Beating down my familiar rush of guilt, I stalked my victim.

"Oh, Miss Peterson. You mean both your fellows are out?" Like something coming from a stranger, my office management voice pierced the corridor. "You said Mr. Petit was at the shore? And Mr. Janowski is late? I wonder . . ."

She caught on before the words were out of my mouth. I saw the quick caution in her eyes, the shoulders pulling back in the classic "turn and flee" stance. I looked away and continued with what was, hands down, the worst part of my job.

"I wonder if you could help me out for a little while. If you could give me a hand with Mr. Decker. Just take a little dictation until I'm able to line someone else up?"

Thurston Kellogg, Esquire, drank. Not heavily. Lightly and steadily. By two P.M. on almost any weekday you could find him holding court in the firm library, sprawled in the one padded armchair, telling rambling, barely coherent war stories to anyone he could corner. The stories always began with, "I don't believe I told you about the time," generally involved "the big boys from Washington," meaning the Federal Trade Commission, and, to the obvious discomfort of his listener, invariably ended with the opposing counsel's figurative dismemberment: "nailed the shyster's balls to the wall . . . son of a bitch's head on a pole . . . ass right where his mouth should have been . . . castrated the bastard!"

As head of Ely Sneed (Messrs. Petit, Sr., and Sneed were dead), Mr. Kellogg, while certainly in a class of his own, was quite a bit less than effective. When his secretary, Rosalie, called to say he wanted to see me in his office that afternoon, I figured he needed a captive audience to hear the brain-deadening details of *FTC* vs. *Gortz Indus.*

Rosalie was filing her nails into crimson talons and chewing a wad of gum the size of a golf ball.

"What's going on in there?"

"Some kind of committee meeting, I think. Decker said it was a crisis." She made a face and shrugged. Rosalie was no fool.

Ely Sneed had committees like gardeners have crabgrass: management committees, picnic committees, efficiency committees. Battle one committee down and another would spring up in its place. As for our crises, they included everything from an outraged custodian's report of shortages in the toilet tissue supply to the onset of one of the firm's periodic purges.

If there had been any conversation going on, it stopped when I opened Mr. Kellogg's door.

Old Mr. K, as he was called by the staff, with no particular affection, was from all accounts a very wealthy man. You wouldn't have suspected it from the condition of that room. It was a big corner one that reeked, perpetually, of dry rot and bourbon. His furniture was a red variation on Ely Sneed's cracked-leather theme, and his rug was worn through to the matting. Shelves of law volumes—circa 1950s and earlier—lined the wall opposite his desk. A permanent blanket of dust covered them. Faded red brocade curtains, always drawn, hung like the tattered, forgotten flag of a defeated enemy. On sunny days the low afternoon light shone through them, tinting the room and everyone in it a raucous, misleading pink.

Old Mr. K actually had a rather grand look about him, that of a turn-of-the-century robber baron. He was portly, with fine posture, flowing white hair, and John L. Lewis eyebrows.

I often thought it was a shame he wasn't a different kind of drinker. Ely Sneed might have been another place if Mr. K had been one of those back-slapping happy drunks who do boozy public relations in the bars at men's clubs. Unfortunately, he was rather infantile and, apart from the stories, reclusive. Stripped of his three-piece suits and his society-page wife, propped up in a West Side doorway, he would have been another rambling, sad old bum.

Wilbur Decker and Miss Peterson were in straight-backed chairs facing Mr. K. Decker, looking like Uriah Heep incarnate, nodded sourly to me. Miss Peterson was pale and subdued. Long faces preceded almost every committee meeting at Ely Sneed, so I had no reason to think anything unusual was going on.

The old man shifted his eyes to me. There was a viscous, unfocused quality to them, like half-set Jell-O. "We're waiting for young Petit . . . ah . . . Gary to call back, Miss . . . young woman," he said. "Called from a phone booth before. Mr. Decker here found that . . . inappropriate." His voice trailed off as he gave Decker a frosty look.

I heard Decker mutter something under his breath.

I sat on the sofa as far from Decker as I could get, and soon found myself slipping into a worn niche in the corner. Surprisingly comfortable, those old leather Chesterfields. What with my Friday afternoon narcolepsy and the hot room, I was on the edge of torpor, fighting to keep my eyes open, when the phone rang.

"The speakerphone, Mr. K," Decker said. The old man looked at him, not comprehending.

"Put the call on the speakerphone so we can all hear."

Mr. K grimaced, made a couple of bumbling stabs, and Gary Petit's disembodied voice crackled through the room.

"Yes? Hello? You there, Mr. K? Hello?"

Mr. K went at that receiver box like it was some hard-of-hearing, stupid opposing counsel. He leaned down with obvious dislike until his mouth was inches from the mesh, and bellowed:

"Yes. I'm here, Gary. Along with Wilbur and Miss Peterson. And that other young lady. Miss . . . Miss . . ." Looking up, he waved his arms at me in frustration. If he had ever known my name, it was long forgotten. "Indermill," I said. "Indermill," he shouted at the receiver. "You know the one. Something to do with the secretaries."

"All right," Gary answered. "You're loud and clear. Now, what's going on?"

"Em . . . Gary . . ." The old man paused as if collecting his thoughts. "My fool son-in-law seems to have . . ." Again he hesitated, then, without warning, he swiveled his chair as far back as it would go and began gazing into space with an expression of total self-absorption.

"Yes? Albert has what?"

For a few moments no one said a word. The old man's rasping breaths joined the hissing radiator in a sleepy invocation. He seemed to have passed out with his eyes open. I leaned back, about to do the same. Then Decker spoke up:

"Gary, I believe we could have something of a firm crisis on our hands. You say Albert didn't meet you at the shore. We've heard nothing from him all day. Miss Peterson called his home this morning and Stephanie had no notion where he might be." Decker gave Mr. K a quick, unpleasant look. The old man's daughter was married to Albert Janowski. "Stephanie left for the Caribbean this morning." He stopped and looked around, waiting for the shocked gasp that never came. "As you know, Gary, it's not my nature to be an alarmist, but this isn't like Albert."

"Are you suggesting . . ." Gary began. "Well, what are you suggesting?"

It was Decker who said it first: "Foul play."

Suddenly I was very much awake, touched by some inexplicable chill. Miss Peterson's eyes met mine, and we stared at each other, bewildered. Her normally flushed cheeks were chalky and her rouge spots stood out, deep red blotches.

Decker continued: "I hesitate to put it that way, but what else?"

"I don't know." That was Gary. "Initially Albert planned to drive out with me yesterday to open up the place, but he canceled at the last minute. Said something had come up. An appointment last night, or maybe this morning. I can't recall. He said he'd call and let me know if he'd be out today, but I never heard from him. I was here by six-thirty and stayed in all evening. I figured . . . well, he's probably trapped at some meeting. Miss Peterson, couldn't you have forgotten something? Think carefully. Are you certain he didn't mention anything to you?"

"No. Not a word." She was crisp, loud, and defensive.

"Well, Mr. K, do you have any suggestions?" Gary was being polite. It was customary to defer to the old man, but we all knew he wasn't going to suggest anything that made sense.

Decker, however, was never at a loss for suggestions. "I most certainly have some ideas. As a matter of fact, I would say that the immediate implementation of a plan of action is called for. Perhaps a committee. . . ."

A derisive snort came from the old man. He lowered himself in his chair, looked around the room like he was sick of the bunch of us, then brayed into the speaker box: "I have many suggestions about my son-in-law, but none of them are fit for mixed company. You boys can handle things any way you wish. For me," he added, his voice suddenly weary, "I would like to be done with this. Why don't you take Wilbur's advice?" A smile spread over his face. "What was it you said, Wilbur? Implement an immediate plan of action?" With that Mr. Kellogg pushed himself from his chair and, using the edge of his desk for support, shuffled to his door. I heard him ask Rosalie to call for his car and say, with a demented laugh, "Perhaps a committee," as the door closed behind him.

Between our "boys," neither of whom would ever see forty again, there was a thinly veiled animosity. Nevertheless, after a few minutes haggling, they agreed to alert the New York City and state police and the Connecticut state police. All this time I had been wondering what my role would be. To my tremendous distress I was named "middleperson."

"In the interest of firm security," Decker said, "to keep the staff from screening calls pertaining to this matter—you know how they talk among themselves—perhaps she"—nodding at me—"should be Ely Sneed's confidential middleman—middleperson, as it were—between the firm and the police. What do you say to that, Gary?"

"She? You mean Bonnie? It's okay with me. Bonnie, how do you feel about it?"

Oh, just wonderful.

Being top secret, Albert Janowski's disappearance was all over the office by quitting time. Everywhere I looked, staff members huddled in tight packs, whispering excitedly. Only the partners appeared unhappy.

I worked late that evening, trying to divert myself from our crisis by going through that pale young man's notes for *The First Hundred Years*. There wasn't much there, and what there was was hardly compelling. The only vaguely interesting things were a couple of photo albums, with pictures of events like Christmas parties and the annual picnics. It was kind of intriguing, seeing how people had changed over the years and seeing if the wives in the old pictures were the same wives in the later ones. I was thumbing through these when I noticed that the young writer had flagged the photos from the 1962 picnic with a yellow stick-on that said: "E.S. drowned." Pretty cryptic, but I knew what he meant.

At the 1962 picnic, Ely Sneed, then one of the senior partners, had drowned in Long Island Sound. You sure couldn't tell that from the photos on that page, though. They made it look as if there had been nothing going on that day but fun in the sun. There was a young Gary Petit in tennis whites, smiling broadly. There was Miss Peterson, spit-curled and dressed to the nines, and Wilbur Decker with his own hair on his head.

Flipping the page, I confronted the stern glare of Mrs. Kotch, our bookkeeper. God! That woman had been born a battle-ax. She looked seventy now; she had looked seventy twenty-five years ago. The photographer had caught her at an especially serious moment, and you can take it from me, Mrs. Kotch's light moments were nothing to laugh about. She, a middle-aged Mr. Kellogg, and Mr. Petit, Senior, made a grim trio near a portable barbecue. It hadn't all been fun in the sun, after all.

I went through a couple more pages, then glanced at the clock. It was already past seven, and I was getting nowhere with *The First Hundred Years*. Slamming the album shut, I picked up a pen. I was holding it, poised, over a lined tablet, waiting for inspiration, when the phone rang.

"Is Miss Indermill there?" It was a nice deep baritone, and just what I needed. Without question, six feet tall with wavy blond hair, a sports car, and a beach house to make the coming summer weekends so much pleasanter.

"This is Detective Anthony LaMarca of Midtown Homicide. We were told to contact you if anything turned up concerning an Albert Janowski."

"Yes?" I responded, thinking all the while, Homicide. No, no! Having begun my day with a mugging, I had no desire to end it with a murder.

"Can you get over to Forty-first and Tenth Avenue right away? I'll have a radio car pick you up if you want."

"No. I'll get a cab."

He gave me the address of the Hotel Central.

H.tel ..ntral, the awning said.

I would have recognized it anyway. There were three police cars and an ambulance in the street, and a mob of curious degenerates milling around the door.

When I stepped into the lobby, a smell of stale beer and ammonia that would have stopped an elephant stampede hit me in the face. The furniture was a ragtag jumble of what was called, in the early sixties, Danish Modern, vandalized beyond any Dane's imagination. To the right was a hedge of faded plastic philodendron and to the left a reception desk. The desk clerk was separated from his clientele by about an inch of shat-

17

terproof Plexiglas. He was an Italian Stallion, if you could believe his T-shirt.

"You lookin' for the cops? You're Miss Inderman? Fifth floor. Take the elevator." He nodded toward a door on the other side of the hedge.

"It's Inder*mill*. Aren't there any stairs?"

"Cops got the stairs closed off."

I would be an analyst's delight. I suffer from an entire textbook of phobias. Elevators are at the top of my list. Not all of them. Just the ones in the subways and those nasty little tombs you find in dilapidated buildings. I have visions of archeologists digging one up some day, a long time from now, and discovering my mummified remains, nails rendered to the quick, encrusted with centuries-old blood shed in my desperate attempts to escape a lonely grave.

I stepped into the box with pounding heart and the doors clattered shut, revealing a roach the size of a small bird. The next thirty seconds was a nightmare of scratching insects and metallic screeches. When the doors finally shuddered open on the fifth floor, I was in a cold sweat on the verge of collapse. For a second I leaned against the corridor wall.

There was the briefest muffled footfall behind me, and then a firm hand gripped my arm. I grabbed my purse and spun in as fierce a stance as I could manage, a scream already building in my throat.

"You all right, Miss?"

Detective Anthony LaMarca. Short, for a policeman, and kind of boxy, with a little thickening around his waist and a gloomy face lengthened by receding dark hair. No sports cars, no beach houses there. He had the resigned look of a man who expected the worst to happen and was seldom surprised.

"The desk clerk said you were on your way up. Thought I better meet you before you walked in there. If I'd known it was going to upset you this much. . . . Maybe we should wait for the father-in-law. I wouldn't want you to go to pieces."

He looked so concerned for me. I suppose that's when it really hit: I was going to have to look at a dead body, and in who-knows-what condition. My stomach turned over. What if it wasn't even Albert Janowski? I would have looked at a dead man for nothing. For a second I thought, *Yes, let's wait for the father-in-law*. But then, what if it *was* Albert Janowski? I was Ely Sneed's middle-person. I straightened my shoulders and drew a deep breath.

"No. I'm all right. Just a little nervous."

"Okay. You want to step back here for a minute?" He indicated the door he had come from.

"Before I do, can you tell me what I can expect to see?"

"We've got a white male, approximately fifty years of age, brown pin-striped suit, balding. No ID on him. My team is in there now, going through the place. The victim was shot twice. Looks like a small-caliber weapon. Dead . . . maybe twenty-four hours or so."

"What makes you think it's Mr. Janowski?" If I was going to look at the body, I thought I deserved the particulars.

"At about eight-thirty this morning, when alternate side parking went into effect, a black 1985 Lincoln with Connecticut plates was towed from down the block. A run through the computer identified it as a car you reported missing earlier today, registered in Janowski's name. Highway Patrol's been looking for it all over New England." He looked kind of severe, like all that wasted manpower was my doing. "We need a positive ID."

As Detective LaMarca opened the door, he turned to me and said, in the best 1950s B-movie style, "He's not a pretty sight right now."

I had to clench my teeth to stop myself from saying the obvious: Albert Janowski was never a pretty sight.

The room was a shambles. That's the first thing I noticed. That, and the terrible smell. All the dresser drawers were pulled out and overturned, the cushions on the chair were unzipped and dumped on the floor, and the unspeakably dirty mattress was stripped and partially off the bed. Even the dime-store rug was pulled up around the edges.

"Your team certainly does a thorough job," I said to LaMarca.

"My team didn't do this."

Keeping his grip on my arm, he led me around some white-coated men who were dusting windowsills and furniture and putting their findings into plastic bags, and then to a horizontal figure on the floor next to the bed. Reaching down, he pulled back the sheet from the torso, and showed me Albert Janowski. I had never admired Albert's appearance, but this! His narrow eyes were mere slits, with only white showing; his lips were drawn back into a snarl, and his pasty skin was almost as white as the sheet covering him. In death, Albert had become a caricature of himself. I turned away from the sight.

"Yes, that's Mr. Janowski," and as I said it, I knew I'd be sick if I didn't get out of that room. I must have been green. The detective quickly steered me back into the hall.

"Thanks for your help, Miss Indermill. Would you mind waiting for me down in the lobby? I'd like to ask you a couple of questions."

"Can I take the stairs?"

"Sure, if you want to."

"You the wife?" The Italian Stallion had come out of his stall. "No? The girl, huh? You're a hell of a lot better looking than that broad he was fooling around with. Christ! That old whore looked like she'd been rid hard and put up dirty, if you know what I mean. She was nothing compared to you. That guy must of been nuts."

The shocks that had been building up so rapidly reached a crescendo then. The clerk's words took my breath away. My knees buckled and I fell into a stained settee.

"A girlfriend, here? Mr. Janowski? You can't be serious."

"Geez, I'm sorry to be the one to tell you. But you know how it is with some guys. Like . . . uh . . . one broad ain't enough. Know what I mean?" He made a significant adjustment to the crotch of his pants, in case I didn't.

I wondered, briefly, if it wasn't all some eerie dream.

Things like this don't happen. Except that it was happening. I was at the point of asking the clerk more about the "other broad" when Detective LaMarca stepped off the elevator.

He spoke to the Stallion first, asking him to be available for further questioning, then turned to me. "Can I offer you a ride home, Miss Indermill? I'd like to ask you a couple questions."

"All right."

The degenerates near the door had been joined by a couple of pushy young men in trench coats, one of them carrying a camera. We brushed past them and I heard the desk clerk say behind us: "Girlfriend. All broke up about it." A flashbulb went off as the detective ushered me into a plain green car.

His questions, as I expected, were about Ely Sneed's office structure. Strangely, I found myself giving the same dry recitation I gave applicants: "Eleven partners, nineteen associates, dealing mainly in the corporate area, with some patent work. A small estates department. . . ."

"Ever do any criminal work?"

"Never."

"This Janowski—as far as you know, did he get along with everyone?"

As far as I knew, Albert Janowski got along with almost no one. All the associates held grudges against him, and most of the staff tried to stay out of his way. But that's not the kind of thing an office manager can say.

"You'll have to ask the people he worked with. I had very little to do with Mr. Janowski."

"Oh?" His voice tilted up in surprise. "I overheard the desk clerk back there say you were Janowski's girlfriend."

"He was mistaken. I most certainly was not Albert Janowski's girlfriend."

"Ah."

Ahead of us, lights over the George Washington Bridge burned in a vast fairyland arc. "Nice view up here," the detective said, and I thought to myself, He doesn't believe me. We finished the ride in silence. When he dropped me at my apartment, he asked if I'd help him by setting up appointments with staff members the following Monday. "Otherwise, I'll have to get a court order. Takes time."

I saw no reason to bother with that, and we decided he would be at Ely Sneed Monday at one.

As I opened the car door, something happened. LaMarca leaned across the seat and put his hand over mine. "You're sure you're going to be okay? We could go get some coffee, or a drink, if you want to talk."

Well, I am no stranger to police television melodrama. The gesture, smacking of freshman psychology, might have worked if Paul Newman had used it on me. Detective LaMarca would have to do better.

"I'll be fine."

Bad news travels fast. I wasn't in my apartment fifteen minutes when Gary Petit called from Southampton.

"Mr. Kellogg just called and told me the police had contacted him," Gary said. "I can't believe it, Bonnie. A sweet guy like Albert." There was a slight choke in his voice.

Until then, I had been dry-eyed and composed. Gary's words took care of that. By no stretch of anybody's imagination, except perhaps Gary's, was Albert a sweet guy, but I began sobbing into the receiver.

"Oh, Bonnie, you poor kid. I'm so sorry you had to get involved in this," Gary said. "Look, I was going to wait until morning to drive into the city, but maybe I should leave now and go straight to your place. You shouldn't be alone."

I pulled myself together fast. "No," I said. "I'm fine."

"There's no traffic now," he continued, conveniently not hearing me. "I can be at your apartment before midnight."

Gary's offer shouldn't have surprised me. In the three years we had known each other, he had made it clear that his feelings for me could easily become more than platonic. For me, though, platonic was as far as things could ever go. I enjoyed my "good buddy" relationship with Gary. I had been to several lovely dinner parties at his apartment; he had been to a couple less sedate parties at mine. Those evenings had always ended with a nice, chaste kiss on the cheek, and that was how I wanted it.

I had never had much trouble deflecting his occasional passes, but that night he was trying to use Albert Janowski's body as a stepping stone into my affection, and making me awfully uncomfortable.

"No," I repeated, a little more decisively. "All I want to do is get some sleep."

I burst into tears again the minute we hung up. Maybe it was for Albert, maybe more for myself, or maybe shock. I don't know. Maybe it was just the kind of day I'd had.

In the days immediately after the murder, our office split into several factions. There were the benevolent spirits, always compelled by conscience or maybe their own fear of the hereafter to say something nice about the dead, who whispered in Ely Sneed's corners that Albert had been a good man, actually, "just a little reserved," and that, perhaps, his wife's well-known peccadilloes drove him to his odd, violent end. Others, less forgiving, or with more to forgive, said that Albert got exactly what he deserved, although how he came to get it in the Hotel Central not even his strongest detractors could imagine. Then there were the uncommitted, who shook their heads and said, "How sad," and couldn't even begin to speculate about what happened. I was part of that group. Even now, having been almost totally immersed in the life and death of Albert Janowski, he remains a stranger to me.

That first night it made no sense at all. I could think of nothing—no suspects, no motives, no clues. I remember lying on the sofa long after midnight, staring at a blank television screen as if Act II would soon begin and clear everything up.

It was not so much the fact that somebody wanted Albert dead. I knew any number of people who couldn't stand the man. But they were almost all lawyers, and to be fair to that bunch, they don't usually shoot their enemies. Unless they're Texans. New York lawyers set out to ruin their enemies, smear their names, steal their clients and maybe even their wives, but they don't shoot them.

Which meant, then, that Albert's murder was sex-related, as early circumstances indicated. Granted, I didn't know Albert well, but from what I did know, that possibility was even more far-fetched than the idea that another lawyer had done it.

The sum of my personal experience with Albert was a brief, puzzling incident we shared on a spring afternoon the year before.

A new grocery had opened across the street from the office. It was a pretentious affair, banking on occasional rumors of neighborhood gentrification. Fake aged-wood shelves, fake sawdust floors, a fake cracker barrel, even a fake friendly neighborhood shopkeeper.

It was lunchtime. I was in the checkout line with my usual—a carton of yogurt and an apple—and Albert was behind me with something. We had exchanged cursory nods. The old woman in front of me paid for her quart of milk with small change and a wary eye on the grocer. I remember that her cuffs were frayed and that she carried with her an air of privation only a lout wouldn't have noticed.

The noonday sun shone through the shop window, casting a glow on the rainbow of fruit beneath it. There was one plump, perfect cluster of grapes. A point of light caught them so that they gleamed like jades in a museum showcase. As the old lady moved to the door, her eye fell on them. The temptation was too much. Her spidery hand darted into their midst and emerged, grapes dangling. They disappeared into her bag as she disappeared out the door.

I looked back at Albert. He had seen the theft, too. His eyes were following the woman down the street. I couldn't tell what he was thinking.

It took the grocer only a second: "Hey! Did you see that old lady take those grapes?" He looked right at me.

"No. I didn't notice anything."

We turned to Albert at the same time. He acted like someone caught on the horns of a monumental moral dilemma. His back stiffened. I heard the deep intake of breath and saw the grimace brush his face. His silence was a condemnation hanging in the air. Finally he grunted a reluctant "No," paid for his purchase, and shouldered his way past me and out the door.

For days neither of us mentioned the incident, until one morning when we found ourselves the only passengers in the elevator. It was probably the slowest elevator in New York. I watched the light ticking off floors as we bumped up together: 5 . . . 6 . . . 7 . . . The thought that we could get stuck crossed my mind.

"I do not approve of that sort of thing. There is no excuse for a lie." That was all he said. He didn't even look at me, and could have been talking to himself, except that I knew exactly what sort of thing he didn't approve of and whose lie he meant.

I was never terrified by Albert the way some staff members were. To me, he always looked like an East European minor bureaucrat. I'm not sure what I mean by that—I've never been to Eastern Europe—but the word that comes to mind is lumpish. His pants were never quite long enough and his jackets always tugged in the back. I wouldn't have been very surprised to see him wearing white socks with his suit.

I am a pragmatist, though, and my concern for my job made any defense of my behavior unthinkable.

"I see," I answered. The floors ticked slowly: 16 . . . 17 . . . 18 . . .

Nothing more was ever said about it.

I woke the next morning to the ring of the phone. My mother's voice chafed through the wire.

"Lord knows we've tried to do right by you, Bonnie Jean. Don't tell me you learned that kind of thing from us. It made me sick to my stomach, I want you to know. Lydia O'Connell brought the paper over first thing this morning. You remember her—Tammy's mother, from next door? She likes to rub it in. Tammy finished her nursing course and married a podiatrist. Finkelstein. A Jew. They make the best husbands. She's got a condominium in Great Neck now, with a microwave oven. And here's my daughter in the papers, involved in a scandal. I don't know what to think any more."

"Mom, what's the matter? What time is it, anyway?"

"You know what's the matter. And you're still in bed. You didn't get that from my side."

"Mom, it's all right. It's not my scandal. I just identified the body."

"You should never have moved there in the first place. Can't tell you a thing. One of these days you're going to come to your senses. . . ."

It was much too early for this. "Mom, I'll call you back later." I cradled the phone.

A thin gray light was filtering through the blinds. Moses dozed next to me, eyes half open. He's overweight, with the face of a thug: dark-rimmed eyes and a voracious square mouth. I rescued him from the bullrushes by the Hudson years ago and have spoiled him shamefully ever since. I pulled him closer and rubbed his belly. He purred, then, always the opportunist, broke my grasp, stretched, leaped from the bed, and headed for the kitchen. Kitty cat nirvana.

From the alley behind my apartment I heard the sounds of Saturday morning—clanking of lids on garbage cans, the creaking of a third-floor clothesline, the sleepy muted voices. It's my favorite time of day, too early for the ghetto blaster set to gather on the sidewalks and for the brawling couple upstairs to work up any steam.

I was out of coffee. In fact, I was out of everything but cat food and a frozen anchovy pizza. Faced with tackling Saturday-morning lines at the supermarket or treating myself to breakfast out, there was no contest.

As I walked from my building, Ethel and Eunice Codwallader, ages sixty-three and sixty-five, respectively, walked in, fixing me with bifocaled evil eyes. Tap dancing, my one hobby, and a pretty harmless one when you think about the things other people in New York amuse themselves with, caused me no end of trouble with the Codwallader sisters.

The morning air was crisp and fresh. Yesterday's rain had formed ice crystals, sparkling on bare limbs. Two black squirrels, early risers from their long winter, scuttered around me, forecasting a warm spring. Albert Janowski was yesterday's sad memory, to become next year's anecdote and finally, someday, a muddy blur. Already I found myself wondering if there had been pain in his expression. All I could remember was the anger.

Washington Heights is not an "in" neighborhood. Anything but. When your battered spirit cries out for the *haut monde* up there, the only game in town is the café at the Cloisters Museum. No self-respecting East Sider would allot it a half star. It is lovely, though, set away from the road, surrounded by towering elm trees and shrubbery. It has a sweeping, unobstructed view of the Bronx, for whatever that's worth. On my way into the café I picked up the morning paper. Then, black coffee and bagel in hand, I settled into a corner booth.

I made Page Five. And Mom was right. It was my scandal. There I was, right under a headline: NAKED ATTORNEY SLAIN IN TIMES SQUARE SEX DEN. At first glance I didn't even recognize the open-mouthed, fuzzy-haired creature gaping at the camera as myself. Detective LaMarca was a hand on my arm and a faceless shadow behind me. The caption named me as Mrs. Mill, girlfriend of the victim, who identified the body, and quoted the desk clerk: "She was all broke up about it."

Of course I had known Albert Janowski's murder would make the papers, but I hadn't thought I would. And the unbridled sensationalism—why hadn't his wife's family done something about that?

The rest of my day was spent on the telephone, first with the *Post*, and then with my mother. The paper promised a retraction only after I threatened a lawsuit. My mother was a bigger problem.

"You know, Bonnie, you bring these things on yourself. Running around with I don't know what. You need a husband to take care of you. Like that nice fellow you brought out here last Christmas. Whatever happened to him? I can't imagine how you let him get away. A lawyer. They make a good living. There he was, on the line. All you had to do was reel him in."

No one is more anxious than my mother that I perpetuate the Ozzie and Harriet myth. Every conversation, regardless of its beginning, leads to that end. For some reason, her language of courtship is peppered with fishing terminology of good catches and slippery ones and, in my case, the big ones that get away.

As I'm sure I mentioned, it's not as if I haven't tried it. I raced into marriage at eighteen like John Wayne racing into battle, with a man of little intelligence and no common sense. He had a then-irresistibly gaunt starving-poet face and a father with enough pull to get him a decent job. I should have married his father.

The scenario read that I was going to be forever cherished by my prize, surrounded into perpetuity by an unshakable white picket fence, golden nasturtiums draping prettily over it. The reality was that within six months I felt qualified to write the definitive manual on martyrdom for young wives. The travesty finally ended when I discovered the answer to my prayers *in flagrante delicto* with the next-door neighbor's seventeen-year-old baby-sitter. It was too much to ignore.

Mother thought I overreacted. "You have to be patient with them, Bonnie Jean. It's just their nature. You've got that nice ranch style there, with a den, even a dishwasher. I'll tell you what; you drive over to the shopping center with me on Saturday. Sears is putting their new no-stick cookware on sale. We'll pick out a few nice pieces. . . ."

Can you imagine the kitchen I'd have by now if I'd listened to her?

MONDAY

APRIL

6

I had once taught kindergarten for a year, at a progressive school in Berkeley. One Friday afternoon we found Elizabeth, our pet white rat, dead in her cage. Elizabeth, in her shoebox coffin, was placed on ice until the following Monday, when we gave her a proper burial.

A dense fog mingled with the morning light. My children and I dug a hole under a tree at the back of the playground. Someone had fashioned a cross. The scene was perfect for reflection, mourning, perhaps a tear. One small boy squeezed his eyelids and balled his fists. I thought he would cry. He looked up at me, grinned, and shrieked: "This is so much fun, Bonnie!" His voice knifed through the fog. Then, spirit subdued by a touch of guilt, he added, "Poor Elizabeth."

That is just about how Ely Sneed's staff reacted to the investigation into Albert's murder.

News of the pending interviews—or interrogations, as the staff preferred calling them—preceded the arrival of the police by several hours. By the time Detective LaMarca and his associate, Sergeant Scott, got to the office, the talk was all rubber hoses and pistol whippings. I think the staff was disappointed by the gloomy detective and his middle-aged sergeant in their dull business suits. However, the men's escort managed to raise a few eyebrows.

She poked her head through my door at about twelve forty-five. For one hysterical moment I thought she was the applicant for the Decker job. "Hi. I'm Brandy, from Hollywood Enterprises." Brandy had waist-length gold ringlets and her makeup looked like it had been applied with a spatula. I was speechless.

"You know, from 24. These fellows wandered in by mistake. We're 2415 and you're 2514." She pulled the two men into my tiny office, a bare proprietary arm around each. Sergeant Scott, a dignified black man, looked mortified. Detective LaMarca was red-faced and didn't meet my eyes.

"Thank you, Brandy. We appreciate it." I intended that as a dismissal, but she clung to the two men.

I looked at Detective LaMarca. "You probably want to get to work now, don't you?"

"The sooner the better."

"Well, then, boys," Brandy gushed, "I'll be running along. Nice meeting you people."

We stood there, the three of us, and watched her retreating form. Her slacks were tighter than my skin. By an awful twist of fate, Decker walked out of the men's room in time to catch Brandy's exit. He did a double take, then turned and glared at me.

The policemen spent the afternoon combing Ely Sneed's offices. Considering the unpleasant nature of their business, the investigation was conducted with a minimum of fuss. When they had completed the interviews I'd arranged, they asked Miss Peterson for Albert Janowski's calendar and for a list of people he had seen during the two weeks before his murder. They gave his office a hands-and-knees microscopic examination. They looked through his list of current clients, asked about his practice: Had he been overheard arguing with any clients or associates, with the staff, with his partners? Was he particularly friendly with anyone in the office?

I bet that by late afternoon their list of suspects numbered several dozen. As far as I know, none of the associates was sorry to see Albert go, and a number of staff members had suffered at his hands. I even wondered how many of Albert's partners would really miss him. From what I gathered, his death was described more in terms of the grieving widow and fatherless son, and how hard Old Mr. K was taking all this, than in sorrow because Albert was gone.

I hadn't put myself on the list of interviewees because I didn't think I knew anything. Detective LaMarca, though, had other ideas. He looked into my office at about five P.M.

"We're through here. I'd like to talk to you for a few minutes, if you don't mind."

The only thing I was concealing at that point was my old distrust of police authority, but I managed to stammer so much you would have thought I put the bullets into Albert.

"Oh, you want to put me under the spotlights? I have a watertight alibi, Detective."

For a moment he looked absolutely blank, then he seemed to force a smile. "No. Please call me Tony. Actually, I wanted to thank you for your help and"—he looked over his shoulder and lowered his voice—"I thought if you're not busy, you'd let me take you to dinner. I know it's kind of early but. . . ."

My immediate feeling was relief, followed by an impulse to say no. There was a Fred Astaire–Ginger Rogers double feature on that night—*Swing Time* and *Top Hat*. But then again, I had seen them before and, as Mom would say, "Any port in a storm, Bonnie Jean. At your age there aren't too many fish left in the sea."

We rode down in an elevator packed with Ely Sneed people. As Tony flagged a cab, Old Mr. K and Mrs. Kotch, our bookkeeper and unparalleled grand-master gossip, stood on the sidewalk in front of the building watching us. Mrs. Kotch had her hands on her hips. I figured that by morning it would be all over the office that I'd been taken in.

Tony seemed ill at ease. He wasn't sure what to do with his hand, and made tentative moves toward my elbow. I wasn't much better. I was pretty sure this was a date and not an interrogation, but I couldn't shake a feeling of dread.

"There's one place, kind of a favorite of mine, if you'd like to try it. It's not far," he added, as if he thought I thought he was going to drag me to Brooklyn or Long Island.

"Oh, that will be fine."

What would a homicide cop's favorite place be, I wondered. I saw two possibilities: one of those bustling all-you-can-eat steak and ale places on Broadway where you have to shout over the canned music, or a rough Irish bar that served heaping, fatty corned-beef sandwiches. Neither prospect appealed to me.

He gave the driver an address in the Village, on Waverly, and we rode in silence, him fidgeting nervously with his digital wristwatch and me watching the pedestrians. Over the years my ability to make small talk has diminished to the point where my cocktail party talk is a series of platitudes and hopefully fetching smiles. Tony LaMarca promised to be equally glib. Once I glanced at him from the corner of my eye and caught him looking at me. We both turned away.

In my life I had spoken to perhaps a half-dozen policemen. One gave me a speeding ticket, a couple gave me directions. Two I remember well.

It happened on a summer day in San Francisco, when the fog had burned off early and you could tell the afternoon would be warm and drowsy. It was 1972. I was with a group of friends at an anti-war rally in Golden Gate Park. STREET ARTISTS AND PERFORMERS AGAINST THE WAR, our placard read. There were seven or eight in our group, sitting on blankets getting light-headed on cheap wine and speculating, between speeches and music, how bluegrass music would fare in Monterey and whether a tap dancer might be welcome on the corners in Santa Cruz.

On a grassy rise to our right were the very vocal representatives of a radical activist group. To our left were two very silent motorcycle policemen. One of them I'll never forget. Everything about him said beefy, sun-reddened power. He wore black boots to his knees. A black helmet with SFPD across its front hung over his forehead and those sunglasses only the wearer can see through covered his eyes. Nothing could be seen of his face but a drooping mustache and a compressed, brutal lower lip. I must be wrong about this, but I picture him with Zapata-type holsters crossed over his chest.

Who knows what started it? I heard the sound of breaking glass below us, and then laughing and clapping on the hill above. I looked down in time to see that big cop make the smallest movement with his wrist. Five seconds later I was in the middle of a screaming battle. There couldn't have been more than the two policemen at first, but it seemed as if a dozen rode us down. Our crime was no more than being at the wrong place at the wrong time, but the experience left me with some very big bruises and a healthy restraint around authority.

We ate in a seafood restaurant on Waverly Place, a candlelit, appealing place on the second floor of a brownstone where a fireplace cast feathery lights over the polished wood floor. By appetizer, I was relaxed; by entree, while still a far cry from "your place or mine," I was interested.

A long time ago I dealt in absolutes. Life after death and White Knights and till death do us part. No more. The years have had their tempering effect. Besides, in a society where single women outnumber single men two to one, specifics are impossible. Standards, sure, but even tarnished knights deserve a chance.

Tony spoke about his work and his three children with comfortable informality. He told me about the strains police work had put on his marriage, about the "friendly" separation from his wife that left him isolated, about his introduction to the Columbus Avenue single bars.

"Went with my lawyer," he said. "He told me it was a

'piece of cake.' But I can't handle that kind of thing. Some of those women looked friendly enough. Almost too friendly. Needy. And when you're so needy yourself, you don't have room for anyone else."

I enjoyed the element of almost buoyant simplicity in the way Tony looked at things. He didn't hint at smoldering secrets and dark, unfulfilled desires. It didn't occur to me that this candor was a little at odds with what had seemed, initially, a rather reserved personality.

"And now?" I asked.

"Now, I've accepted. My relationship with the kids has straightened out and . . . but here I keep talking about myself. What about you?"

"What about me?"

"Okay, your job. You like it? That place seems kind of . . ."

"Seedy?"

"I was going to say 'not so prosperous.' They deal in patent law? Isn't there money there?"

"Actually, they've been trying to edge away from patents and into corporate work. Years ago—many years ago—the patent work was really profitable, but now most patents are held by big corporations and, well, I just can't see IBM and Wang knocking on Ely Sneed's doors. They had tunnel vision. They kept the specialty but didn't grow with it. But you don't have to worry about any of them starving to death. There's a lot of old family money around that place."

"And how about you?"

"Not a nickel."

"That's not what I meant."

I knew exactly what he meant. "It's my first real permanent job." I said it low, looking at my plate. I must have been loose that night; it was something I seldom told strangers.

"Your first permanent job, did you say?" His look was incredulous.

"That's what I said." I began the horrible rote monotone

explanation I had made so often. God, how I hated it. Six months student nursing, a year student teaching, so many law-firm temp jobs I'd lost count. All the while the dancing: street bands, auditions, showcases. I don't mean I had hated the life. What I hated was trying to explain it to people with grave faces and unions and pension plans.

". . . and I finally had to face facts. I was thirty-three years old and I wasn't any better than the chorus line, if that. I was lucky when Gary offered me the job at Ely Sneed."

"That's Gary Petit?"

"Right. I was doing temp work as his secretary, and Ely Sneed's office manager died. Gary was impressed by my work—"

"I'd say he's pretty impressed with you," Tony said.

"What do you mean?"

"When I talked to him, I got the impression that you two had a kind of . . . relationship."

"You must have misunderstood him," I said. "In any event, he recommended me for the job. And now, in two years I'll be fully vested in the retirement plan and I can look forward to spending the rest of my working life there and then retiring into semi-poverty." By then we were both grinning; it was too awful a prospect to take seriously.

"Actually," I went on, "I've been holding out until I've been there over three years. It will look better on my résumé."

"I guess so, but right now I'd think twice about mentioning the place. How about some coffee? I really did want to ask you a few questions about the firm."

Coffee? Love it. Questions? Why not? Can there be any doubt what was happening? That devilish infatuation had once again trampled my angel of common sense and restraint. In the fire's warm light Tony's dark lashes made lush etchings on his cheekbones. He wasn't married, he wasn't gay, he seemed to be a light drinker, he had fathered three children and was, or at least had been, capable of sexual intercourse, and he was not part of that vast army of forty-five-year-old single men who live with their mothers in Brooklyn.

36

"I'll tell you what we've got first. The victim—Janowski—left the office about three forty-five Thursday. Didn't say anything about where he was going. Picked up his car at a garage on Twenty-second Street at four. The desk clerk at the Hotel Central thinks he remembers seeing him go in about five-twenty or five-thirty. If he's right, that's an hour and a quarter to drive one mile." He paused to let the significance of this sink in.

"That means Albert must have stopped somewhere else first."

He nodded. "Supposedly, Janowski had been there at least once before, a few days earlier. Tuesday. Took out a Miss D. Smith, then went back to her room with her later that evening. No one saw him leave, but that doesn't mean he didn't. There's a lot of action in that place in the evening. This D. Smith had checked in on Monday, late in the day. Paid cash by the day until Thursday, when she skipped out. Took her luggage with her."

"Was she there the evening Albert was killed?"

"Yes. We have two witnesses who remember seeing her go up to her room around four-thirty. Apparently she was what you'd call 'visible.' About forty, flashy dresser, red-headed, thin, about five-foot-six. Heavy smoker. Sound like anyone you've seen Janowski with? Someone around the office? Maybe a temporary secretary?"

"What she sounds like is 'Hi, I'm Brandy.'"

Tony smiled back at me. "Too young. She was probably a hooker. There have been lots of problems at that hotel. Prostitution, drugs. Nothing real big time, but a lot of small pushers and pimps. A couple years ago a Colombian couple who had been staying there were gunned down in a rental car in Queens. A friend of mine in Narcotics said they'd been skimming off more than their cut in a cocaine smuggling—why are you shaking your head like that?"

"Because none of that can have anything to do with Albert Janowski."

"No? You never noticed any irrational behavior from the guy? Mood swings?"

"Of course. He was a lawyer. But drugs had nothing to do with it. He was as straight as an arrow. A prostitute, maybe. Who can say? But I can't imagine him hanging around the Hotel Central. The Algonquin would be more like it, and the woman would be about as flashy as Eleanor Roosevelt."

"You can never tell about that. You may be right about the drugs, though. Nothing showed up in the PM."

"PM?"

"Postmortem examination."

It is one thing to have an abstract over-dinner discussion about the murder of a man you didn't know well, another to get into the flesh-and-blood realities. Strangely, the notion of the coroner's knife doing its work bothered me more than that of the two .38-caliber bullets. Tony and I watched the fire for a few minutes, not speaking, before he went on.

"Apparently the perpetrator was looking for something. Janowski was robbed. Wallet missing. But most robbers, after killing someone, would panic and get out. They wouldn't spend time searching a dive like that unless they thought something was hidden there."

"Is it possible Albert searched the room himself? Or maybe he found someone else searching it and was killed because of that?"

"Almost anything's possible, but as far as Janowski searching the room himself, his prints only showed up in places he would have left them in the ordinary course of moving around the room: the doorknob, the bathroom door, on his briefcase." He counted these off on his fingers. I couldn't help noticing how nice they looked, strong, with blunted tips. Competent hands.

"It's hard to believe Janowski walked around there without his gloves, then put them on to search the room. Your other point is a possibility," he continued. "He could have walked in on someone searching the room, who then shot him and, as an afterthought, robbed him. Also, it's possible the killer meant to shoot Janowski, that he or she waited there for him and after shooting him ransacked the room to make it look like something else was going on."

"What about other prints?"

"Impossible. There were latents—readable prints—all over the room. The cleaning woman's, prior occupants. The woman's—D. Smith—we've figured out which are hers. She wasn't the one who searched the room, unless she put on gloves to do it. Her prints were everywhere else, though. And I mean everywhere. It looks as if she even climbed out on the fire escape."

"What about the shots? Didn't anyone hear them?"

"If they did, they're not saying. Look, it was a top-floor front room next to the bus station at rush hour. There's an eighty-three-year-old man downstairs, almost totally deaf. A couple of—professional women—use the room next door. They never hear anything."

I remembered one thing I wanted to ask. "Tony, you know what the *Post* said. In that article, it said, 'Naked attorney.' From what I saw when you pulled down the sheet, Albert was dressed. Right?"

"He was sort of half dressed."

"Sort of half dressed?" I repeated. That didn't satisfy me. "Which half? Why am I even asking? It had to be the bottom half that was undressed. I mean, I saw his suit jacket. You're telling me he didn't have pants on?" One thing about being an ex–flower child second-string chorus-line girl: "naked" in itself, by itself, doesn't carry much punch. I wanted more. Tony drained his coffee cup.

"Janowski's trousers and shorts had been removed. He had his shoes and socks on."

I asked one more, obvious question. "Was there any sign of sexual intercourse? They can tell, can't they?"

"None. No sexual relations within the twelve hours preceding death."

"Don't you think that's strange?"

Tony shrugged. "Not necessarily. I've gotten used to it."

I pretended I hadn't heard that. "What I'm saying is, to be found like that—and not even—well, it's a shame that if that's what got him killed, he never even made it."

"I hadn't thought about it that way." He paused like he was trying to make up his mind about something. "I suppose I can tell you the really strange part. You want to hear this? We haven't given it to the papers."

Did I? I was fascinated. And flattered. He trusted me with this confidential information.

"His feet were tied to the leg of the bed, with his belt. Not tight. I mean, it didn't look as he was really being restrained. Probably some kind of bondage thing."

"You're kidding. Bondage?"

Tony just shrugged.

"Do you have any idea why? Maybe I'm naive, but what kind of high would you get out of that? And why didn't they at least get on the bed?"

"Don't ask me. I'm not in Vice anymore."

"You were in Vice?"

"For a while. That's another story. What I'm saying is, you can't imagine some of the things people do to themselves, and to each other. We found the woman's prints on his belt."

"Son of a gun." My mind raced with the possibilities unleashed by all this, and I couldn't think of a thing to say. Finally Tony broke the silence.

"There are a few things you may be able to help me with. The first is, do you know anything about that business twenty-five years ago?" He had pulled a little black notepad from his pocket. "August 1962?"

"No. I don't know what you're talking about."

"One of the partners drowned at the firm picnic. A man named Sneed."

"Oh, sure. Everyone knows about that. It was an accident. At least I *think* it was an accident. Wasn't it?"

"Far as I know. Just that there had been some bad blood between Sneed and Janowski, and Sneed's widow went around making accusations to anyone who would listen, accusing Janowski of killing her husband. Nothing ever came of it. Struck me as strange, though. This Janowski, straight as an arrow like you said, hit by murder twice in his life."

His eyes followed a page to the bottom. He flipped it over methodically. "A number of people I talked to at your office said Janowski wasn't well liked. Said he married the boss's daughter years ago. About the time of Sneed's drowning, if I recall."

Tony was asking me for more than a yes or no. He wanted information about the Kellogg family, about Albert's rise in the firm hierarchy. I told him I knew very little about the partners. Actually, I could have spent hours telling him the gossip but that didn't seem like a good idea.

"Anything you want to know about Albert's position you can get from Mr. Kellogg or Mrs. Janowski," I told him.

"I will, if I ever catch him sober, or if she decides to come back from the Islands."

"Stephanie hasn't come home?"

"No. I talked to her by phone yesterday. Said she hadn't wanted to cut her weekend short." His expression was like Miss Peterson's: brows up, lips pursed. "Said she'd fly back tonight. Fond of the guy, I'd say."

I made one of my noncommittal gestures.

"Don't worry. I'm not going to quote you. What about you? You ever have any problems with Janowski?"

"No. Nothing worth mentioning. He didn't pay attention to me. His bad reputation around the firm is, or was, based mostly on his dealing with the associates. He was responsible for their work. Overseeing assignments, quality. Sometimes he could be pretty rough."

"Do you remember anyone having a bad problem with him?"

"Not bad enough to kill him. There are a couple of things.

Last Wednesday he fired someone. One of the messengers. We're part of a city program where we hire parolees. Gary Petit's in charge. We employ one or two of them at a time. Albert caught one of them rummaging through his desk. We've had a lot of trouble with petty theft at the office. Calculators, purses. Albert let the fellow go on the spot. Tate was his name, Andrew Tate. He wasn't there long enough to get on the payroll. You'll have to check with Gary about him."

Tony wrote a couple of quick lines in his notebook.

"There's something else, now that I think about it," I added. "It must have been almost three years ago, right after I started. I got a temporary secretary for Albert. I don't remember what the problem was, but she threatened him. Said she was going to have her brothers 'beat the shit out of him.' Those were her exact words. I'll get her name if you want."

He nodded, then looked straight into my eyes. "As far as you know, those were the only threats against Janowski?"

I had known, of course, that what was coming was inevitable, yet had deceived myself, thinking, But it was so insignificant. They'd never suspect . . .

"I was told that you witnessed an incident last summer at the firm picnic involving an associate, Emory Hightower. Must be quite the picnics that place has." He flipped the notebook pages back. "Here it is. The Friday before Labor Day. This Hightower and Janowski had a scene. A threat was made by Hightower."

"No, no. There was no threat." I can hardly believe what I did next, much less explain it. I lied on.

"You must mean what happened by the pool. I'd forgotten all about it until now."

"See if you can remember."

Was it my imagination, or was there something slightly menacing in his voice? He seemed unperturbed, quietly waiting for me to collect my thoughts. Unconsciously, my right hand slid across the table and began picking at the nails on my left. His eyes fell, observant, filing away my nervous ticks. I forced my hands down, then began trying to explain the incident, omitting, as I did, the fact that there indeed had been a threat.

I explained to Tony that each of Ely Sneed's partners was in charge of one administrative area, and Albert Janowski headed the firm's associate program. Temperamentally it was a job that probably wouldn't have suited him under the best conditions. Albert was not an easy man to talk to. Add to this his wife's inclinations toward younger men—"She's quite charming," is the way I put it to Tony—and Albert's job performance in this area could be called tyrannical. He naturally had a great deal to say about who made partner. In law firms, that's the pot of gold at the end of the rainbow. The big, prestigious firms have their unspoken laws—if you haven't made it by your seventh or eighth year, you never will. Some of those firms even have automatic termination, though I suspect it isn't necessary. The devastation of finding yourself a permanent associate is doubtless enough to crucify the strongest ego. At Ely Sneed, however, if an associate was fortunate enough to be related to one of the partners, or to a client, he would have to be a total dimwit not to make it.

"And what about this Hightower?" Tony said.

"I'm getting to that. Emory came to the firm with some experience already. Foreign corporate work. He'd lived in Europe. He was older than most of the associates, he spoke a couple of languages—French, Italian. Knew the right people. He was promised an early partnership. I understand Albert never wanted him there. Emory was very polished. He came from some old Southern aristocracy—impoverished—but his demeanor got on Albert's nerves. He carried himself well, dressed well, had a certain style. You understand what I mean?"

"Sure. Like me." He smiled.

"Exactly." I smiled back. "Emory stood out in a crowd. Particularly a crowd of Ely Sneed attorneys. The morning of the picnic Emory had turned in a draft brief to Albert. A little later Albert came flying out of his office waving Emory's papers in his hand. He couldn't find Emory, but he found his secretary and some other people at the copy machine. I was one of them. I remember that Albert looked wild. The veins were popping out of his forehead. He went into a tirade and said something like, 'You tell that moron to see me the minute he shows up. Where did that asshole learn to write a legal brief?' That's what he said. I don't know what happened when he caught up with Emory, but I'm sure Emory didn't feel much like going to a picnic that afternoon."

"You were at the pool when the incident occurred?"

"Yes. But it wasn't really an incident, or a threat. Albert wasn't even there. Emory just said the kind of thing people always say when they want to let off steam, like 'I could just shoot that guy,' or something. Nobody really means things like that. It's a harmless way of striking back."

It was Tony's turn to be noncommittal. He looked up from the notebook and studied my face. What was he seeing? A congenital liar? Was my nose growing like Pinocchio's? I couldn't keep my eyes on his and looked down. Nothing could have surprised me more than his next words.

"You like old movies?"

"Old movies?"

"Forties. Fifties. I was thinking maybe you'd like to go to a double feature with me Friday night." It kind of spilled out, a rehearsed line.

I was seesawing between surprise, dread, and that nagging awareness that, under it all, he and I probably had the same thing in mind, and it didn't have anything to do with Albert Janowski. "Yes," I said.

He made a final note in his book, possibly "unreliable witness," and snapped it closed.

It was still early and I had Tony drop me at the IND station on 14th Street.

"Funny, isn't it," he said as I opened the taxi door.

"Funny?"

"You can remember what a temporary secretary said three years ago, word for word, but you're not that clear on something last summer." While he spoke his eyes followed a pair of punks stalking a fur-coated matron.

"It's not so funny. I'd had a couple drinks that afternoon. It was hot and I was half asleep."

"Ah, I see."

Would he jot "witness drinks" in his book later? Did he understand how little I had to do with any of this? If he had, I wondered, would he have asked me out?

"I'll pick you up about seven Friday. We can get something to eat after the show. How's that?"

"Fine. I'll look forward to it." There's nothing like the prospect of a grilling to brighten your weekend.

There is nothing at all wrong with my memory. I can remember that picnic like it was yesterday: how the summer heat rose in waves off the parched Manhattan pavement as Ely Sneed's staff boarded a country-bound bus. I recall my delight at the vast green lawns of the Kellogg estate and at the gigantic rippling pool. I can almost smell the chlorine and the fresh-cut grass now. And Emory Hightower's threat is etched into my memory as if it was chiseled in granite.

The firm's yearly picnic was planned, no doubt, with good will, but in my experience it was more endured than enjoyed. It was probably typical of things of that sort, when a group of repressed people with little in common are thrown together on a hot day with a limitless supply of liquor. There was little mingling. The file clerks and messengers formed a beer-drinking clique around a gigantic transistor radio, the secretaries drifted cautiously around the place, amoeba-like, sending out occasional tentacles of two or three to the powder room, a duo to the food. The associates took over the tennis court. From time to time one or another of those madcaps, buoyed by a winning set or a few drinks, dared to approach the partners' enclave on the shaded terrace.

Old Mr. K, looking like a Palm Beach gangland chieftain in white slacks and a Panama hat, made a brave try as host, wandering blurry-eyed from one group to the next. It seemed hard for him; he was not, by nature, a good old boy.

I, having a pronounced aversion to sweaty games involving balls and nets, found myself a comfortable chair by the pool and buried myself in *The Great Gatsby*.

A flawless beauty I am not, but I look all right in a bathing suit. That can be a surprise to people who work with me, given the way I tend to dress for the office.

Gary Petit took a chair next to me, from which he cast furtive glances at my bosom. Mrs. Kotch, of all people, was sitting on Gary's other side. After a time, Emory and a couple of other associates, tiring of flailing at tennis balls and having no immediate heart for fawning on the terrace, leaped into the pool. Emory swam a bit, nicely, golden arms slicing the water without a splash, then hoisted himself onto the deck directly in front of me, near enough to drop chlorinated water on my ankles.

In retrospect I can only describe the look he gave me as a leer, but then, with the sun and the gin and tonic, and the absolute lack of excitement in my life, I saw standing before me a physical elegance that defies my ability to explain it. Sex appeal is too simple, suave too oily, and "all-American" way off the mark. I must face it. Emory looked like one of those magazine-profile Wasps who never bother with women like me. He should have had a pedigreed flawless beauty on his arm.

"Well, F. Scott, I see." There was a touch of cynical intimacy in his voice, as if there was something about good old F. Scott that he knew, some dark secret he'd promised he'd never reveal. Emory did that, I came to realize—conferred familiarity on the rich and famous, as if he could step into their lives that way. He could tell you about the mayor's new wife and how she had locked up the liquor. He knew about a Broadway leading man's proclivity for adolescent boys. He had once dined with Mimi Sheridan, and could have told you the name of her absolutely favorite restaurant, except that she'd asked him not to. Most of this was probably gleaned from the pages of the same weekly gossip sheets we all read in the supermarket lines, and ordinarily I would never have been fooled by his name-dropping, but at the time . . .

He pulled a chair to my side, and there I sat, flanked by two single men. Lawyers, at that. Mom would have loved it.

"I would have thought you preferred more modern writers," Emory continued.

I don't kid myself here. He meant I seemed like someone who wallowed in trash, which I do on occasion, but I didn't take it that way then.

There was a wayward lock of golden blond hair falling rakishly over his high, tanned, lightly furrowed brow. A few, just a few, manly crinkles accented his blue eyes, as if a fancy Brazilian plastic surgeon had given him just the right number for a thirty-four-year-old man-about-town. He had the bland, blond features that those of us who were raised in trailer parks associate with the aristocracy. More important, he had a literary bent. I was flattered by his attention.

Emory was not your everyday Ely Sneed associate. As I had told Tony, he was a little older, having come to the firm after what was probably an undistinguished career in Paris. And he looked good enough for one of the better firms, those Wall Street and Park Avenue giants that hire shiny, fresh-faced, eager young Ivy League things, pure of mind, sound of body, and thrilled at the prospect of working fourteen hours a day. Apart from Emory, Ely Sneed hired two associates during my time there: an underweight, lank-haired Ichabod Crane whose fiery weals of acne were so heightened by Albert Janowski's tirades that his face appeared constantly aflame, and a grossly overweight, effeminate young man who emerged from his three-month review in tears, left for lunch, and was never seen again.

For a while that picnic afternoon Gary and Emory vied for my attention. That an associate would compete with a partner for anything, including a woman, says something. What Emory may have lacked in common sense he compensated for with ego strength. The pair of them parried over me—I mean that literally, back and forth across my supine body—playing oneupmanship with Fitzgerald, and then Hemingway, all for my benefit, I'm sure, while I sipped a drink and made what I hoped were intelligent, amusing comments.

Of course it was bound to end. The conversation drifted to the law, as it must among lawyers, and I promptly began drifting in and out of catnaps. I don't recall what brought Albert Janowski's name into the conversation—no doubt it was something he and Gary were working on—but Emory's mood took a strange turn.

"What an animal that one is," I heard him say. I woke up, fast, and saw that he had leaned back in his chair and gripped his arms behind his neck. "Someday I'm going to pay Albert back. Life's a long time and I'll never forget the way he spoke to me. The day is going to come when he grovels in front of me and I'm going to chop him down and let him get a good look at what hit him before he falls." Emory's expression was introspective and his words were said with more conviction than anger.

As you might expect, there went Emory's partnership, not to mention the conversation, which gasped to a stop. Wide awake then, and completely flabbergasted, I tried to defuse things by laughing it off. The two associates sitting by the edge of the pool slipped like quiet eels back into the water, lest they be tainted by association. Gary, pretending it had all gone right past him, suddenly remembered something he had to do somewhere else. Mrs. Kotch, a lemon-sucking look on her face, was right behind him.

I considered following the exodus, but, frankly, my temporary infatuation had welded me to my chair. And there were other things: only a week earlier I had attended a dear friend's second wedding and had been momentarily besotted by the microwave/Tupperware fantasy; and my mother was in the middle of a big push for me to reel in a big one. But the crux of the matter is, I'm light-skinned, with reddish-blond hair and blue eyes, and tend to burn easily, and Emory chose that moment to swing around and face me. "You're burning," he said, with that secret-joke voice of his, and he began rubbing my shoulders with sunscreen. I couldn't have gotten out of the way if Albert had come after Emory with a horsewhip.

I won't bore you with all the particulars of the relationship that followed, and believe me, most of them would bore you. Some of it, though, is so vivid.

He didn't like driving in New York. "And anyway," he said, with the facile nuttiness I found so logical for a while, "Paris has the only streets I'm comfortable on." So, with my expired California license, I chauffeured us around Manhattan in his white antique Porsche, right-hand drive, stalling at every intersection and creating countless traffic jams, while he smoked a Sherlock Holmes pipe and told me funny uncensored stories of the old Louisiana plantation (sold for taxes), of boarding school (Switzerland), prep school (England), of a French mother who married four times, descending the social scale until she now found herself—a woman of a certain age, little means, and endless style—giving solace to a penniless Italian count with nothing to recommend him but his title and what sounded like a peculiar extended family.

Emory talked about his forced indenture into the law. "It's not for me," he said, sipping designer-bottled water with a wedge of lime from a long-stemmed glass. "What I should be doing is writing."

We dined like we rode, in the with-it mode of Manhattan pseudo-elegance, and the whole time he talked about the novel—his Novel. "I feel it in me," Emory said over poached salmon in a Soho restaurant of black walls, astronomical prices, and such tastefully manicured indifference I wondered if they wanted us there at all. "A story is in me. A great one, I think. If only I could find the place, the right atmosphere, to get it started. I almost hear the words, like a beautiful song heard in the distance, not quite able to make itself clear. What I need is ambience."

By then it was the end of November. Winter's sting was in

the city air. Emory popped the question: "Bonnie, how would you feel about going to an island for a week?"

I had immediate, overwhelming visions of myself, bikini-clad on a palmy beach, shopping in sunny markets, dancing until dawn in my never-worn off-the-shoulder flowered silk, returning with a radiant tan so everyone would know I'd made it to the Caribbean.

"Look at these pictures," he said. "I discovered this article in a *National Geographic*. Isn't this your idea of a writer's paradise?"

We went by car, then ferry, to an island off the Massachusetts coast, a place of "stark, unspoiled beauty," peopled by the descendants of nineteenth-century whalers. Believe me, nineteenth-century whalers were not into creature comforts.

It was damp, and when it wasn't damp, it was bitter cold. The wind blew relentlessly. Our cabin, "within an easy walk of all the conveniences," was a mile from the tourist-deserted town, and stood on a bluff overlooking the churning Atlantic to the north and an endless, bleak stretch of scrub pine to the south.

Emory was delighted. "What melancholy. Think of it, Bonnie. The anguish this place has seen. The romance. Like the Brontës' moors. Yes. I think I'll be able to work here."

For six days he worked. Created, I should say, alternately typing, then brooding, head in his hands. His sighs mingled with the wind; the cabin became a chamber of whispers and whooshes. He would pace from time to time, and then: "Ah, yes. That's it."

I passed my time trying to stay warm, reading thrillers, and doing hand laundry, the island's laundromat being closed for the season. Our underwear froze solid on the sun deck.

In the evenings we walked into town, through cold, stinging whirlwinds of sand and pine needles, to the only restaurant open out of season, Smitties' Bar and Grill.

"Just look at these faces, Bonnie." Emory gestured toward a bunch of boozy fishermen arguing around an electronic pinball machine. "Real workers' faces. This is marvelous; what life is really all about. Man against the elements. Although," he said, lowering his voice, "the shrimp in this bouillabaisse are not fresh. For the best, of course, you'd have to go to Marseilles, but in this country . . . New Orleans. A little place in the French Quarter. Not a tourist trap," he added.

I had, by that point, made it clear that I would have preferred the tawdry comforts of a tourist trap. Next time, he promised.

It had been our plan that he would create and then I, being bright enough but hopelessly mechanical, would edit. At the end of the sixth day, over dinner, Emory handed me fourteen badly typed pages. I remember being surprised by how few there were, considering the suffering that had gone into them.

I settled myself into the booth and began reading while Emory studied the real life around him.

It was the beginning of a story of an Australian sheep farmer's son, for reasons I can't recall, one-legged, who, "in the full flush of youth," hobbles off with a traveling circus and, on a "raging, stormy night, the sky shrouded with ebony clouds of passion," falls into the eager arms of a wealthy older woman ex-aerialist, who offers him not only the vast wealth concealed between her well-muscled thighs but "the entire world. It's yours, Emile." How she planned to accomplish this was not explained. There was much heaving of breasts and pounding of hearts in rapture. For the life of me, I didn't know what to say.

"Why Australia, Emory?" That seemed a safe starting point.

"Why Australia?"

"Yeah. Why Australia? You don't know anything about Australia. And the name—Emile. Do you think that's right?"

He drew back and looked at me as if he couldn't quite believe he'd heard my shortsighted, pedestrian response, as if a reappraisal of my judgment, if not my entire character, was called for.

"It's not about Australia, Bonnie. It's about man colliding

with society's barriers and tearing them down. I'm trying to capture the similarities of life and the artistic endeavor. I would have thought that was obvious." He made an angry stab at one of his pre-cooked shrimp. "The name is symbolic."

I thought it best to leave that alone. "Well, as it now stands," I said, as if fourteen pages of anything could be said to stand, "it's not completely credible. It's . . . shaky. Like it needs an anchor. Maybe if you set it in a place you're familiar with—like Paris or New Orleans—it would ring truer."

His expression told me I'd gone too far already, that I could kiss that tourist trap goodbye.

"Shaky, Bonnie? I think the word you're looking for is audacious. How many people do you suppose thought Beckett and Joyce were shaky? What they were was bold stylistic pioneers with the courage of their impertinence. You," he added, his voice rising, "should learn to be more open-minded, particularly about the creative process."

I saw one of the men at the bar turn our way and elbow the fellow next to him. "Perhaps you're right," I said.

We boarded an early ferry for the mainland the next morning, sleepy, grouchy, and cold. Emory, after staring out the window for an eternity, drew his manuscript from his suitcase and began looking it over, carefully avoiding my eyes.

"I've thought about what you said. In one way, Bonnie, you're right. It would never do for the society we're living in. It wouldn't translate"—finally his look met mine—"into television." And with that, he left his seat and, head bent, manuscript in hand, opened the door and climbed onto the open upper deck. I raced after him.

The wind was terrible and the deck slick with salt water. "What are you doing?" I had to shout over the gale.

"It's a waste of my talent. No publisher would touch something like this. It's too complex. An experimental reflection of . . ." He was bellowing like Brontë's Heathcliff.

I screamed back: "You shouldn't take my word for it. I'm not the last word in literature, you know."

He turned cynical, ever-so-bemused eyes to me. "Ah, but

53

you are." There was a quick grand gesture with his right arm and the pages were airborne, floating among the gulls.

"It is finished," he said.

It wasn't, quite. We returned to our chairs, wet, miserable, and silent. And there, plastered by the sea and storm against the window by my seat, pointing the finger of guilt at me, was page thirteen: "He could feel the heat from her swollen breasts as she pressed her womanflesh against him. 'Emile, I've never felt this way before.' Her hands, sure and deft, sent messages to his very being. 'Take me,' Camille moaned, and he moved to join them in that most ancient ceremony." Mercifully, a strong gust washed the thing away.

It was the end, of course. We hung on for the two weeks until Christmas, out of habit, I think, and that peculiar, universal need to be wanted during the holidays. On Christmas morning he gave me a briefcase I didn't need, being disinclined to carrying work home. I gave us tickets to a musical he didn't enjoy: "Terribly self-conscious; trivial, in fact. But fun, Bonnie. I'm glad we went."

On my part I can say I gave it my best, which included résumé typing services to help in Emory's eventually fruitful job hunt, numerous buttons and pockets sewn, and occasional home-cooked, though by no means gourmet, meals. Emory's best consisted of a shakedown of my wardrobe ("Surely you can afford better") and a drunken Christmas-night critique of my family ("They're rednecks!"). Needless to say, my mother found Emory positively enchanting: "I just love that accent. So refined. That's a good catch there, Bonnie Jean."

In case you think I'm being too hard on Emory, you're probably right. I've tried to maintain objectivity, but it's hard with ex-boyfriends. I find I either lapse into drooling sentimentality or take vengeance in self-inflating sarcasm. In Emory's favor he had a ready wit from which he didn't always exclude himself, except where the Novel was concerned, and often made me laugh. He could be depended on to use the right fork, and never wore anything that would make people stare at us on the street. Our four-month involvement was not the worst thing I've ever done to myself.

There is one thing I'd like to clear up here. In the end it was I who said, "This isn't going to work. Let's be friends," and Emory who said, "Keep the keys to my place. You'll come to your senses."

Was Emory capable of murder? I didn't think so. If anything, he was too vain for murder. It's a dirty business. Certainly he was capable of the dramatic gesture, and his threat against Albert had been real enough, but it was open to interpretation.

So was my reason for lying to Detective LaMarca about it. Was it some neurotic need to belittle his authority? Or a misplaced loyalty to Emory? Maybe an understandable reluctance to face the fact that I had carried on an affair with a murderer? I wonder if I would ultimately be one of those sweethearts/co-workers/wives who, after the capture of some hideous criminal, exclaim in shock, "He was such a lovely person. Sang in the Methodist choir. And so good to his mother."

WEDNESDAY

APRIL

8

"**K**eeping in mind that Ely Sneed's dress code (a copy of which is attached to facilitate ready reference) was formulated in the interest of a high standard of professionalism . . ." The confidential memorandum from the Protocol Committee, a.k.a. Wilbur Decker, went on to suggest I cease giving Ely Sneed's business to the personnel agency which had supplied the scantily clad temp seen near my office Monday at one.

The other envelope on my desk contained a black-rimmed announcement of a memorial service for Albert Janowski, to be held that afternoon. Decker had personalized my copy with a scrawl making it clear that my presence as the representative of non-legal management was not only invited, but demanded.

When it came to burying Ely Sneed's dead, Decker, a natural for flagellation anyway, was in his glory. I remember my unfortunate predecessor's funeral. In return for thirty-five unblemished years' service, she merited a half-day office closing, a memo calling for one hundred percent staff participation, and black limousines for all. I've been told that Decker made her life on earth hell, but you can be sure she went to the hereafter like a head of state. Ely Sneed's wreath looked like something for the neck of a Kentucky Derby winner.

The chief mourner himself, flushed with morbid excitement, poked his head in on me before noon. "I personally would have preferred something with more dignity," he said, his "tsk tsk" almost audible, "but the way in which Mr. Janowski left us precludes that." He turned to go, then wheeled back. "By the way, Miss Indermill. I'm sure you understand. I'm not sure how far you've gotten"—here the simpering and hand-wringing began—"but there's no reason to include this in *The First Hundred Years*. It's not the kind of thing the firm . . . you understand."

"Of course, Mr. Decker," I simpered back. It was a moot point anyway. I had yet to flog as much as one syllable out of Ely Sneed's filthy history.

I took a noon train to Stamford and a cab to Albert Janowski's church. It was modern and prosperous-looking, built on a wooded hillside with a tree-lined circular drive winding up to it.

Beads of perspiration broke out across my forehead as soon as I walked through the door. It's a reaction I sometimes have in churches. This one had an austere, unadorned quality—I suspect this was more in the name of architectural modernism than ascetic self-denial—with none of the mystery I remembered from churches of my childhood. No statues, no stained glass, and no incense permeating every pore of the old wooden pews, emanating its sweet magic to fire young imaginations into confessions and penitence. Albert's church smelled of lemon-spray furniture polish.

Family members sat in the first few rows. Behind them were Miss Peterson and Rosalie, Gary Petit, Decker, and the rest of the partners. Only a sprinkling of associates were there.

Without thinking I sat in an empty row at the back, by an open window. Almost immediately a wave of chilling self-consciousness swept over me. Would I appear too aloof? Should I move closer? No, I decided. That would make things worse. I sat like an outsider, hoping my self-imposed exile would pass for piety, and sure everyone else would get something out of the service—some communal cleansing—that I was going to miss.

Then the priest walked out to the altar, and it was too late to move anyway. I remembered the priests from rural Maryland and New Jersey I knew as a child: red-faced men with heavy jowls and paunches who recited their Latin in musical Irish brogues. Albert Janowski's priest looked like a man you might find steering an America Cup entry at Newport or skiing St. Moritz. At the very least, he jogged. His remarks—what I recall of them—concentrated on the terrible loss to community and family, and tactfully avoided any mention of the crime. I saw Miss Peterson and Gary wipe their eyes, and felt strangely at odds with my surroundings.

Hoping to catch a fresh breeze, I slid closer to the open window. There was no breeze, but I witnessed a brief, bewildering drama. A small, light blue car was coming up the long drive. As it drew nearer, I picked out the Buick emblem. A boy of perhaps seventeen was driving and an older woman was in the passenger seat. Late arrivals, I thought. The car stopped in the parking lot about twenty feet from me. The boy left the engine running while the woman opened her door, stepped out, and walked around to the driver's side, nearer the church. The boy, in turn, opened his door and watched her with a curious tension. She was a sweet-looking woman of seventy or so, your storybook perfect grandmother, her hair piled in a beauty-shop blue bouffant, her face pleasantly lined.

She took a few steps toward the church. The boy stepped from his door, placed his hands on her shoulders, and seemed to be trying to force her back to the car. Shaking off his hands, she turned as if to comply. Then, to my shock, she wheeled around, faced the church, and spat at it. Rage contorted her face. The boy gripped her by the arm and pushed her back into the car. As they drove off, because of my intense curiosity, I memorized the license number.

"Let us pray." The congregation shifted to its knees, taking me by surprise. I knelt and tried to force my thoughts onto something more contemplative. Then I saw Rosalie stifle a yawn and one of the partners sneak a look at his watch, and felt better about having had no catharsis.

We waited on the church steps later, under a dismal slate sky in quiet groups of three or four, none of us knowing what to say or do.

Stephanie Kellogg Janowski was among the last to leave the church. She stepped into the cold surrounded by elderly people in black: Old Mr. K and his ever-stylish wife, and a gray, dowdy couple who I thought must be Albert's parents.

Wilbur Decker, standing by my side, had a sure instinct for making an ass of himself. He elbowed me in the ribs: "Come on, Miss Indermill. Let's pay our respects." I held my ground, but he managed to recruit a few others and led a twitching dance macabre into the family group. I wouldn't have been surprised if he'd started pounding his breast and wailing. Stephanie broke away from the group almost immediately. She stood alone for a moment, facing the woods in a posture I thought of as quietly grieved. Then she raised a black-gloved hand and drew away her veil. There was just the faintest smile on her lips. I'd expected the ravages of something—if not grief, at least guilt. But the widow Janowski looked better than ever. Calm, radiant, in fact. She had the tan that always eludes me, her eyes were clear and her countenance . . . content. I don't know what else to call it.

Part of my difficulty in describing Stephanie Janowski must stem from the fact that I dislike her so, but it goes further. Long ago, even before she threatened me, my reaction to her physical presence was totally at odds with that of all our mutual male acquaintances. When I looked at Stephanie on those church steps, I saw a tall, angular, well-groomed, expensively dressed, and absolutely unremarkable woman. When men looked at Stephanie, they saw stolen weekends, heavy breathing, steaming sheets, black satin, and mirrored ceilings, the personification of all the fuzzy fantastic promises of Sex with a capital S.

Her smile broadened when she saw me staring at her.

"Bonnie. How nice you're here."

She walked toward me like a guest at a cocktail party greeting an old friend.

"It's been so long, hasn't it? Since last year's picnic? What naughty girls we are. We should try to get together more often."

Under the circumstances, finding the right thing to say wasn't easy. I finally settled on an out-and-out lie about how much we were all going to miss Albert.

"Oh, bullshit." She giggled then, and put her hand over her mouth in one of those cute oh-bad-me gestures. "But I do know better, Bonnie. I'll bet most of them"—the expansive sweep of her arm took in all the mourners—"are here to be sure he's not coming back. My husband was not a popular man."

Stephanie had a way of staring into your eyes and not letting go. She was making me uncomfortable and enjoying it.

"And by the way," she said, "you needn't bother explaining that headline in the *Post*. I have faith in your taste in men. You wouldn't have looked twice at Albert."

What a thing to say at your husband's funeral. And what did she know about my taste in men, anyway? Her smile indicated it was a lot. She saved me the trouble of groping for a polite response to that one.

"I have an idea. Do you have to go straight back to the city? I wouldn't mind getting away from this for a while. There's a nice restaurant in Weston, by the lake. I can tell you all about Aruba. Have you ever been there? No? You've got to go sometime."

Like the spitting grandmother, Stephanie apparently intended to deal with her grief in her own way. I watched while she spoke to her parents. It was a muted conversation, all mumbles and small, sharp gestures. I saw Old Mr. K give a heave of his shoulders and turn his back on his daughter. She stared at him for a second, then walked back to me.

"So much for that. Guess we'll have to make it some other time. They're determined to drag this thing out to its bitter end." Her eyes rolled in exasperation. "You know how parents are."

"Oh yes."

"Perhaps we can get together some Saturday when I go in shopping. Brunch, maybe?"

I agreed, of course, but expected nothing of it. Stephanie and I were barely acquaintances, hardly friends.

When Gary Petit offered me a ride back to the city, I accepted, but not without reservations. As I mentioned, I sometimes had difficulty shaking the feeling that Gary was only waiting for the right moment to try to make more out of our relationship than was there.

I won't deny giving Gary a quick look when we first met, either. He wasn't an unattractive man; just a bit ungainly, with awkward long limbs that never seemed comfortable and a homely face that almost always did.

One problem was that, at forty-three, Gary was still in an almost adolescent state of self-improvement, as if some unknown male perfection lay just out of his grasp. This search was marked by fluctuations in appearance and speech. Nothing drastic, but one month there might be a mustache and hair growing over his collar, and when you'd gotten used to that, the spirit of the sea would jettison his closet of everything but deck shoes and navy blazers. These parts seldom came together in a whole. The swinging single with ten pounds of gold hanging around his neck was as likely to say, "Let's shove off, Matie," as the guy in Wimbledon whites was to call me a "foxy chick." If all this had been done with the humor of a good-natured impulse buyer, I might have looked at it differently, but Gary chased his ideal with solemn doggedness.

But beyond all that, even if I'd found Gary wildly attractive, it would have taken only one ride in his car to cool me off completely. He was, hands down, the most aggressive driver I've ever ridden with. It was as if, when he slid behind the wheel, he went through a Jekyll to Hyde transformation. He drove a huge, supercharged metallic Mercury with a garish silver stripe. A car for a rampaging teenager. When I accepted his offer that afternoon, I naively figured that the sobering effect of Albert's funeral would run over into Gary's driving. As it turned out, I was mistaken.

He started the engine, gunned it, and then, white-faced, eyes red and haunted, looked at me. "I feel so damned guilty. I might have prevented this."

Before I had the chance to ask what he meant, he slammed the gearshift into reverse and shot from his parking place. So much for sobriety. I tightened my seat belt until it cut into my lap.

"I should have pursued whatever it was Albert had going with that woman," he said. We roared down the driveway and pulled into traffic without bothering to slow down. My chest tightened as a white delivery van hit the shoulder to avoid us. The driver leaned on his horn, and when I looked back, he was shaking a middle finger at us. Gary glared into the rear-view mirror. "That son of a bitch should have yielded."

I let out the breath I'd been holding. "Gary, I bought a round-trip ticket. I don't want you to go out of your way. Why don't you drop me at the train station."

"Don't be silly. You're going back to the office, aren't you? So am I. The thing is, Bonnie, I didn't want to embarrass Albert—try to get into his personal space, if you know what I mean. But he should have known I'd understand. After all, his marriage was on the rocks. Could you believe Stephanie today? Already on the make." He shook his head. "I wouldn't touch her with a stick. She's scary. Who could blame Albert for fooling around?"

"Are you saying that Albert told you this woman was his girlfriend?" I asked. "You know, Gary, from the way the desk clerk at that hotel desk described Miss D. Smith, I can't imagine how she and Albert ever got together."

He leaned toward me. I watched the steering wheel swivel in his hand. The car veered to the left. A screech of brakes and a blaring horn grabbed his attention. He rolled his window part way down and shouted through it: "Asshole!" before turning back to me. "No, Albert didn't say in so many words, 'I'm having an affair with D. Smith,' but when you've known a guy as long as I've known Albert, you learn to read between the lines. Something had been on his mind for a while, and last Thursday night, when he was supposed to drive out to the beach place with me, he decided to see Miss Smith instead. Said it was personal. That should tell you something."

"Personal? That doesn't tell me anything. But even if he was having an affair, you didn't see the Hotel Central. A real Times Square dump. The kind of place where you hold your nose when you walk past the door. One step above sleeping on the subway. Can you imagine Albert going to a place like that? According to Tony, there have been prostitution and drug problems there, too."

"From what I hear, there have been prostitution and drug problems at the Waldorf. Who's Tony?"

"Detective LaMarca. I . . . well, we had dinner the other night."

"Oh." He tapped the accelerator, throwing the car into overdrive and flattening me against my seat. Connecticut's blossoming countryside flashed past in quick frames of pale green. I took a breath and pushed on.

"Tony says that a few years ago there was a drug-related murder at the hotel. Central Americans who had been staying there. . . ."

"Tony says." Gary gave a sigh and shook his head. "I think it's off the point to go on about the hotel. Albert and his lady friend probably didn't know what it was like when they made the resevations. Maybe once they got there, they thought it was kinky. Jesus, Bonnie—what if Albert died because he was embarrassed to ask if he could use my apartment? What a horrible thought!"

He was one horrible thought ahead of me. I was still on

"kinky." Gary didn't seem to have any trouble mentioning Albert and "kinky" in the same breath. Maybe there was something to Tony's bondage theory.

"Albert was a pretty cool dude, Bonnie, when you got to know him. He'd had several relationships I knew about. Once, before your time, there was even a woman at the office. A good-looking gal. Don't ever repeat this. It was serious for a while. They used to borrow my apartment. He had to be careful, you know, with his father-in-law around. With men," Gary added, an arch look my way, "sometimes what you don't see is as important as what you do."

I answered that with a grunt. As far as I was concerned, with Albert Janowski, what you saw was undoubtedly what you got.

"This past January"—Gary's voice fell to the level I'd come to recognize, confessional—"Albert and I went to a seminar in Miami. He was speaking on the Lanham Act."

I remembered it well. I'd helped Miss Peterson type some of his notes. "Section 43 (a) and a Consideration of Trade Container Infringement." She and I had made the usual jokes— how it was a real knee-slapper, how he'd have them shouting "Bravo" and "Encore."

"I was a panel moderator," Gary said. "Got to write the whole trip off. Anyway, that first night Albert and I went out on the town, kind of tomcatting around, rapping with different people. At about the third place we met these two chicks—stewardesses—from Atlanta. Great-looking gals. After a few drinks . . . Why are you smiling?"

I shook my head. He was off again. Frankly, I never understood why Gary told me these things. Perhaps it was because I wasn't very judgmental. Whatever the reason, I eventually heard all about all Gary's forays into sex and consciousness raising. When I withheld comment or censure or whatever it was he was looking for from me, he would pick from a grab-bag of psychological mumbo-jumbo and tell me why a particular woman, a new guru, vegetarianism, whatever, hadn't lived up to his expectations.

". . . just the four of us," he was saying. "Middle of the night. Had to climb a fence to get out to the water. Our hotel wasn't on the beach. All of us three sheets to the wind. Loaded. The gals had some coke. Stews always do. Bonnie. . . ."

"What?" I'd been half-listening.

"You're not going to tell anyone about this, are you?"

"Of course not. Who would I tell?"

"We ran down to the waves, all holding onto each other. All of us snorted coke. That's how I want to remember Albert. Holding his shoes in one hand, his other arm around that gorgeous gal, his pants legs rolled up, playing in the surf, trying to remember the words to 'Yellow Submarine.' The moon was terrific that night. Have you ever noticed how much closer the sky seems when you're in the South?"

"No."

"I'm sure he made it with her later. But you know Albert. I couldn't pry it out of him. He did tell me she was going to get him a free flight to Maui, though. They had talked about meeting there."

"You've got to be kidding," I said.

"Kidding? Why do you say that? Women loved Albert, once they got to know him. He was one of the great lovers of all time, next to yours truly, of course."

"Of course." This was unbelievable. Everything I knew about Albert resisted the notion of Albert the swinger. Skinny Gary the rakehell was hard enough to picture. Tubby Albert, impossible. Cavorting in the surf with gorgeous women in moonlight saturnalias? Albert Janowski, the man who disapproved of my lie about two dollars' worth of grapes, the great ladies' man of all time, snorting coke, no less? Was I so dense, so unperceptive, so much in my own small world that an essential part of Albert's character had slipped right by me? Maybe so. Gary had no reason to make these things up.

"Oh, God!" he said suddenly. Without even glancing in his side mirror, much less giving a turn signal, he whipped the car across a lane and into a roadside rest area. We screeched to a gravel-spraying stop inches from a concrete picnic bench.

Unconsciously I had stiffened my back and braced my feet against the floorboard, ready for the impact. "What's the matter?" My voice was shrill with panic.

He looked at me as if he was surprised to find me there. "I'm sorry," he said after a moment. "I guess this whole thing has filled me with intimations of my own mortality."

"I've had intimations of my own mortality since I got in this car," I shot back.

"I'm serious, Bonnie. Damn!" he said angrily. Clenching his fists, he slammed them into the steering wheel so hard the entire dashboard vibrated.

This was awful. Was he going to have some sort of breakdown, right there at the rest stop? I looked around for a telephone, but there was none in sight.

Gary had leaned forward into the steering wheel. Gripping it, he pushed back, stretching his arms. "My grandfather, and his father before him, they were the kind of men who shaped the world they lived in. Then my father. . . ." He shook his head. "Oh, he tried too. And now, it's my turn. I should have taken a more active part from the beginning. Instead, I sat on the sidelines letting Mr. K drag us down. What a mess the firm is now."

"Why are you being so hard on yourself? Nobody's job is perfect." I said that from experience.

He glared at me. "Job! I don't have a job. I have an inherited position. Do you know what I want most? I want to return the firm to what it was when my grandfather was my age. I want us to have the kind of prestige we had then. If I ever have children, I want something of value to pass on to them, the same way my father wanted something of value to pass on to me."

Gary wanted me to understand his ambitions, but they were alien to me. I felt a bit squeamish, like a voyeur peeking into emotions I couldn't share. "You have a very nice practice," I said without much conviction.

He waved his hand impatiently. "I don't want nice. I want great. I want to consult with heads of industry. With Presidents! Bonnie, I was born into a prominent family, I went to the best schools. I was handed a law-firm partnership by a father who wanted the best for me. And now I owe him something in return. Wherever he is, if there is a chance he can look back on the firm, I want him to see it hasn't been a total loss."

I didn't think there was much chance of Gary's father being able to look back, but Gary wasn't interested in debating the possibility of an afterlife. I felt sorry for him. Love and duty were all mixed up inside him, churning around. Albert's death had had a strange effect. He was bent over the wheel, his head resting in his hands. "Would you like me to drive?" I finally asked.

"No, no. I'm fine." Straightening, he looked at his watch. "You're right, though. We better get going. It wouldn't do for me to disappear for the afternoon with my office manager, would it? Might shock my partners."

I settled back into my seat, bracing for a jackrabbit takeoff.

"Although, Bonnie, I am the boss." The smile he gave me looked forced. "If you'd like, we could forget about the office for the afternoon. Maybe get something to eat, have a drink. One for the road, for Albert."

What a depressing idea that was. Gary had tried to make the invitation sound lighthearted, but he didn't succeed. His words and the expression on his face were packed with longing.

"I better get straight back to the office," I said. My voice was overly stern, and right away I felt guilty.

"I can't talk you into it?"

"Not today. I'll take a rain check, though."

"Good enough," he said. "Maybe dinner one night?"

"Great," I said, with more enthusiasm than I felt.

We pulled back onto the highway, and whatever was going on in Gary's fevered imagination soon excited him to the point where we were crossing the Bronx at about ninety miles an hour, changing lanes at random.

"Gary, would you mind driving a little slower. You're frightening me."

"Come on, Bonnie. I know how to handle a car. Fast cars and fast women." He chuckled at his little joke. The black cloud of despair that had hovered over him moments before seemed to have dissipated. As we drove into Manhattan, heavy traffic forced him to slow up. "Just look at that skyline," he said. "Nothing like it. Have you ever heard that expression, 'If you can make it in New York, you can make it anywhere'?"

I nodded absently.

"Well, Bonnie, I have the feeling my time has come to make it here. Big! By the way, how are you feeling about the city these days? Liking it any more than you used to? I remember when you were ready to throw in the towel with New York and head for the suburbs?"

Boy, he was manic that afternoon. His thoughts were jumping all over the place. My occasional fear and loathing of New York City was something I'd sort of stopped talking about. The thing is, if there is one subject guaranteed to provoke a bout of self-pity in me, it is the all-too-likely prospect of my penniless old age, spent in the most expensive, dangerous city on earth. In my blackest moments I picture myself doddering, drooling, maneuvering my walker through empty whiskey bottles onto the median strip between the lanes on Broadway to take my daily air surrounded by bus exhaust, winos, and thieves.

I shrugged. "I must be getting used to it. It doesn't seem so scary anymore. Not that I wouldn't like a nice little house in the country, with a lawn, but it would probably take something awful to get me to make a move like that."

"Well, let's hope nothing like that ever happens. You know, I'll bet that's why you went out with that detective. Your subconscious need for protection," he said thoughtfully. "I better warn you. The only cops who ever make any money are the ones on the take. Awful hours, too. No home lives."

"Gary, all I did was have dinner with the guy." Gary had done a complete about-face. We were once again in "good buddy" mode, and from the direction he was trying to steer this conversation in, I could tell I was about to get some brotherly advice, like it or not.

"Like I've said before, you're old enough to know what you're doing, but I can't understand why you continue to choose men who are bound to disappoint you. Like that last character. Hightower. The polo wimp. Say, do you remember the time Emory threatened to kill Albert?"

"He didn't threaten to kill him. Let's talk about something else." Good grief! Fifteen minutes earlier it had looked like I was going to have to call the men with butterfly nets to take Gary away, and now here he was, playing the wise elder with me.

"Sure, Bonnie," he said. "But I wouldn't be your friend if I didn't warn you about cops. From what I've heard, they won't hesitate to take advantage of women. Use them for their own ends. With someone as vulnerable as you are. . . ."

To my relief, we had finally hit the familiar streets of midtown. For me, this ride had been one unbroken misery. "Would you cut it out!" I snapped. "I'm not as dumb as you think. Everything you say has already occurred to me. But you know what? I enjoyed talking about the case—the body, prints, all the rest of it. After all, I didn't kill Albert. I'd like to see the murderer caught, too."

"What's 'the rest of it'?"

Tony had asked me not to say anything about the condition Albert's body had been in when found. It wasn't something I would have discussed with Gary anyway. Experience had taught me to avoid any mention of the undressed human body with him. God knows, even a dead one might have set him off.

"Nothing much." I told him, then, about this idea I'd had—

that we might try role-playing at the office, going through Albert's movements on that last day, maybe with Miss Peterson's help. "We might even find out where he could have hidden something."

"What makes you think he hid something?"

"Whoever searched the hotel room didn't do it for nothing. I wonder if the police thought to search Albert's car? It was right out there on the street."

"I should hope so. That's their job. I wouldn't be surprised if it was drugs. No particular reason, but can't you see a guy like Albert, getting older, deciding to experience life while he could?"

"Maybe." I didn't believe drugs for a minute, but Gary obviously wanted to preserve Albert's memory as a "pretty cool dude."

We were pulling into the garage near the office when I remembered the spitting grandmother. I repeated the story to Gary.

"And? What's that supposed to mean?"

"Don't you see? She may be someone connected with the murder."

Gary laughed. "We've been working you too hard, Bonnie. She was probably someone with a grudge against the priest or someone with a right-of-way gripe. That church is sitting on a gold mine. Property values in Connecticut are out of sight. Or it could be—"

"Enough! Just one more thing," I said as we walked across Lexington. "What about the reward? I haven't heard anything."

"I wasn't aware there was one. Is there?"

"There has to be, with his family, and the firm. There's always a reward when someone rich is killed. How could there not be a reward?"

"Very easily. And, Bonnie"—Gary touched my elbow—"let's talk later, to firm up dinner. You know, there are a lot of places in this city I'm sure you haven't tried. And a lot of things," he added suggestively.

"Sure," I said. Like necrophilia, slam dancing, swimming in the East River . . .

That afternoon I did one thing of note. It occurred to me as I was locking up my desk for the day. I dialed Stamford Information and got the number for the Connecticut Department of Motor Vehicles. The phone there rang a dozen times and I was about to forget it when an unpleasant man answered. I know he had his jacket on and was about to step out the door.

"My car was struck in a parking lot today. The other driver drove away but I got the license number," I said. "Can I get you to check the owner?"

"Not now, lady. Give me your name and address and the plate number and we'll send you the information."

As far as first dates go, I've run into so many aberrations that I no longer entertain high hopes. Still, I can't simply give up.

6:55 P.M.: I buzzed Tony into the building, and opened my door a minute later to a moderately attractive, reasonably dressed, and perfectly respectable first date. At the same time, the Codwalladers' door opened and Eunice walked into the hall carrying an oversized bag of garbage to the incinerator room. She wore pink scuffs and had a lavender net around her hair. She looked at Tony. He looked back at her. "Umph!" she said. I quickly hustled him in and closed the door behind him.

"What do you suppose 'Umph' means?" he asked, grinning at me.

"I think a loose translation is 'Disgraceful.'"

"That's what I thought." He walked into my living room. "Nice place you have here. Great view. And a big cat. Friendly, too." Moses was already trying to climb up Tony's pants leg. "What's his name?"

"Moses. Just push him off."

"No. That's all right. I like cats. Named after someone you knew?"

"Very funny. I found him in the weeds by the Hudson."

"I had a cat until recently. A little orange fellow. Friendly, like this guy. Not an ounce of meanness in him." Tony stooped down to scratch Moses' head. Moses, who knows a good thing when he sees one, collapsed onto his back so he could get his fat tummy rubbed.

"And?" I asked as I slipped on my jacket.

"He died." It seemed for a second as if he was going to go on, but then, suddenly, he stood up and shook his head. "You must think I'm a lot of fun. Everything I talk about is dead."

I laughed. "I guess it gets to be a habit."

We were on our way out when the phone rang. It was my mother. I think she has this sixth sense that lets her know when I have a man in my apartment.

"Bonnie Jean. I'm glad I got you at home. I wanted to tell you the good news about Raymond and Noreen. I tried to get you earlier."

"I work, Mom. Remember? What's his holiness done now?" Raymond is my younger brother. He's at heaven's door, if you listen to my mother.

"Oh, the way you talk! They're expecting again. He and Noreen. That boy. He makes me so proud." Her voice had a musical lilt in it.

"Again! That's three times in four years. How awful. She's nothing but a brood mare. Haven't they heard of birth control out there?"

"Bonnie Jean, it's no wonder you never remarried. Men don't like attitudes like yours. Raymond's a fine provider. He's got a good thing going with that garage. If you had any sense . . . you remember a few years back, when Ronnie Bosgrave from the grocery store was interested in you? He was a good catch. He owns it all now. Bought out the old man who ran it."

Ronnie Bosgrave had red hair, green freckles, and ears that

stuck out at right angles from his head. The last time he showed any interest in me was when he asked me to the senior prom. I went, instead, with a Marlon Brando—type who rode a Harley Davidson. Mom tells me he came to a bad end.

"Ronnie married that Filbrook girl. Ugly as sin. You could have hooked him if . . ."

Tony had retreated to the kitchen. Moses was right on his heels.

". . . and Raymond wants you to come for Easter dinner, with a date."

"Sure, Mom. Can I call you in the morning? I've got company."

"Company? A date? Is he nice? What does he do for a living?"

"He's a brain surgeon, Mom." I heard Tony guffaw. We were both laughing as we left the apartment.

We drove to a small art theater in the Village for a double feature: *Kiss Me Deadly* and *Kiss of Death*. Three hours of kissing and dying, and to be honest, that part of the evening was such a shock to me I couldn't have told you the first thing about either movie ten minutes after we left the theater.

What happened is, we ran into Emory Hightower. I'm usually pretty blasé about potentially embarrassing public confrontations, having brazened my way through many of them, but I wasn't prepared for this encounter with the object of my earlier lie. I never thought I'd run into Emory at a detective double feature anyway. His disdain for detective fiction was no secret. I guess what tripped me up was that these movies were old enough to qualify as art.

The first feature, whatever it was, was all right. A little ponderous, actually, but I didn't care. Tony shifted and bumbled a bit, until his fingertips rested lightly on my shoulder. It was a feeling I thought I might be able to get used to. When intermission came we strolled out to the refreshment counter, chatting easily about the film. I was beginning to feel comfortable with him. We were standing in line waiting to buy popcorn and sodas, talking, flirting with the delicate shifts in mood you find in new relationships. Then, behind me, I heard an all-too-familiar honey-drool male voice:

"Princess," it drawled, "why don't you go ahead and get us seats. I'll get the popcorn. On the right aisle. And be sure they're clean this time. It took two dry cleanings to get that gum off. . . ."

Glancing back over my shoulder, I caught a brief glimpse—enough to recognize the vision in tweed as Emory Hightower. The smart thing for me to do would have been to keep my back to him, get the popcorn, and skulk back to my seat, but I wanted so badly to get a look at this "Princess" of his that I turned and stared, transfixed, until Emory noticed me. Princess was long gone.

"Why, Bonnie! How nice to see you." He stepped out of line and pushed his way in behind us. That guy had so much nerve. "And Detective LaMarca?" Emory's double take didn't become him. "I didn't expect to see you again this soon. Particularly not in such charming company. What a pleasant surprise."

I'll just bet it was. He bent to give me a brotherly kiss on the cheek, then extended his hand to Tony. As he did, I noticed that he stretched himself up to his tallest, putting him a good four inches over Tony. Tony, in turn, straightened his shoulders and narrowed the gap by a couple of inches. Suddenly I was in the land of the giants.

"You're in good company here, Detective. Bonnie's quite a girl."

What pap. I was probably beet red. Tony said, "Yes, I know," and placed a protective arm of ownership around my waist. Emory averted his eyes. Then the three of us stood there, trapped in this paralysis of good will until the woman at the concession stand broke it up.

"Next. *Next!*"

"You know," Emory said, "they have the most marvelous popcorn here."

"But not like that popcorn in Marseilles," I responded. Blinking lights announced the start of the next feature.

"How 'marvelous' can popcorn be?" Tony asked as we returned to our seats.

"That's the way he talks." We settled down to watch the next feature. I guess Tony watched. It was completely lost on me. I spent the entire time taking surreptitious looks around the rows of darkened seats, hoping to spot Emory and the Princess. I never did.

Tony took my hand as we left the theater. What a nice gesture it seemed, for a minute. Until he surprised me:

"When you were going out with Hightower, did you ever hear him say anything about Janowski? Other than what you told me?"

His hand tightened on mine. He probably thought I was going to run. Actually, I was startled into near honesty.

"Not much more than any of the other associates said. Emory didn't like Albert, but none of the other associates did, either."

"And that scene at the swimming pool, that happened just the way you told me? And then you went out with Hightower for months and never heard him say anything else about Janowski?" Tony stopped walking, turned, and looked at me. "Bonnie, is there a reason for you to feel protective?"

"Of course not." No getting around it; he'd caught my lie. I've always heard the best defensive is a good offensive. I counterattacked: "How did you find out, anyway?"

"At least three people at your office told me, one of my men showed Hightower's picture to your neighbors and they recognized him, Hightower's super recognized a picture of you, Mrs. Janowski said you and Hightower had gone down to the Islands on vacation. . . ." His voice was so casual we might have been discussing the weather instead of my past, but we had once again crossed that fine line between romance and interrogation. I should have been feeling guilty, but I felt like the injured party, and I was furious. I yanked my hand out of his and looked at him with narrowed eyes.

"Down to the Islands? Stephanie told you that? It was up. Up to one nasty little island. And I never told anyone at the office but Gary. What a bunch of damned gossips. And what are you doing running around showing my picture to everyone in town? Those old biddies down the hall would swear under oath that I entertained the Marquis de Sade, and Emory's super is usually so drunk he wouldn't recognize his own mother."

"I'm sorry you're so upset, Bonnie, but if you'd been honest with me from the start, I wouldn't have been flashing your picture around."

"Oh, I know." I started walking again, fast. Tony caught up with me. "Frankly, I still don't think Emory did it," I said. "He isn't the type to kill someone. It's not his style. The fact that I went out with him has nothing to do with that."

"I didn't say he did it. I'm only doing my job. This is as hard for me as it is for you."

"Sure it is." Softening my tone a little, I asked, "Does Emory have an alibi?"

"Alibi? Everyone always has an alibi. He said he was doing research, at the Bar Association Library. The librarian said she might have seen him, but she's not sure. A guy like that, looks like a million other guys."

Emory didn't look like a million other guys to me, but the Bar Association Library bit was definitely baloney. Emory didn't know where the Bar Association was, and if he had, he would have avoided it like the plague.

"What about the other people I told you about: that secretary and the messenger?"

"Nothing there. The secretary is married now. Moved to Philly eighteen months ago. The messenger—Tate—we've got a yellow sheet on him a mile long. Mostly small stuff, though. Burglary. He was uptown with his parole officer from five-thirty to almost seven that evening, then he met two other guys. Had a couple beers at a bar on Eighth Avenue and then went to a Rangers' game."

It was a cold trail, he told me, and getting colder. "New

cases every day, not enough men. You keep spreading yourself thinner and thinner, trying to break things that look like repeaters. Something like Janowski—seems like a one-time thing—gets put aside pretty fast."

We started walking, more slowly this time. Once again he took my hand. "You still mad?" he said.

"I'm not sure."

A warm scent of spring hung on the night air, and the Village street was dotted with couples laughing and necking on stairways. The smell of marijuana floated past us. Tony didn't seem to notice. There were some backless benches in a little park near the New School. Tony guided me to one and we sat down. He swung his leg over the bench so that he faced me. His eyes were deep brown pools and I could feel his pulse beating in his palm. He brushed my hair from my forehead and the air between us was suddenly charged.

It may be the oldest police ploy in the world, but he swept away my anger and resentment, as easily and quietly as a mist from the Hudson sweeps across Manhattan. I repeated Emory's threat, verbatim. I told about driving without a license, about that miserable island. I confessed that Emory's hound's-tooth sports jacket, with the suede elbows, was still in my foyer closet. Tony didn't take any notes while I talked. He just kept looking at me with those big brown eyes. Who knows? Maybe I'm just the biggest sucker in the world. I finished by trying to explain myself: "The thing is, I didn't want you to think I'd gone out with a murderer."

"Oh. So you do think Emory did it." Tony's fingers rubbed against mine, kneading softly. Generally I don't have much trouble deciphering gestures like that, but I was confused.

"No. But I thought you did."

"I never said that. You don't happen to know if he had a gun around, do you? Ever see one at his place?"

"Yes!" I remembered it suddenly. "Yes, he did. I'd forgotten. Really."

"I believe you."

"It had been his great-grandfather's. He claimed three carpetbaggers had been killed with it. 'The Colonel's Revenge,' Emory called it."

"I don't think that's what we're looking for. Janowski was killed with a .38-caliber Smith and Wesson, the kind of gun you can pick up on the street if you have a connection. Did Hightower ever use drugs, that you know of?"

"No. He didn't use drugs. Just wine. Emory is kind of a wine snob."

"I'll bet." Tony stood up, pulling me after him. "What's your favorite food?"

"Lobster. Up at the Cape, or the Maine coast."

"Right. With waves slapping against the wharf, and the smell of salt water in the air."

"You've got it," I said.

"Well"—he looked at his watch—"at eleven-thirty on a Friday night, in the middle of Manhattan, how do you feel about pizza?"

"Pizza's my second favorite."

We were as quiet as two human beings could be getting off the elevator and walking down the hall to my apartment. At least two human beings who've demolished one small pizza and one big carafe of red wine. Certainly not quiet enough for the Codwallader sisters. As I put my key in the lock, I heard their door open as far as their safety chain would allow. Maybe since the police had visited them, they'd decided to keep a log on my comings and goings.

"A drink?" I asked. "Or coffee?"

"Depends." Tony opened the door to the foyer closet and instantly picked Emory's jacket out. "This it?" He started going through the pockets.

"What do you think you're going to find?" I walked over next to him.

"I don't know. Maybe I'll find some money. This is an expensive jacket." He rubbed the wool.

"You won't find any money because I already looked for that. There was a token. I took it. Depends on what?"

"What depends on what?" He looked at me, baffled.

"What? We sound like Abbott and Costello. I asked you if you wanted a drink or coffee, and you said, 'Depends.'"

It was dim in the foyer. Tony dropped the jacket and put his arms on my shoulders. "Depends on whether I'm going to be doing any more driving tonight."

"I'll fix us drinks."

As somebody once said, the rest is history.

Through the blinds the morning light was soft butter yellow. I turned over and curled myself around Tony's body. He was warm and solid. I felt better than I had in a long time. He opened one eye, then slipped his arm around me.

"What time is it?"

I squinted over his shoulder. "A little before nine. Why?"

"I have to pick up my kids at noon."

"Yuck!"

"Hey! They're not bad kids. You got something against kids?" Rolling over, he pinned me down and started tickling me.

To make a long story short, he didn't leave my apartment until eleven forty-five.

As we were saying goodbye, he asked me if I'd do something for him. He tried to make it look like it had just occurred to him, but even in my gaga state, I knew better.

"Could you talk to that woman in your office—Peterson? The one who's been there forever. See if you can find out anything about the picnic. . . ."

"I've told you everything."

"No. Not last year's picnic. The 1962 picnic, when Sneed drowned. I'm curious. Just pick her mind a little. She seems willing enough to talk."

"Miss Peterson's more than willing to talk. And I should do this without letting her know I'm doing it. Right? Like an undercover agent?" This was sounding better and better.

"Sure. But don't go too far. You don't have to wear a false

nose or anything." He gave me a long kiss. "Tomorrow I have to fly up to Buffalo."

"Buffalo?"

"I'm testifying at a trial up there on Monday. I'll call you tomorrow night from my hotel. Okay?"

"Okay."

Someone finally came up with a few dollars reward money. And don't think for a second it was Albert's tightwad firm or his heartbroken family. A notice was buried on the last page of the *Sunday Times* Metropolitan Section: "A twenty-thousand dollar reward has been offered by the Association of the Bar of the City of New York for information leading to the arrest and conviction. . . ." The notice mentioned that another $10,000 had been put up by Albert Janowski's club.

I was drinking a cup of coffee and wondering, just in case, whether that $30,000 was tax-free when my new best friend on earth, Stephanie Kellogg Janowski, called.

"Hi, Bonnie. Did I get you up?" How chipper she was. Her one week of grieving was obviously over.

"No. I get up early."

"I was thinking about how much we wanted to get together. Do you ride?"

"Ride?" Certainly not, and I didn't remember us wanting to get together all that much, either.

"Horses. Some friends of mine are in the Orient. They asked if I'd exercise their horses for them. In Central Park. It's a gorgeous day. Would you like to join me?"

"Thanks, Stephanie, but I better not. I haven't been on a horse in years. I'd probably break my neck. And I was planning to clean my oven today." That, in fact, was true.

"Come on, Bonnie. Ovens clean themselves. I won't take no for an answer. Maxi's gentle as a lamb. An old plow horse. You'll see. We can have lunch at the Tavern. What do you say?"

The boss's daughter, the dead man's wife, and me with my new interest in detection. I told her yes. She said she'd pick me up in an hour.

From the beginning the outing had disaster written all over it. I do not ride. When pressed, I will sit on a horse and allow it to do with me as it will, but I get no satisfaction from trying to assert myself over foul-tempered, smelly animals that outweigh me by a ton. And those people who ride in the Park are not your good old down-on-the-farm set. They wear boots that cost more than my winter wardrobe. As for the Tavern, those of you who are unfamiliar with New York City may be picturing a homey little inn where the gang sits around pitchers of beer swapping horse stories. It is nothing like that. Tavern on the Green is one of the spiffiest places around. I'd always wanted to go there, though not necessarily with Stephanie Janowski.

Could it be that Stephanie was lonely? That she relished my company? That she was suffering from cabin fever and needed to get away for a few hours and I was the only person she could come up with who was willing to get on a horse? None of those reasons sounded right to me.

An hour later we were roaring down Riverside Drive in Stephanie's wonderful little yellow sports car, the wind blowing our hair. Like she had promised, it was a beautiful day, the air warm and clear. Stephanie kept up the easy banter of someone accustomed to making polite conversation.

". . . and you wouldn't believe the bathing suits down there, Bonnie. Absolutely nothing to them. I was positively obese. I'm thinking of joining a spa. You know, when you get to be our age. . . ."

Which of our ages she referred to I wasn't sure, but I giggled and grinned my way through the ride downtown.

We turned onto West 89th Street and Stephanie parked the car. As I followed her across the street to the stable I noticed how perfect her outfit was, from the top of her little jockey cap to the tip of her handmade boots. In deference to the occasion I had tucked my cords into my boots, but I wouldn't have fooled a soul.

The young man at the stable greeted Stephanie warmly. Rumor said she lacked "standards," and certainly nobody would have looked twice at her dead husband, but in her defense this was a very attractive young man. Possibly a college student; not much older. They giggled together for a moment out of my hearing, over some private joke.

"Bonnie, I'm going to the office and get something settled here about . . . the Von Lapps' horses. I'll only be a minute. You can go take a look at Maxi if you want. He's over there."

She waved her arm to the right and disappeared with the young man through a door marked "Private," to consult over the Von Lapps' accounts, I have no doubt.

The day promised, at best, to be one of those bizarre ones when you're forced to smile until your jaw feels arthritic. I'm not sure what Miss Manners has to say about mourning periods, and I'm aware that social strictures have relaxed during the last half century, but Stephanie's husband of twenty-some years had been in the ground less than a week and here she was tooling around Manhattan with the happy abandon of a madcap heiress in search of the good life.

I wandered back in the direction she had indicated. On either side were stalls, some empty, others with horses doing horse things, mostly eating. Each stall had a name plaque: ARGONAUT, RANGER, PRISSIE. I examined each one in search of Maxi.

THE BARON MAXIMILIAN VON LAPP. A terrible dread swept over me. Where I come from people name their plow horses Dusty or Sugar, not The Baron something. When I was a kid, Raymond and I used to ride Minnie, the neighbor's horse. We would climb on double and kick and yell like fiends to get Minnie to the far end of the pasture away from her oats. When we gave the raging beast her head, she—seventeen, fat, and always hungry—would make a lumbering U-turn and trot, stiff-legged, head low, back to the barn. Now, there was a real plow horse.

A good look at the Baron Maxi did little to comfort me. True, he had a little paunch, and there was a comfortable-looking sway to his back, but the problem was, he was a big horse, one of the tallest in the stable. Also, he was black as midnight. That struck me as ominous.

It was love at first sight for Baron Maxi. The moment he saw me, he turned his giant body around, stuck his head over the railing, and began slobbering on my shoulder. I was having none of that. I jumped back. Too late. There was a big smear of horse drool on my sweater.

"Great. You found him." Stephanie and the young man were walking toward me carrying saddles. Her cheeks were pink and I don't think it was the weight of the saddle. I wiped at the drool with my sleeve.

"What do you think? Isn't he a beauty?"

"I'm not sure. How big is the other one?"

I was dead serious but it struck the pair of them as hilarious.

"Size has nothing to do with it, Bonnie."

Ha!

Stephanie was riding the delicate, doe-eyed Prissie. I cast an envious look her way.

"You wouldn't want to trade. Trust me, Bonnie. Maxi's a lamb."

I doubted that very much. I had to be helped into the little English saddle, and once up there, I found there was nothing to hold on to. Stephanie's friend made a big production of adjusting my stirrups. He thought they were about right when my knees were level with my waist.

Stephanie waved goodbye to him and we were off.

"Peter's good-looking, isn't he?" she said.

"Sure is," I answered, Peter totally forgotten. Fear leaves no room for other feelings. From my precarious perch the ground looked a mile away.

In all fairness to Maxi, he behaved himself like the old gentleman he was. Stephanie and Prissie danced and stirred up dust around us. They raced ahead and then back in a maniac sweaty frenzy. "Use the switch, Bonnie. He'll move. You have to switch him."

"No thanks. We'll just stroll along for a while." I patted Maxi on the neck and he turned and smeared my pants with more dribble. We were establishing a nice rapport.

"All right," she said. "I'm going to go on ahead. I'll meet you at the Tavern in a few minutes."

Maxi had a nice rolling walk, like a comfortable old rocking chair. The sun, shining through the canopy of branches over me, warmed my back. Now I was never, for a minute, silly enough to think I was part of that world. Yet it was so easy to slip into a fantasy. None of the passersby knew it was a borrowed horse. "Look at her," I imagined them saying. "Must be filthy rich." I took a chance and smiled at one of those grim, skinny joggers you see everywhere. He smiled back.

Stephanie had probably been waiting ten minutes. I saw her before she saw me, through the hedge at the back of the Tavern in a pretty frame of green. She was pacing the restaurant entrance and slapping her boot with her whip like a Luftwaffe ace. Her expression was hostile and tense.

"Well, here you are." The Junior League smile returned with a skeletal stretch.

There was a bottleneck by the restaurant door. A birthday party, all expensive dark suits, spring pastels, and good cheer, pushed me into an unwelcome intimacy with the widow. She scowled at the birthday boy and I think she must have shoved him because he turned around and looked at her, brows set in an indignant line.

"They shouldn't allow children in here," she said, not bothering to lower her voice. "By the way, Bonnie"—she paused to exchange glares with the boy's mother—"how's your new boyfriend? Detective LaMarca? Dad says you're a 'hot item.' That's his expression, not mine. He's not bad-looking. I've always heard Italian men are good in bed." Her shrill boarding-school voice rose with every syllable. The boy and his mother both looked at me this time.

"He's fine." It was all I could manage. Unless my apartment was bugged, Old Mr. K thought we were a "hot item" on the basis of an afternoon cab ride. I wouldn't have put it past Gary to say something like that to Mr. K, but Gary couldn't have known I'd gone out with Tony a second time.

"Well, enjoy," she said. "Underpaid civil servants are not for me."

It hadn't entered my mind that Stephanie and I were in competition, but I was not so dazzled by my surroundings that I missed her suggestion. Was Tony hers for the asking? Had he too gone all mushy at whatever it was she had?

"Did he tell you he thinks I killed my husband?"

That one left me speechless. I was staring into space, already terribly sorry I wasn't cleaning my oven, when she attracted the maitre d's attention.

"Why, Mrs. Janowski. How lovely to see you again." Almost as an afterthought he drew his face out to the proper length and said, "So sorry about poor Mr. Janowski. An incredible loss. Tragic."

That seemed to be a matter of opinion, but Stephanie managed to put on an appropriately long face for a second.

"Let me see." He consulted a list. "We have a window table in the Garden Room. Will that be satisfactory?"

Satisfactory? If I had been with anyone else, it would have been like walking into Nirvana. The room glimmered with the incandescence of crystal chandeliers reflecting through frosted mirrors and polished brass fixtures. Fresh flowers were everywhere. Our table was by a corner L in the building, so that through the window in front of me I could catch glimpses of the birthday party in the next room, and hear the faint echo of their music.

Our waiter was young and imperious. "May I recommend the cold poached salmon" was proffered with a disdainful tone and an expression that suggested he wouldn't have touched the nasty fish himself.

Stephanie ordered that, "and a bloody Mary, now please."

"Scrambled eggs and bacon," I said, "and a white wine spritzer." It was the cheapest thing on the menu and promptly stamped me as petty bourgeoise.

"I want you to understand, Bonnie, that I didn't kill him." She stopped toying with a crystal vase of daffodils on the table to pull a gold cigarette case from her pocket.

"I'm sure you didn't."

"Your boyfriend isn't, is he?"

"We haven't discussed it." What with him being Italian and so good in bed, there just hasn't been time . . .

"What about you, Bonnie? Who do you suspect?"

"Stephanie, it's something I haven't thought about." By then I was not kidding myself about having fun. With "Happy Birthday to Danny" coming from the next room, I was starting to feel like a guest at the mad tea party.

"I didn't care enough about Albert to kill him." She beat her cigarette on the table a moment before a waiter appeared out of nowhere to light it. When he had gone, she took a long drag and went on. "Albert and I went our own ways. To kill someone, there has to be feeling. Unless you're a psychopath. Don't you agree?"

It's something I hadn't given much thought to, but I nodded. She turned to look through the window at the party, giving me a chance to study her. Mid-forties, maybe. A cap of short, gray-flecked brown hair, light eyes, a face made of angles and planes, a vicious little bit of an overbite, and a surprisingly pugnacious chin. A carefully dieted, expensively groomed package that did nothing at all for me.

"Remember the girls who 'had to get married'? Does that

bring back your cheerleader days, Bonnie? Well, I was one of them. Seventeen, going to a private school in Virginia with a reputation for dealing with difficult young women. Unfortunately, I ran into my greatest difficulty there. A visiting chemistry instructor. He was married. This story's such a cliché, isn't it?"

I said nothing.

"I remember standing in a phone booth, crying, telling my parents. 'That's all right, Stephanie. We'll take care of it.' That's what my father said. I thought he meant a year abroad. But what do you suppose I found waiting for me when I got home, standing there in the living room like he owned the place? Albert. The first time I saw him, he was outlined by the sunset through the terrace window, and I thought he looked like a big white garden slug. I can't imagine how many rocks they turned over before they dug him out. The son of a client, third-year law. . . ."

She stopped, which was fine with me. With the most unobtrusive movements, the stuffy waiter was sliding our lunches onto the table.

"Doesn't this look good," I said. It looked like a million other plates of eggs and bacon, but I carried on about it, hoping to change the subject.

"Our honeymoon! Fourteen days on St. Thomas. I'd thought I'd go crazy."

"How's your salmon?"

An impatient look crossed her face. "Bonnie, I cannot tell you. . . ."

She certainly tried hard enough, repeating her disagreeable story as if there was something special about it. A difficult pregnancy, a cranky baby, the problem finding a reliable nursemaid, and then, that done, the deadening boredom of her marriage.

As she spoke, I could feel, hear, even see some fundamental change in her. Her voice hardened, lines deepened at the corners of her eyes. Everything about her melded into something bitter and ugly. For a moment it chilled me. Finally she snuffed the cigarette roughly in the ash tray and began picking at her salmon.

"For the first year my mother and I decorated. You know what that's like? Three months you shop for the perfect sofa, and then six for the perfect painting to go over it. You take trips—little galleries you've heard about in Massachusetts. You comb through Soho and Fifty-seventh Street. And when you finally find it, you're afraid to buy it because if you do you won't be able to look for it anymore. And one day— you've dreaded it without knowing why—the house is finished. Filled up. And then you know why. I took up hobbies. Golf, tennis, throwing pots, for God's sake!" She flipped her hand through the air; another drink was there in seconds.

If her tale of woe was a cry for sympathy from me, it wasn't working. I've known too many women who haven't had nursemaids, reliable or otherwise, who've been back at their desks six weeks after the baby was born. She told me Albert was a pitiful lover, and had "no game of tennis at all." I wondered how it would have been if he'd been a pitiful worker, with no salary at all. What about the powerlessness poverty might have added to her boredom? Perfect paintings, indeed!

"Did you ever think of finding a job?" I think I said it nicely, trying to sound concerned rather than disgusted.

"A job?" Her eyebrows shot up. "Hardly!"

She went on: "One day I was at my parents' place, sitting on the terrace, aimless. They had a gardener. A Greek kid. I watched him for a while. He took off his shirt. The sun was on his back and I could see the shine of his sweat. My husband's skin always felt like something that had just come out of the refrigerator. A Jell-O mold. Cold and clammy. I visited my mother a lot after that. Spent hours peeking through the curtains at the kid like I was some crazy old woman. I was nineteen years old. One morning when Mother had gone out, I got up my nerve." She was rubbing her hands then, thumbs against the flat of her fingers. "I called to him out one of the bedroom windows and asked if he'd come up and help me fix something. He did.

"Later, by the time I was mature enough to consider a divorce, Albert was a partner in the firm. It would have been so messy. So, I went my way and he went his."

I had hardly touched my meal, but my appetite was gone. Through the corner window I could see the party next door. It was getting lively. Strains of an Israeli folk song drifted through the air and dancers flashed by in pastel twirls.

"He was such a jerk," she went on, "right to the end. Do you know what he told me? He said he had information that was going to 'shake the skeletons out of Ely Sneed's closets.' After all the firm had done for him. What an ingrate!"

"When did Albert say that?"

The grin she gave me was almost a sneer. "I see LaMarca doesn't tell you everything, after all. Well, the Tuesday before he was killed, Albert got home late, all worked up about something. That's when he said it, right out of the blue. I spoke to my father later that night and told him. Dad said he couldn't imagine what Albert's problem was." She laughed bitterly. "Apart from the obvious, of course. Albert was such a tight-ass. Who knows! Maybe he caught one of the associates charging an extra taxi ride to the firm. Boy, I'll bet they're glad he's gone. None of them could stand him. Nobody could."

"I liked him, and he and Gary were close." The first was a lie, but I had this crazy desire to defend Albert.

"You didn't. You couldn't have. He was repulsive. And Gary! One big walking wet dream. He'll never grow up. What a fine pair they were: the perpetual adolescent with his yoga and all that other nonsense. You know, Bonnie, Gary Petit is the only man I ever knew who actually bought a Nehru jacket. And Albert? The man was geriatric when he was twenty-five."

I was tired of pretending this was a conversation. "Shall I ask for our checks?"

"Before you do, I'd like to suggest something. Your detective friend, LaMarca"—she leaned across the table; not intimately, aggressively—"when he called me in Aruba and told me what had happened to Albert, my reaction was, What a damned embarrassment. And then I started thinking about it. You know, I can have a nice life now, Bonnie. I'm the wronged wife whose husband was killed cheating on her. Maybe I can make something new for myself. The kid is in college. I can manage the respectable widow business for a while, and then maybe a better marriage. Something more appropriate. I have simple needs. Maybe I'll busy myself in the arts. Or travel. There are a lot of options for a respectable widow with money. But the key is reputation. I don't want to be laughed at. I don't want my name in the papers again unless it's on the society page. Do you understand now?"

"No, as a matter of fact, I don't know why you're telling me any of this." I half-stood and looked for our waiter.

"Your detective friend questioned me with less than good manners about where I was the night my husband was killed. I didn't care to tell him."

The edge in her voice made me look down at her. She was clutching the arms of her chair, white-knuckled with an expression of primitive, cold fury. I almost expected her to leap across the table and try to strangle me.

"What some boorish cop thinks of me is not important. What is important is my future. I intend to endure no more bad publicity in connection with my name, and if your boyfriend isn't willing to accept what is obvious to everyone else—that Albert got himself killed going to hookers—Detective LaMarca may find himself back in Vice where he started. And you can also tell him that the woman he's had following me isn't very good at her work."

I waved frantically to our waiter. When he finally looked my way, I drew a big check in the air with my hand. The corners of his mouth sank.

"He may be taking the Captain's Test, you know, Bonnie.

You'd be surprised at how much influence my family still has, and it's foolish of him, and you, to assume we're in the same position as the firm. You like your job, don't you? Then don't underestimate me. Think of it as a sign of our friendship. You use your influence to keep LaMarca out of my hair, away from my friends, and I'll use mine to keep him where he is and you where you are. And when the Captain's Test comes around, who knows. . . ."

We left the Tavern in a frosty silence. I would have walked straight to the subway but for two things: I couldn't afford to lose my job, and I felt some responsibility for Maxi.

Rain clouds from the west were blowing across the sky and a cold wind ripped through my jacket. We mounted up. I was slow, having to let the stirrups down to reach them, and then pull them back up.

"Can you move a little faster, Bonnie? I'm in kind of a hurry."

I had no intention of moving any faster than a walk. I thought—hoped—that Stephanie would run ahead and meet me at the stable. No luck. We rode abreast for a time, without speaking. Then at a narrow place on the trail she tightened her reins and dropped back.

Under oath I couldn't swear to what happened next, but I feel it in my bones. There was a sharp sound, a snap, close behind my ear. Maybe a low-lying branch, or the buzz of an insect, but I'm convinced that it was Stephanie hitting poor Baron Maxi a hard one on his backside. Whatever did it, the old boy jumped about ten feet and took off. He thrashed along at some awful jarring gait while I clung to the tiny saddle with one hand and pulled on the reins with the other. I lost one stirrup and felt myself sliding to the side. Branches slapped across my face and dust clouded around me. And then it stopped, as quickly as it had started. Maxi stood and stretched his neck into some leaves as if nothing had happened.

I straightened in the saddle and turned, shaking with anger

and fear. Stephanie was right behind me, a malignant smirk on her face.

"Why did you do that? It was stupid. I could have been hurt."

"What on earth are you talking about? Looks to me as if you're catching on. You'll be ready for the hunt in no time at all, Bonnie."

"I think I'm already ready for the hunt, Stephanie."

Her smile hardened into a block of ice.

Peter was by the stable door talking to a pretty young blonde. The breeze whipped her long hair across her face, and I saw him raise his hand and pull it back, touching her skin as he did.

"Don't they make a cute young couple?" I asked Stephanie, a heavy emphasis on "young."

After that we wasted not one breath on courtesy.

"Bonnie," she said, "I've got to get a few things settled here. If you want a ride home, you'll have to wait."

"No. I've got to do some shopping on Broadway. Thanks for the lovely day."

"You're welcome. We'll have to do it again sometime."

"Sure, Stephanie." Over my dead body. I walked toward Broadway, leaving her to settle her few things, Peter's hash probably among them. There is no sight like hindsight. I was furious with myself for not saying more than I had, and afraid I had already said too much.

Tony, as good as his word, called me that night.

"I'm sure she did it," I told him. "You should have heard her. She's crazy."

"Oh, come on. You really think she did it?" He was flirtatious and bantering, not taking me seriously. "I'd hate to think that. A good-looking woman like Mrs. Janowski, going to jail."

"Good-looking? She's hideous, black-hearted, nasty. . . . And by the way, you didn't tell me Albert had said to Stephanie that he was going to 'rattle Ely Sneed's skeletons.'"

"It slipped my mind. And I'm kidding about Mrs. Jan-owski. I miss you. I wish I was with you right now."

That sounded so good I scratched the demerit I'd just given him for "good-looking."

"It's possible I'll be up here a few days," he said. "Soon as I get back, I'll call. Probably Wednesday night. If you get a chance, don't forget to check into that thing I mentioned—the picnic."

I promised I would, but as far as I was concerned, there was no question about the murderer's identity.

"Now , if you ask me, the firm would be better off today if Mr. Sneed was still with us. I know some people didn't care for his methods, but he wouldn't have tolerated this sort of thing for a minute." Miss Peterson popped a curled carrot stick into her mouth, leaving me to decide what sort of thing she meant: surely not the restaurant.

Convinced I knew who the murderer was, and that it was only a matter of time before Stephanie Janowski was hauled off in a straitjacket, I was nevertheless, for the third time in a week, sitting in a restaurant talking about dead men. Probing Miss Peterson's vivid memory about the Sneed drowning was a joy after brunch with Stephanie. Unfortunately for me, or my wallet, when I suggested a hamburger at the Rose of Killarney, where I planned to ply Miss P with cheap liquor, she had surprised me by countering with a new, pricy little health-food place on First Avenue. "That's how I've kept my figure," she had said, smoothing double knit over nonexistent hips. "And the walk will do us good."

"Cut quite a swath with the girls, I'll tell you that. You can see it in that portrait—an awful-looking thing, isn't it?—but Mr. Sneed was a real ladies' man. Why, I remember when I won the dance contest at the Christmas party in 1961. We had live bands then. Mr. Sneed would never have settled for a record player. Well, there I was, walking up to the bandstand to pick up my prize. Dinner for two at Luchows. And what do you suppose?"

I shook my head.

"I saw him lean over and whisper something to the band leader, and they struck up 'The Most Beautiful Girl in the World.'" Her fingertips were pressed to her throat. Did her pulse race? Had there been something between Sneed and Miss Peterson? No. I battled down that idea.

"And you were there the day Mr. Sneed drowned," I said. "How awful for you." I was forking my way through a tofu grain thing that tasted even nastier than it looked.

"Yes. For all of us. Tragic. And such a scandal."

"Scandal?"

"My, yes. With poor Mr. Janowski, and . . . all."

"All?"

"Well, we were asked not to talk about it. The Management Committee, you know. But it's been so long, and I guess since it's for Mr. Decker's history . . . though I do wonder why he wants to use this. Maybe he's doing it to add color. The fact is, Mr. Sneed simply couldn't stand Mr. Janowski. Naturally, Mr. Kellogg wanted his son-in-law to become a partner, and Mr. Sneed's confidential secretary—she's no longer with us—she told me that once, during a partners' meeting, Mr. Sneed said that Mr. Janowski graduated at the bottom of his class at a fourth-rate law school, and that the firm already had enough dead wood. That man said what he thought." She blinked. "I always admire that in a man. And then, there was that incident on the day of the picnic."

"Oh?"

"This certainly isn't going to look good in the history. I can't imagine what the clients will think." She was examining a spinach leaf like she'd found something funny on it. "Rich in iron. I can only hope Mr. Decker will use some discretion. There had been such . . . bad blood, you could call it . . .

97

between Mr. Sneed and Mr. Janowski. Then, the day of the picnic, not long after we got out to the Kelloggs' home—isn't it lovely out there, Bonnie?"

"Beautiful."

"They had this little altercation. Mr. Janowski and Mr. Sneed."

"A fight?"

"Oh, I don't know if I'd call it a fight. Some of the lawyers were playing croquet in the shady spot by the terrace and Mr. Janowski accused Mr. Sneed of kicking his ball closer to the wicket. Mr. Sneed raised his mallet over his head and threatened to split poor Mr. Janowski's skull with it. Why, Bonnie, you look surprised. It was nothing like what you're thinking. No one got hurt. Mr. Sneed"—Miss Peterson began smiling at the memory—"he said Mr. Janowski had such a fat head and such a pea brain he couldn't do any damage anyway. That's all it amounted to. Exciting for the staff, though. It's not every day we get to see something like that."

"Hardly." And hardly all it amounted to, either; a few hours later one of the combatants had turned up dead.

"Then . . . oh, my. Did you see that tray of desserts? Don't they look nice. Maybe. . . ."

I pushed my tofu mess away. "Good idea, Miss Peterson. It must have been a terrible shock to all of you when Mr. Sneed drowned."

"You have no idea. It was later that afternoon. Actually, he hadn't been missed until his wife started looking for him. Please don't ever repeat this, but Mrs. Sneed was never good enough for her husband. We all suspected that she tippled. I'm sure the reason she was so worried about her husband was because she thought he was with his confidential secretary. They were rumored to be lovers. Nothing to it. I knew.

"Later on, near dark, Mr. Sneed's secretary turned up with her husband. I mean, her own husband. They had been on the golf course the entire time. People started getting worried. For a while we couldn't find Stephanie, either. Wouldn't that have been something? But," she sighed, disappointment apparent, "she turned up after a while. She had been at the greenhouse helping the gardener with his seedlings.

"We broke into little groups and searched the grounds. Finally, at around ten that night, Mr. Kellogg called the police. That's when Mrs. Sneed—no self-control at all—right there in front of the police and the whole office accused poor Mr. Janowski of murdering her husband. Stood there shaking her finger at him and screaming. And Mr. Janowski. A more upright man never lived. Oh. Now, would you look at that. What a small world it is." Her voice rose, she rose, her napkin rose and flapped through the air. "Yoo-hoo! Look, Bonnie. Do you think we could make room? The entire office is here."

It certainly was. Gary, Wilbur Decker, one of the other partners, and another gentleman, a stranger to me, had just walked in.

"Ladies." Decker, that fool, bowed from the waist when they stopped by our table. Gary, keeping in form, put a hand on my shoulder and gave a squeeze that didn't escape Miss Peterson's eagle eye.

"Heard this was quite nice," Decker said. "We thought we'd give it a try. As they say, you are what you eat."

"So true, Mr. Decker," Miss Peterson said. "Bonnie and I are enjoying this so much. Perhaps you'd like to join us? I was just telling Bonnie about Mr. Sneed's tragic accident."

A trio of lawyer mouths united in tight disapproval. The stranger watched them, then turned to us, a question on his face.

"We were talking about the history, Mr. Decker, and it kind of led around to that," I said.

"Humph. Well. . . ." Decker looked like he wanted to say something, but Gary suddenly grabbed the stranger by the arm.

"Look. There's one by the window. Let's get it before someone else does." He took off across the room, the strange man in tow. Decker and the other partner followed.

Miss Peterson nodded at the stranger. "That's Mr. Kramer,

Vice President at Fidelity Mutual Bank. Mr. Petit says Mr. Kramer's money is very important to us right now." She hesitated, then looked behind her. When she went on, it was with her voice lowered. "I'll bet you never heard about the vicious rumor that went around the firm right after Mr. Sneed died? Now"—she cautioned—"this has to remain between the two of us."

"Certainly, Miss Peterson. I wouldn't breathe a word."

"Mr. Sneed's confidential secretary told me . . ."

Miss Peterson was whispering now. I leaned over the table to hear her.

". . . there was evidence that the money the firm was holding in probate trusts had been mismanaged. After Mr. Sneed's death, a story went around that Mr. Sneed killed himself after he was caught red-handed dipping into the trusts."

Wow! This was juicy stuff, if it was true. "So whatever happened about that? How was it cleared up?"

She seemed surprised I'd asked. "Why, Bonnie, it was only gossip. No one who knew Mr. Sneed believed it. It disappeared, the way gossip always does. Never heard another word." She looked around the room absently. "You know something, Bonnie?"

Her voice was lower than ever. I couldn't wait to hear what other bomb she was going to drop.

"I do think we should have dessert. I'm going to try to catch our waitress."

It was clear Miss Peterson had nothing more to say about the trust mismanagement rumor, but I figured there was still some mileage left in Sneed's death. "You were talking about the accident."

"Was I? Oh, yes. Well, that's all there was to it. Except that Mr. Sneed's body was recovered the next afternoon. The current carried it all the way to Norwalk. Can you imagine? And that was that. And we have to remember there are two ways of looking at it, Bonnie," she added, with unexpected philosophical vacillation. "If Mr. Sneed hadn't drowned, there wouldn't be an Ely Sneed, Kellogg & Petit any more. Isn't that a paradox?"

"What do you mean?"

The story of Ely Sneed's association with Kellogg and Petit unfolded over squares of carrot cake, mine topped with a big glob of whipped cream. Mr. Sneed joined the firm in 1949 after serving as a deputy counsel to the U.S. Patent Office, and as something of a war hero in the Pacific campaign. According to Miss Peterson, he brought to the firm numerous high-level connections and a considerable reputation for derring-do.

"Rode in an open car down Fifth Avenue in a ticker-tape parade after Japan surrendered. He was right there on the *Missouri* in Tokyo Bay. Unconditional surrender."

From the look on her face you'd have thought Sneed won the war in the Pacific by himself. "I'm sure that's why they put his name first," she continued. "Reputation. Um . . . delicious, isn't it? Could I just taste that whipped cream? Bad for my weight, but. . . ."

She told me that for the first few years the firm ran smoothly. It was later, in the late fifties, when things began to sour.

"You're too young to remember, Bonnie, but there was a lot of business expansion in those days. Mr. Sneed was such a go-getter. He wanted to change things. 'Move Ely Sneed into the twentieth century.' Mr. Kellogg and Mr. Petit didn't care for that at all. They had old-fashioned ideas about doing business. Not that they weren't excellent lawyers," she went on. "In their own way they were very impressive. They thought there was something . . . tawdry . . . about Mr. Sneed's methods. Mr. Petit—he was Gary's father—said Mr. Sneed had the ethics of an ambulance chaser."

Miss Peterson said she didn't know all the details, but from what she did tell me, it was apparent that Mr. Sneed's confidential secretary hadn't taken the confidential part of her title too seriously.

"Mr. Sneed was threatening to pull out of the firm. And naturally, he would have taken so many of the clients with him. By that time he was the most respected member of the practice. There would have been nothing left. And what would you and I be doing? Why, I can't imagine life without the firm. Can you?"

"Um. . . ." There are some lies even I cannot tell.

Ely Sneed, Kellogg & Petit's first hundred years have been distinguished by a level of legal expertise and professional ethics. . . .

   The history of Ely Sneed, Kellogg & Petit is one of unparalleled achievement stretching over a full century. In 1883, when Henry Garrett Petit began his legal practice, little did he suspect . . .

. . . what an abysmal concern would carry his name a century later. I put down my pen. Like most lazy people, I am capable of working pretty quickly when faced with a job that won't go away. But I could see the pale young graduate student's point: I just couldn't get into it, either, and nothing Decker had prodded me with had been sufficient to make me "attempt" Ely Sneed's dreary past. I stuffed all the notes into a shopping bag, thinking that the subway, that groaning, crawling, broken-backed beast, might provide atmosphere.

On the way out that evening I stopped and took another look at the portrait in the lobby. Ely Sneed. Ladies' man, war hero, go-getter, rumored embezzler, caught for posterity as a little dandy with a rusty carnation in his pocket.

Heel-toe-heel-toe-heel-toe-shuffle-ball-change
Heel-toe-and-list-en-to-the-music-change

Tap dancing. I'm kidding myself when I say I do it for exercise. It may be all that stands between me and stylish stouts, but there's a lot more to it; accomplishment, rhythm, a buoyant joyfulness that takes you away from your memos and your typewriter and carries you, for an hour or two, to a place where there's nothing but the movement and the music and the beat. You can't worry and tap at the same time.

There was a time—now it seems like a hundred years ago, or something I dreamed—when I actually earned my living at it. A precarious one, true, but in the sweet security of retrospection I remember that lighthearted period when we roamed Northern California—a troop of traveling musicians and dancers—in an aging VW van held together by hope, rope, and an optimistic, it-will-be-all-right attitude that somehow never let us down, playing for quarters on street corners and in cool small-town parks. We were refugees from frying pans and textbooks, and our futures stretched only as far as the next tank of gas would take us.

That kind of abandon is hard to recapture in New York City. It's a place for ambitions and worries. Sometimes on rare evenings I would find myself driven out of control by a bit of an old song, or a Gene Kelly movie, drag my kitchen stepstool into my apartment hallway, and proceed to bring the Codwallader sisters to the edge of apoplexy with my feet. Mostly, though, around the time Albert Janowski was killed, my tapping was limited to Tuesday nights, when I taught a beginners' class.

It was an eclectic group: office workers, several college students, a married couple, a remarkably spry retired schoolteacher. No Broadway aspirants. Just a handful of enthusiastic people who strive for that moment when suddenly all eight or ten or twenty feet move in unison. It's the most elusive thing in the world, an almost physical impossibility. You know you can never do it, and then in a brilliant, shimmering second it happens—and there is nothing quite like it. Then one pair breaks stride, and another, and everyone dissolves in laughter and starts over again.

These classes were held on the first floor of a semiconverted warehouse in an industrial part of lower Manhattan. The loft movement hadn't hit there yet. No artists' studios had been fashioned out of seedy storage areas, no fern bars brought to life on the corners. The neighborhood wasn't particularly dangerous, actually. There was nothing open at night to attract those who prey on others—no shops, no restaurants; it was just empty and lonely.

Our lesson was from six to eight P.M. In the summer that wasn't bad. There was still light when we left and walked the three blocks to the subway. Sometimes we took our time, playing in the empty streets, hearing our laughter bounce off the canyon of walls around us. In the winter, it was another story. The streets were dark and we left in a tight little knot, huddled together talking in gruff voices to frighten away evil spirits.

I was tired that Tuesday night; the class had run longer than usual. We were sitting around on the old crates that lined the room, changing into street clothes, when I heard the phone in the upstairs office ringing. I tried ignoring it, but when it persisted, changed my mind. It wasn't likely to be for me, but a number of people knew I taught that class on Tuesdays. Leaving my street clothes in a heap, still in my tap shoes, I went up the stairs and down a corridor into the empty office.

"Hello?"

There was a silence on the other end of the line, and then an unfamiliar voice.

"Is this the teacher?"

"Yes?"

At that moment someone from the class called to me from the lower floor.

"Just a second," I said into the receiver. Leaning out the office door, I shouted down the stairwell: "Go ahead; I'll catch up at the corner."

That was a big mistake. As I put the receiver back to my ear, I heard the unmistakable sound of a dozen feet walking across a wooden floor. The building door opened, and then slammed shut.

"Hello," I said again. This time there was nothing but those indistinguishable hollow noises that come from an open line. I sat down in the office chair, and after a moment the voice returned:

"Hello, Miss?"

"Yes?"

"My, my. You're all alone in there now, aren't you? I've been watching you." It was an unnatural, rasping whisper. "You sure look cute in those shorts. You know what I'd like to do with you?" He began to tell me, in graphic detail, while I clutched the phone in shock. Finally I slammed it down. Not a second later, the building's lights dimmed and went out.

I felt a quick tightening across my chest. When I was able to force air into my lungs, it came with a choking gasp that knifed through the palpable quiet in the dark, empty room. Making myself get out of the chair, I walked to the office door, closed it quietly, and clicked the lock shut.

I tried to reason myself out of my terror. Maybe someone in the class left through the basement and extinguished the lights from there. The caller was a crank; and aren't crank callers harmless? What made me think there was anyone in the building anyway? But fear doesn't yield to logic. Irrational solutions raced through my mind. I would spend the night in the office. But the top half of the door was glass and easily broken. Go out the office window. Onto what? It was a two-story drop into a dark alley.

The telephone—of course! My own sigh of relief startled me. I picked up the receiver and dialed 911, the police emergency number. There was no dial tone, no ringing—nothing. Just dead, dead quiet. I thought I was dead if I stayed where I was.

I walked back to the office door and put my ear to it. What are the sounds of a deserted warehouse? The creak of a rotting staircase, the moan of an ancient foundation, the whisper of wind through broken windowpanes. The stuff horror movies are made of. Quietly, I took off my tap shoes, then walked back from the faint gray light coming through the door. I looked around for a weapon, and in the dim light saw a steel letter opener on the desk. When it was clenched in my fist, I took a deep breath, flung open the office door, and ran for the stairs.

It was almost pitch dark, and I could feel a hundred hands reaching out to grab me. I went down the stairs in a panic, half sliding and hanging onto the handrail, shoes under my arm, letter opener cutting into my fingers. I knew I was making too much noise, but I couldn't stop myself. I opened the door at the bottom of the stairs, raced across the dance floor, and threw myself at the street door. It held fast. It had been bolted from the outside.

Did I hear someone—a scuffling noise—outside the building? Did I only think I did? There was no time to have a debate with myself. I had to get away from that door.

At the far corner of the room was a steel ladder, half obscured by old furniture and storage crates. It led to a catwalk above the floor. Still clutching my shoes and the letter opener, I maneuvered myself through the dirty furniture, grasped the first rung of the worn steel ladder with my free hand, and started to climb. The ladder trembled as I moved toward the distant ceiling, and its rust coated the skin of my hands. I was almost at the top when the street door cracked, and then opened.

A tall, slender figure stood in the door, outlined by the yellow glow of the streetlights. His shadow reached halfway across the floor. He stepped inside and closed the door behind him, plunging the room back into darkness.

"Okay, Momma. We're going to play hide-and-seek. I'm it."

A beam of light flashed around the room beneath me, illuminating the packing crates and abandoned machinery. He was still for a moment, then he walked to the stairway, stooped, and stared up at the hall above him. A second later he mounted the stairs and climbed, quiet as a cat, until he disappeared.

I almost fell. My hands were sweaty, my arms weak, and my pulse racing. I gripped the ladder and managed to pull myself the last few feet. The corrugated steel floor of the catwalk was coated with years of accumulated grime. I started crawling away from the ladder, hoping for a hiding place. The man's footsteps echoed in the distance as he searched the building for me.

The warehouse was large and crowded; it would take him at least an hour to do a thorough search upstairs. If I could get down the ladder fast—and quietly—I might have a chance at reaching the door . . .

I started backing up. My foot was on the top rung when the letter opener slipped from my hand and clattered to the floor. A horrible quiet, then the man thundering down the stairs. I pulled myself back just as he slashed the floor with his light. On the far side of the room there was a noise, the slightest rustle. The man moved softly closer to it. Suddenly a rat jumped from behind a crate and ran across the floor, trying to outrun the light.

"Aw, fuck it. Not worth my time . . ."

I thought I must be hearing things. The man sounded bored with it all. He walked to the street door, opened it, and left the building. The lock clicked on the outside and then there was silence.

I felt my way along the catwalk until my hand found a doorstop. Rising to a crouch, I groped blindly, found a bolt, and pushed it back. The fire door opened and wet night air washed over me. Ahead was the roof, flat, shining with broad puddles from the rain. There was a fire escape on the other side. I crawled over to it and looked down. It ended in the alley behind the warehouse. I started down slowly. When I reached the bottom of the ladder, there was an eight-foot drop to the pavement. Shards of glass were everywhere. I put my shoes back on, climbed to the edge, closed my eyes, told my quaking body to relax, and dropped to the pavement. My taps slid and I crashed to my side. A stab of pain shot from my knee. When I touched my leg, my hand came back warm and wet. Forcing myself to my feet, I limped toward the front of the building.

Mott Street was as quiet as a tomb, and almost as dark. I began walking toward the closest intersection half a block away. Then, through the mist, first one and then another figure appeared out of the shadows and stood in the funnel of light cast by a street lamp. I heard laughter and the crash of a breaking bottle. Kids? Harmless drunks? Nothing was harmless to me. Making a quiet turn, I headed away from the corner, staying as close to the dark side of a building as I could. South Broadway was two blocks down. I'd be safe there.

Reaching the first corner, I saw a traffic light at a heavily traveled intersection several blocks to my left. I began to trot in that direction. Wet asphalt shone pale and sinister in my path. I know I was limping, but if there was pain I was hardly aware of it. The blinking caution light ahead looked warm and motherly, and I thought about being a little girl, remembered being tucked in at night, feeling warm and safe. It was all right. I was safe. I slowed down and caught my breath.

"Momma, I thought I lost you. Where have you been?"

He was on the other side of the street a little ahead of me. The voice was tinny and unreal; little more than a whisper. I strained to see, but there was nothing more than a hint of gray shadow on a building wall, then a flicker of movement in the half-dark. Then there was a damp footfall and he was crossing the street. My heart began pounding with such force that my chest knocked.

He was a dozen feet in front of me when I saw bright lights turn into the street. A car crawled my way, inching through the light rain.

I came to life, animated by something primitive and powerful. With a blood-curdling scream, I ran for the light, right toward the stranger. We collided and I lashed at him in a terror-filled frenzy, pounding with my fists, kicking, screaming all the time. He moved aside. As I ran, the sound of his laughter followed me.

I was hysterical, and what happened next comes back in telegraphic flashes with no continuity.

I threw myself at the hood of the car, grabbing hold of the windshield wipers. I remember the warmth of the hood on my stomach, the feeling of panic when the car tried to pull away from me, the terrified Oriental woman in the passenger seat.

The driver backed wildly down the narrow street, through the caution light and into racing city traffic. A taxi cab swerved, narrowly missing us. The cab driver pulled abruptly to the curb. As he leaped from his cab and advanced on us, swinging a wrench and cursing "God-damned foreigners," I slipped weak-kneed to the pavement.

"I'll tell you something, Miss. I've got a daughter a little younger than you. I'd never let her go out into that part of town at night. She doesn't even ride the subway after seven."

He was a tough old sergeant, and not sympathetic.

"This is New York City, lady. How long have you lived here? There's always going to be some nut on the street. Don't you know better than to stay away from that kind of neighborhood at night? This isn't Rockefeller Center down here. Women don't go walking around alone."

"I told you," I insisted. "He wasn't just some nut. He was after me. *Me.* He called me on the phone. He kept me late so I'd be alone. He did something to the phone."

"But he never asked for you by name. He asked for the teacher. Don't you see? Any woman would have done. Or maybe he'd seen you, picked you out. He works in the neighborhood, sees the girls going to class, week after week, dressed like that. . . ."

"It's a leotard. And I don't dress like this on the street."

"Yeah."

I rode back to the warehouse with the police—four of them. Two waited in the car with me while the others used my master key to let themselves in. A few minutes later they returned, carrying my handbag and street clothes.

"Nobody in the place," one reported.

"Did you check the phone?" I asked.

"Somebody cut the wire." He didn't look at me.

Nothing on earth could have persuaded me to go home to my empty apartment right then. We were on Third Avenue in the Gramercy Park area near Gary Petit's apartment, so I had the police drop me there.

Gary's experience with women in high emotional distress may have been limited, but he saw himself as the rational protective male, and for some reason it worked for me. Less than an hour later I was calmed and coherent enough to have formed what seemed a plausible theory.

"Gary, I'm sure Stephanie's responsible for this. I had lunch with her on Sunday."

"I know." He handed me a mug filled with a thick white liquid. An oily scum floated on its surface. "Drink this."

"It looks disgusting. What is it? Eggnog? And how do you know we had lunch, anyway?"

"Your essential amino acids in a raw milk base. I know because she told her father and her father told me."

"Isn't she a little old to be telling Daddy everything she does?" I sipped at the drink, then made a face. "I'm feeling a lot better already. I don't need . . ."

"Down the hatch."

I downed it in a couple of torturous gulps and handed him the glass. "What I'd really like is some brandy. Lots of brandy. A tumbler full."

That night the theme was the Far East. He was wearing a black Japanese-style kimono with a bright yellow obi sash. When I'd finished my shower, a white kimono, red sash, had been waiting for me. We looked like the Anglo contingent of some strange, colorful sect. On his coffee table was an open book. It looked new. *Yoga Sutras of Patanjali, Abridged*.

"The eight steps to supreme consciousness, Bonnie," he told me. "I'm really getting into it." A thin wailing chant came from the stereo, sending chills up my spine.

"I'll get the brandy myself. And would you mind turning that down? I've had an awful experience."

"I'll get it. I wish you'd open yourself to more spiritual ideas. Meditation is the great healer, you know."

"Liquor's quicker."

On his way to the kitchen he switched off the music and shouted over his shoulder, "Some flower child you must have been."

I heard the sound of cabinets opening and glasses tinkling, then he pushed back through the swinging door, balancing crystal glasses on a silver tray. "Here we go. The first step," he said, settling himself down next to me, "is yarma, the restraint from vice. Then you carry that further with niyama. The removal of uncontrollable desires."

From the corner of my eye I saw his arm begin a leisurely slide along the back of the sofa. One encouraging move from me and niyama would go right out the window.

"Gary, I'm glad you've discovered this . . . thing. But I'd like to talk about Stephanie. She's dangerous. I'm sure she's trying to kill me. If you'd heard her Sunday. She threatened Tony's job and mine, too."

Gary looked like someone trying not to laugh at a too-serious child. "I think you're overreacting. Maybe she meant your job was going to kill you. You've always said you were dying from boredom there."

"Not so funny. What about the horse? I know damned well she hit it."

"If that's the worst she's going to do, you can relax." He inched nearer to me, ready to renew his romantic attack. The ambience was right; I was in a weakened condition, surrounded by the trappings of inherited wealth, drinking aged brandy and essential amino acids while the light rain patted a lulling mantra on the windowpanes. I stood up and began pacing in front of him.

"It's more than what she said. It was in her tone. If we hadn't been in public, she would have attacked me."

"This is ridiculous. Stephanie is capable of a lot of things, but that business tonight doesn't make sense. I expect that she's afraid your friend Tony is going to dig up something about her. She just got a little heavy-handed on Sunday. Maybe she was with another man when Albert was killed. And besides, you said it was a man tonight. Whatever Stephanie is, she's not a man."

He couldn't grasp, or refused to consider, what seemed to be so obvious to me.

"You want to hear what I think?" He probably didn't, but I didn't give him time to answer. "Stephanie has a lover. They want to get married. Albert has no money of his own and the firm is no big money maker, so he wants to hang on to Stephanie. He refuses to give her a quiet divorce. Threatens to drag her precious name through the mud. So they—Stephanie and this man—hire a woman, an actress maybe, and work out a scam. Some kind of trap, to catch Albert in a compromising situation at the Hotel Central. That way he'll be forced to bow out gracefully. But something goes wrong. He catches on, and they panic and shoot him."

Gary answered without looking at me. "Pretty damned

melodramatic. I think you're watching too many movies. Isn't that *Double Indemnity?*"

"Not even close."

"All right. For sake of argument let's assume Stephanie has this lover and this plot and they kill Albert. And I want you to know I feel like a nut even talking like this. But if you're right, where do you come in? Why threaten the office manager?"

"Because they know I went out with Tony. How they know that is beyond me, but they're afraid that since I'm an insider and I'm familiar with the personalities involved, I'll keep picking away and maybe come up with something. Like where she was the night Albert was killed. If she's innocent, why is it such a secret? That business tonight was supposed to scare me off. Or make the police think I'm some kind of crackpot. You know, that guy could have caught me if he'd wanted to. He didn't even half try . . ."

Somewhere in the cavernous apartment a phone rang. Gary stood up. "I've been expecting a client to call. I'll take it in the kitchen."

"Bring some more brandy when you come back," I called after him. "Bring the bottle."

The wildest notion had begun clanking around in my head. I hadn't expected Gary to agree with me—not right away, anyway—but wasn't he being pretty enthusiastic about supporting a woman he claimed he disliked? Was there something between Stephanie and Gary, maybe? Miss Peterson had known Stephanie had a new man, but she hadn't known who. Had Gary been hustling the grieving widow out his service door while I was pounding at the front? She called him a walking wet dream, he said she was scary. Did they both protest too much? But then, who chased me? An accomplice? Ridiculous.

I could hear Gary mumbling on the telephone. It sounded like it was going to be a long conversation. I started thumbing through the *Yoga Sutras*, but soon gave up. Even abridged, it was incomprehensible. Trying to force myself to relax, I leaned back into the sofa. There was something wrong with it—a hard lump disturbing the cushion under me. I slid my hand between the rich velvet and my fingertips brushed a conical wad. In a further burst of imagination it became the missing .38-caliber automatic pistol. I eased the cylinder from under the cushion. *The One Hundred and One Positions of Love, in Full Laser Color*, rolled up, dog-eared, and absolutely unabridged.

A quick look showed me several things far more interesting than the *Yoga Sutras* ever would. There was even one that showed a man in a position something like the one Albert Janowski had been discovered in. Believe me, that gave me a minute's pause. Not too long a minute, though; I wasn't about to let Gary catch me poring over his dirty pictures. I quickly returned the *Positions* to its hiding place. Between that and the eight steps to supreme consciousness, he had his work cut out.

He was taking his time with the phone, and my brandy. I was filled with nervous energy and started snooping around Gary's living room, picking up mementos, examining the bottoms of silver pitchers for trademarks, looking for signatures on paintings.

I felt a kind of ancestral soul in that Old World apartment. His family had lived in it for generations, and you could almost imagine a living spirit, a stirring in Great Aunt Agatha's sideboard, a movement in Uncle Howard's chair.

My father is a machinist and my mother a housewife who still "puts up" vegetables and makes do, with some complaint. They followed a migration from the impoverished deep South in the late thirties, first to Maryland, and then, in the fifties, to northern New Jersey where, having aspired to the middle class for many years, they cinched it with the purchase of a house. Until then, home was a series of trailer parks. We never felt true poverty—starvation, rats, and leaking roofs—but there is, I imagine, a small poverty that happens in a break in the familial tempo, when the fixtures and memories of the past aren't there.

With Gary's rich, musty past around me, I felt a longing, as I often do in the presence of concurrent history. On his piano were photographs of old-fashioned, elegant men and women sitting in carriages and standing on rolling lawns. The women shielded their complexions from the sun with lacy white parasols and the men showed their affluence in their round stomachs. There was one picture standing apart from the others. Franklin Roosevelt and an older man who looked a little like Gary. They were leaning on the railing at the bow of a yacht. I was holding the picture to the light when Gary came back.

"You look nice here," he said. "Like you belong by that piano."

"What do you mean?"

"You know. You fit right in. You've never been here when there wasn't a crowd, have you?"

I shook my head.

"Well, I hate what it took to get you here, but I wasn't sorry to see you at my door. You fill up the place, Bonnie. You bring it a brightness it needs."

He was looking straight into my eyes. This was quite embarrassing. I thrust the picture I was holding toward him. "This is your grandfather, isn't it?"

"Yes. People tell me I look like him."

I looked closer. "Sort of."

"He was a great lawyer. You would have liked him. All these other ladies and gentlemen, too. Some impressive people here, Bonnie," he added, nodding at the photos. "Up to the time my father and Mr. K took over, the firm was at the pinnacle." He picked up another picture, one of himself as a child, hand in hand with a man I recognized as his father. "In my grandfather's eyes I suppose my father would be a bigger failure than I am. He's the one who allowed things to slide."

"If you can see that," I said, thinking I was being supportive, "then you must realize you can't blame yourself for something your father did."

He slammed the photo back on the piano. "My father tried. He may not always have made the right decisions, but at least he tried. And he was always good to me, Bonnie. That's something I can't forget. No matter how busy he was, he always took time for me. Now it is my turn to take the time for him."

Gary's love-hate relationship with his past was becoming a real fixation. I had stopped at his apartment with my own troubles, and here I was listening to his. And his, in my opinion, didn't hold a candle to mine.

Finally he turned to me. "Why don't we sit down again. I want to talk to you about something. Besides Albert Janowski."

He sounded serious. He patted a spot beside him on the sofa. I pretended not to notice and sat in a side chair.

"You know what the firm is," he began. "You're not dumb. You've done temp work in other firms. As Ely Sneed stands now, it's virtually finished. It's going to take money, energy, a recruiting program, and a major change in focus if we're going to continue. I don't know if we can pull it off. If we can, terrific. But there's a chance we won't."

His eyes held mine, and I felt an awful sensation that I was going to have even more to worry about. "Are you telling me the firm's going to fold? That's just what I need."

"No, I'm not saying that. At least not tomorrow. But now, more than ever, you should be looking around for something else. We stand to lose a lot of business if we're not careful, with the kind of publicity we've had. What we have to find is direction. We've been like a rudderless boat in a tornado. No guidance. I'm going to try taking a stronger hand in running things, but who knows what will happen."

He was staring at his glass, rotating the brandy round and round in his hand. The leaded-glass lamp next to him gave his skin a mottled, tired look.

"Sneed saw it coming thirty years ago. The way we're practicing law is obsolete. My great-grandfather—Henry Garrett Petit—you want to know who his clients were? Thomas Alva Edison and the Pearl Street plant. Bonnie, that was the first electric-power plant in the world. George Westinghouse. The railroads. Garrett Petit was consulted on the Sherman Antitrust Act, and when he was almost seventy years old he wrote an amicus brief in *E. C. Knight* that knocked the feet from under *Sherman*. Teddy Roosevelt sat right in this room arguing trust with my grandfather and Garrett. And tomorrow morning, Bonnie, at nine-thirty, I'm having a meeting with Louie Siegal of FunTyme Enterprises about his new line of party favors. Whoopee cushions, Bonnie. In a hundred years we've gone from major utilities and the Supreme Court to whoopee cushions and dribble cups."

It wasn't the first time I'd heard this speech, but this time I took it seriously. "If you're trying to scare me, it's working."

"Good. I want to." He paused for a second. "There's something . . . I'm not even supposed to talk to you about this, but there's been talk of dispensing with your function altogether. Dividing it between some of the other staff. I can't say what will come of it, if anything, but you should consider yourself warned. Frankly," he continued, leaning over to refill my glass, "I don't know why you're still there. You've got that big-shot uncle in New Jersey. Couldn't he help you find something?"

"Maybe. I don't know, Gary. Ely Sneed—well, at least it's there. I've had so many temp jobs and so many false starts. This is the first time I've ever been anywhere long enough to tell the truth on my résumé. I've started feeling . . . secure, I guess."

"Security. There are many kinds of security." He paused, then smiled at me. "You must know that I've always had a great deal of affection for you, Bonnie. A great deal. We have a lot in common. Sometimes I start imagining how things would be if you and I . . ."

He was on the verge of saying something I didn't want to hear, something that would virtually end our friendship. I rose hastily and gathered our glasses from the tabletop. "I'll rinse these out. I'm going to use your kitchen phone to call a cab."

My spurt of activity startled him. "Oh. You feeling better now? You're going to go home?"

"Sure. All better." The truth was, I felt terrible. Not fearful, like I had earlier, but depressed. Sad for Gary, trying hard to live up to the expectations of a lot of dead people; sad for myself, my wasted past, my dismal future. Sad for the whole world.

I let the kitchen door close behind me before dialing Queens Information for Tony's number. One Anthony C. LaMarca in Forest Hills. The phone rang a couple of times, and then, "Hello?"

A woman's voice. Not a baby-sitter voice, or an elderly aunt voice, but a woman woman. I hung up, telling myself that I'd dialed the wrong number. I did it slowly, carefully, the next time.

"Yes?" The woman's voice was pitched lower, with caution in it. I knew I was frightening her and I wanted to hang up, but I couldn't. There was this fleeting vision, like the blink of an aperture, when I thought I saw her, a pretty woman, regular features, dark shoulder-length hair, the tight worried lines around her mouth of a wife waiting up.

The noise of a television program filled the background behind the silent woman. Then an adolescent boy's voice called: "Mom, if that's Dad, I wanna talk to him." Every bit of paranoia I'd ever suppressed, every slight abuse, real or imagined, that I'd ever suffered at a lover's hands, came back to me, and I wanted to scream into the receiver, pound it on the countertop.

Hanging up, I took a deep breath and called a cab.

As I had expected, Gary tried to get me to stay over.

"The guest room is all made up," he said, with a longing expression that I found so profoundly depressing it made me want to cry.

"No. I'm fine now," I told him with false cheer as I hurried out his door. "All better."

Once home, I unplugged my phone and fell into a restless sleep, filled with moving shadows and faceless, nameless fears.

THURSDAY

APRIL

16

I found my first real clue the same day I lost my job.

Albert's murder was none of my business, I had convinced myself. Frankly, the only thing I'd really pursued with any vigor was the investigating detective, and with him out of the picture I would have no trouble putting Albert's corpse to rest. I had also decided, on the basis of Gary's sage advice, to call my uncle in New Jersey, to update my résumé, to buy a "dressed for success" suit, and get my lethargic fanny out of Ely Sneed for good.

And in the meantime, spurred by Gary's warning, I was going to fling myself into managing Ely Sneed's ragtag offices with a passion and, for the present, march in the ranks of the unhappy bureaucrats, those who had preceded me and those who would follow: a form for everything and every form in triplicate and in its proper file. I would, by God, blend in.

I wore my brown suit that morning, with a tan blouse. The overall effect was that of a Russian tank officer. I was fifteen minutes early and carried two containers of black coffee to my desk to keep myself jumping.

Wilbur Decker was my first visitor. His jaw dropped several inches when he saw me. For some unfathomable reason he had taken to roaming the halls with a clipboard under his arm. In his hand I saw one of those nasty little "From the desk of . . ." notes. He crumpled it and shoved it into his pocket.

"Miss Indermill. I didn't expect you. So early. I'd like to see you in my office at some point this morning."

I started to stand.

"No, no. Relax. Finish your coffee. Absolutely no rush. I'll call you. Maybe about ten-ish." Mr. Congeniality. I could only suppose that he was cheered by the circles under my eyes and my brown suit. No complaints about his new secretary? No boiling blood? Did a new era of detente lie ahead?

I turned, then, to a job that made me sick—literally. Every month, without fail, I ended up with a pounding headache. Ely Sneed had several copying machines around the office, and on each machine was a pad of yellow charge slips, so that copies could be billed to the correct client. Naturally, most of the staff ignored them. I did, too. Nevertheless, by the end of the month there was generally a foot-high stack to be entered in the various accounts. When I tried to get our bookkeeper, Mrs. Kotch, to do it, she informed me in no uncertain terms that she was no clerk, and threatened to see Old Mr. K about it. I tried giving the job to Rosalie, who had nothing to do all day but paint her nails and pick up occasional bottles of bourbon for the old man. She said she lost all the slips. I suspect she threw them out. So, for lack of anyone else, the miserable job fell to me.

About nine-thirty A.M., when I was a quarter-inch through the stack and beginning to nod, Miss Peterson dropped in and broke the tedium in her own special way. Her eyes were red. She clutched a shredded, soggy tissue in her clenched fist.

"He called me . . . Mr. Petit called me . . ." she began, and the tears poured out, choking her.

"Sit down, Miss Peterson. Here." I pushed out my side chair. "Tell me what's wrong."

She collapsed into the seat. "He called me a nosy old bat! Can you imagine? He said to me, 'Get out of here, you nosy old bat.' To me. After all these years . . . That kind of abuse.

Bonnie, I'm a nervous woman." And to prove it, she once again dissolved into tears.

"Please, Miss Peterson. Try to compose yourself so you can tell me what happened. Here's another tissue."

She dabbed her eyes and drew a quivering breath.

"I was a few minutes late this morning. You know how the trains are. Well, he's just ridiculous about that. I realize you're one of Mr. Petit's greatest admirers, but he is unreasonable when it comes to punctuality. This morning that got him started. Not even a 'Good morning' when I got here. He just glared at me and slammed the door in my face." Her eyes filled to brimming. I pushed another tissue at her.

"About ten minutes later he got a call. A perfect boor, the man was. It never fails to amaze me, Bonnie, that these men in such high positions . . . Well, this one, when I asked his name, he said, 'Just let me talk to Petit.' As you know, I always screen Mr. Petit's calls. It's a point of pride with me. I said to this man, 'I must insist on your name,' and do you know, he called me a name! The nerve! I won't repeat it, but you can imagine. So, what was I to do? I buzzed Mr. Petit and he took the call.

"I thought that while he was on the phone I'd slip in and take the work from his 'To do' box. That's when he yelled at me. I opened his door and Mr. Petit . . . he screamed: 'Get out of here, you nosy old bat!' Now, Bonnie, what do you say to that?"

Her back was stiff, her brows raised, and she was looking at me as if I, as one of Mr. Petit's greatest admirers, had played a part in this outrage.

"Miss Peterson, I don't know what to think. I imagine the call was of a very personal nature. Otherwise . . . Well, I can't see Mr. Petit acting like that." I really couldn't. Gary could be as difficult as any other lawyer at the firm, but his particular lunacy was, as Miss Peterson said, punctuality. The screaming was definitely out of character. I thought of the *One Hundred and One Positions*, and it crossed my mind that perhaps one or two of them had involved other men.

"It sounds to me, Miss Peterson, as if you deserve an apology, and I don't blame you for being angry. But please try to understand that everyone at Ely Sneed has been under a strain lately. Particularly Mr. Petit." My bureaucratic machine was well oiled that morning. "Now, do you think you could go back to your desk? I'll speak to Mr. Petit and see what we can work out."

She nodded, and with a resolute blow of her nose, pulled herself to her feet, stretched her five-feet zero-inch frame to its sternest, and marched, chin up, back into the fray.

Gary's extension was busy, so I went back to the yellow copy slips. I was shuffling through, jotting numbers in various columns and cursing Ely Sneed for not using a computer, when something on one of them caught my eye. It was a slip written in Albert Janowski's hand. I started to make a mental drama of it—a voice from the silent grave and all that—but stopped myself before I wandered too far afield. All business, I jotted down the figures in their proper column, put Albert's yellow slip in the "done" stack, and picked up the next one. Then something struck me. I retrieved Albert's slip from the pile: 4/1/87. He had filled it out the day before he was murdered.

It was unusual for a senior partner to make copies for himself, especially an elitist like Albert. I wouldn't have thought he knew how the copy machine worked. And strangely, the copies were charged to one of our old file numbers, as opposed to the ones in our new, so-called modern system. The ostensible purpose of charging copies, or for that matter anything else, to these old files was that if, by chance, any money remained in trust, these charges could come out of it. In theory, that was fine; in practice, it meant spending about twenty dollars worth of my time finding out if some long-dead client's escrow fund could absorb twenty cents' worth of copies.

What I generally did was simply charge the copies back to the office, and I had every intention of doing that with Albert's piddling copy charge. I read his hasty, jagged hand: ESKP(F)363. The day before he died, Albert made two copies of two pages having something to do with this old file. I was fingering the slip, wondering what to make of it, when my phone rang.

"Wilbur Decker here, Miss Indermill. Are you free now, for our chat?"

"Certainly, Mr. Decker." I stuck Albert's charge slip into my desk drawer.

"A cluttered desk is the sure sign of a cluttered mind" was one of Decker's favorite sayings. That philosophy was reflected in his office. The top of his desk was swept clear of all but immediate papers. There were no files stacked on his credenza, much less on his floor. He wasn't much for knick-knacks, either. On one wall were some framed diplomas from little-known schools, and on another a framed print, one of José Orozco's toiling peasants, bent double under a massive basket of fruit.

"Have a seat, Miss Indermill. That green chair is the most comfortable."

Goodwill oozed. Pulling open his middle desk drawer, Decker withdrew a slim, unlabeled file, opened it, and began fingering the contents, all the time never looking at me.

"Now, let me see. Ah . . . I'd almost forgotten. Before we get to the matter at hand"—his little ferret eyes struggled to meet mine—"I want to ask you about our special little project." He said what I'd feared he would. "*The First Hundred Years*. I assume you're functioning on that? I'd like to see what you have. Perhaps we can begin the . . . editorial process."

"Oh," I said, snapping my fingers and puckering my brow in distress—"it's at home, on my kitchen table. I've been working on it at night, Mr. Decker, when I have fewer interruptions."

"Oh. Well, splendid. I'm looking forward to reading the fruits of all your labors. Perhaps . . . yes. Miss Indermill, I've always wondered if your talents didn't lie in a different. . . ." His words faded away.

"Yes, Mr. Decker?"

"Yes, let's get on here. Now, let me see. Ah . . . Here we

are." His eyes followed his finger down a paper he had pulled from the slim file. It seemed to be a list—of my sins, I suppose.

"You've been with us . . ."

"Three years and two months."

"And you began as Mr. Petit's temporary secretary."

"Yes. That's right."

"Well, Miss Indermill, the thing is . . ." He took off his glasses, held them up to the light, and began cleaning them off with his cuff. "As I was saying, the thing is, we, the Management Committee, have come to a decision . . . um. . . ."

He returned the glasses to his nose and leaned back in his chair, so that he faced the ceiling.

"Yes, Mr. Decker?"

"Growth, you must realize. To grow with the times. We've been rather lax here at Ely Sneed, continuing with old methods, not keeping pace with technology. The . . . um . . . state of the art, in a manner of speaking."

Coming from Decker, this sounded like a foreign language. He launched into a fantastic speech about computerized word-processing systems and call forwarding, babbling about electronic mail, file retrieval, and how you have to spend money to make money. I experienced a wild stab of hope; maybe we were going to modernize.

". . . and, to implement this renewal . . . a giant step into the twenty-first century . . . we feel an, um . . . management professional is needed."

This last tumbled out so quickly I thought I'd misunderstood him.

"Pardon me?"

"A management professional, Miss Indermill. Perhaps an MBA. We plan to interview a number of candidates from various . . . ahem . . . disciplines, as it were, before making a decision. We're hoping to get this program on the right track . . . implemented, as they say in the field . . . perhaps as early as June. Eventually, this may even involve a move to more prestigious quarters. We've got fine legal minds here at Ely

Sneed, and it's high time they were utilized to their fullest capacity."

"Bullshit" is what was on the tip of my tongue, but I thought better of it. "Mr. Decker, I really don't understand what you're saying. Are you telling me I'm going to be replaced by someone, or will this new . . . management professional . . . be in addition to me?"

He placed his fingertips together, as if in prayer, and weighed his words. "Miss Indermill, you must realize . . . the self-taught office manager like yourself and your predecessor, Miss Osgood . . . you were fine when things were done in the old way, by hand. But times have changed. This is the age of technology. The world is passing Ely Sneed by. Administration of law firms is no longer just a job, my dear." His lips twisted into his idea of a fatherly smile. "It's a highly skilled profession."

There was a tight knot in the pit of my stomach. The world seemed to be developing a vicious sense of humor at my expense.

"So I am being replaced? Is that what you're trying to say?"

"No, no. I wouldn't want to say that. You've done some quite decent work for us. I, for one, have certainly enjoyed our association. We'd be happy to keep you on, perhaps as assistant to this new manager. Actually," he continued, referring to the page in front of him, "you'd be doing much the same work you're doing now: the bills, some of the interviewing, securing temporary secretaries—though we should change agencies there. None of those women have been satisfactory. And, of course, the history, Miss Indermill. *The First Hundred Years* is your baby."

"Big damned deal, Mr. Decker. I can't understand this." My knees began knocking uncontrollably. "I remember suggesting almost three years ago that we look into computerized word processing. I remember getting all the information. I still have it. I suggested sending some of the secretaries to class. I wanted to go myself. You said no." By then I was shouting. I stood up, sending the green chair slamming into the credenza. "When I wanted to bring in a decorator to do something about this place, you and the rest of the so-called Office Aesthetics Committee almost had a collective seizure when you saw what it would cost!"

The sniveling old hypocrite was scared. He rolled his chair back away from his desk, looked anxiously at the closed door, then at me. "Miss Indermill, you seem a little upset right now. Perhaps it would be best if you thought things over. If you choose to leave us, you can have all the time you need to find something more suitable."

He knew damn well I was going to leave. My hand was on his doorknob when he took his parting shot. "And don't forget, Miss Indermill. The history. I must insist. Perhaps tomorrow we can go over it together."

As I stumbled back to my office, Miss Peterson confronted me in the hall. She was in far better shape than I.

"Bonnie. Have you had a chance to speak to Mr. Petit? I've thought it over and I've decided I'm not going to say another word to him until I've had an apology. I refuse to be treated like that. After all my years of loyal service, all I get . . ."

"After all your years of loyal service, all you've got is yourself to depend on, Miss Peterson. I'll tell you what; if you've got something to say to Mr. Petit, why don't you just march into his office and tell him yourself? Just tell him to . . . shove it!"

Poor Miss Peterson. I was in a vile mood, ready to attack anything in my way. She blinked, incredulous. I bolted into my office, slammed the door, locked it, and started to cry, in great sobs and gulps. The yellow copy slips wrinkled under my torrent. I knew it wasn't just my job. It was all of it— looking at Albert's body, Stephanie's threats, Tony's faithlessness, the maniac who'd chased me, even my sainted brother Raymond and his cow wife and those ghastly children. All those things poured out.

There was a knock on my door. The knob jiggled. "Bonnie? It's me, Gary. Would you let me in? Please?"

"Miss Peterson told me to shove it." He handed me another tissue. "I thought I recognized your fine touch in that. I apologized to her." His smile met with a stony silence from me.

"I tried to tell you," he said.

"So why didn't you, instead of just hinting? What kind of crap is that? Who's on this Management Committee, anyway? The last I heard, I sat in on Management Committee meetings."

"Bonnie, my first loyalty is to the firm. When we spoke the other night, the committee had been tossing the idea around. Yesterday we decided to go through with it. Put some money into Ely Sneed. Come on, Bonnie. You were planning to look for something anyway. Things like this sometimes happen for the best, don't they? Now, where's that pretty smile? You weren't fired, you know. You can stay here forever, if you want. You've got to admit, though, that we do need some expert management around here."

"You said it." I managed a watery, painful smirk.

"Now, that's better." He wiped my cheeks. "I've been wondering what happened to the old Bonnie. Where's the Bonnie who earned her living tap-dancing on street corners in San Francisco? Where's the Bonnie who lived for a year in Europe on a thousand dollars?"

"It was six months. And that old Bonnie was twelve years younger than this one. How many women my age earn their living tap-dancing on street corners? Can't you see me tap-dancing in front of Ely Sneed? In front of their new offices, maybe? You and Decker can toss your spare change into my tin cup." This was no time for Gary's Pollyanna charity. I was well on the road to realizing my recurring nightmare—a penniless old age.

After a bit of hovering and cajoling, my despair gave way to a momentary anger, and with that, thankfully, came some sort of "good old Bonnie" self-reliance.

"Listen, Gary. I want to stay here a few more weeks. I need

that next paycheck. But then, do you think the firm would be willing to lay me off? I think Decker wants me to quit so they don't have to pay me unemployment."

Guilt was etched all over Gary's long face. He and Decker had had the same notion. After a bit he recovered himself. "Sure. Of course. I'll guarantee it. Count on me."

"And something else. I'd like to use you as a reference. Is that okay? I don't want to use Decker's name. I can imagine what he'd say."

Gary looked wounded. "How can you even ask that? Have them call me. I'll give you a recommendation that will get you into heaven. I'm surprised you even mention it. We've been friends for years."

I had no friends.

The first thing on my mind when I was finally alone in my office was money. My financial situation was bad, but it wasn't a total disaster: $170 a week unemployment is almost $700 a month, minus $558 rent, minus $30 utilities and I'd have to keep the phone for job hunting, and maybe take up fasting and put Moses on a diet, which wouldn't hurt either of us, and I might make it for a while if I dipped into my savings.

The yellow copy slips were still on my desk. Mindlessly, for lack of anything else to do, I resumed my posting. Right through lunch, mechanically, the way I imagine people work on assembly lines. After about three hours of it, when I felt the tension in the back of my neck mounting, I paused, stretched, and looked over the little domain I was so afraid to leave. About eight by ten feet, no window, a carpet with holes in it, a 1940s wooden desk, one of the drawers varnished shut, a broken swivel chair and a wobbly side chair, one ballet poster (mine), and about six inches of unposted copy charge slips.

A thrill of defiance ran through me. Opening my briefcase, which I'd started using to lug *The First Hundred Years* notes back and forth, I stuffed the unposted yellow sheets into it.

That seemed such a good idea that after just a second's thought, I stuffed all the posted slips in too, and then crammed my completed ledger pages in and headed for the ladies' room.

It took nine flushes to get rid of them all. Several times the retching toilet threatened to overflow and spew a volcano of yellow copy slips onto the ladies'-room floor. I could have cheered when the last of the yellow pages swirled into the bowels of the Hayworth Building. By then I was so elated it was all I could do to keep from dumping the wretched *Hundred Years* in, too.

My headache had disappeared, and the lump in the pit of my stomach was gone. I splashed water on my face and returned to my office.

Under stress, people do funny things. I began straightening my desk—getting it all nice for my successor, the management professional. Albert Janowski's yellow slip in the top drawer was the first thing I saw.

I wadded it into a ball, threw it into the trash, and began plowing through the three-year accumulation in the drawer. There must have been twenty matchbooks from the Rose of Killarney, and a hundred old New York lottery ticket stubs. Not a winner in the bunch. Then something began gnawing at me, just a little: Albert Janowski, the consummate company man. One day from death and filling out charge slips for a few crummy copies. There was something so compulsive, so narrow about it. Me, of course, I'm a genius. It wasn't until late that afternoon when the thing that had been gnawing at me finally hit.

The old file! Why not? An obsessive nut like Albert would probably have sent one copy to the file. He did everything else by the book. Even sex, according to his wife.

I picked up the phone and started to dial the file room. Then I caught myself. If Albert had made that copy himself, there was a chance he hadn't wanted anyone else to see it. That meant that he would have filed it himself, too. Once the copies were filed in one of the old files, there was almost no chance they'd ever be seen again. The "closed files" section of Ely Sneed's file room was the firm's answer to the Black Hole of Calcutta. Also, the $30,000 reward was sounding better by the minute. I didn't want to risk having to share it. I decided to wait until the file clerks left and get the file myself.

The long-absent Detective LaMarca chose that afternoon to call.

"Bonnie, it's me, Tony. I just got back."

"Really." I hadn't known I had it in me, to put that much ice in my voice.

"Well . . . yes. I've got a long weekend coming up. I thought maybe you'd like to go out to Montauk. My brother and I own a place out there. It's nice this time of year. Quiet."

"Thanks," I said, "but I have other plans."

It took him a couple of seconds to recover. "Bonnie, what's wrong? Do you think I didn't try to get you? I did. I tried Tuesday night until after midnight. You know, I was really busy up there."

"I had a date Tuesday night. That's why you couldn't get me."

"Oh."

"Look, I'm terribly busy here. I have to get back to work. Sorry about this weekend. Why don't you ask someone else?"

"Maybe I will."

"Do that. Goodbye."

"Goodbye."

That episode unleashed a flood of tears that would have done Miss Peterson proud.

Ely Sneed's main file room was one big, dreary mess. A high-ceilinged, windowless shoebox with peeling olive drab walls, bare fluorescent lights, and row upon row of old-fashioned army green file cabinets. I felt guilty whenever I hired a file clerk. They never stayed long.

Beyond this room was the one where the old, closed files were stored. That room was, to put it mildly, a shambles. Over the years, pieces of no longer usable office furniture had been shoved into it, on top of the cabinets and between them, until it was a minefield of dangling chair legs and jutting drawers. The room was never cleaned, and on the few occasions I'd gone into it, the half-inch of dust that coated everything never failed to set me into a sneezing frenzy.

This time was no exception. Tissue in hand, I squeezed between one cabinet after another, dodging chairs, stepping over fifty-odd years worth of office discards. The F-300s began in the bottom drawer of one cabinet and continued to the top of another, so that I had to squat until my knees almost gave out and then, when that drawer yielded nothing, stand on a wobbling three-legged stool. The cabinet was covered with dust, but I noticed handprints on its top. Within the last few weeks someone had been in there.

F-363 was right where it should have been. Its label read: "Smithfield, Milton, General Matters." I was going to look through it right there until I heard voices outside in the hall calling goodnights to each other. I probably wasn't persona non grata around Ely Sneed yet, but after what had happened earlier, my presence here, digging around in the old files, might have been questioned. And, too, my run through Soho's dark streets had left me with a monumental case of jitters. I didn't want to be left alone, the only person in the office.

The file was thin. Without looking at its contents, I stuffed the whole thing into my briefcase. As an afterthought, I took a stab at making the cabinet look undisturbed by blowing dust all over it and dragging the stool away.

It wasn't hard to find what I was looking for. It was the top item in the file, a copy of a letter and an envelope, with F-363 jotted in the upper-right-hand corner in Albert's hand. The letter was sloppily handwritten, and the copy was pale. I moved it under a lamp on my kitchen table to read it, shooing Moses away at the same time.

May 12, 1972

My Dear Little Girl,

You're not so little anymore. You're a grown woman now. I apologize for the infrequence of my correspondence, but these days I don't feel good. Sometimes my medicine makes me sick. I think that fat faced nurse puts poison in it. At the moment I'm fine.

I'm not a rich man and you shouldn't think I am and come to me for money, because I don't have any. One or two of my investments turned out though, especially one in particular that I can thank the attorney Lawrence G. Petit for. We share a secret I do not want to die with me. You see the negatives I've clipped to this letter. They can help you like they helped me, but be very careful and hide them.

The nurse watches me all the time. She wants my money too, just like all of them. I saw her hide the scissors. She is planning to kill me. I will give this to that colored boy to mail before she gets back. I can't trust him, but he will do it if I give him a quarter.

Cordially yours,
Your Father,
Milton Smithfield

I read it through three times. It sounded crazier every time. The ravings of a lunatic. There were no negatives in the file. I examined the front of the file folder, where the legend of its Ely Sneed history was recorded. "Opened: November 1956; Billing Partner TK (for Thurston Kellogg); Associate: (there was a long series of initials here).

This was the sort of insignificant client many junior associates would work on, but no one would want to commandeer for his own. ARJ (Albert Janowski) had been one of many. The file was sent to the closed section in 1975. In 1985, EDH

(Emory DesMoulins Hightower) had reviewed it and recommended it be destroyed, noting that the client has been dead over ten years and, even if there were additional charges, there was no money held in escrow to collect from. I couldn't attach much importance to the fact that the file wasn't destroyed. With Ely Sneed's office processes, anything was possible.

It could all be coincidence, I realized. Maybe Albert just came across that letter while cleaning out some old papers. Maybe he just happened to be walking past a copy machine. Maybe, maybe. I was pretty sure of one thing, though. There was nothing coincidental about the things that had been happening to me. In one week I had been threatened by Albert's widow, chased by a madman, duped by a married man, and fired for what I considered trumped-up reasons. My life was reading like a penny-dreadful novel. Okay, the thing with Tony could be put down to my own gullibility, but any one of those other three mishaps would have been as much bad luck as I'd ordinarily have in a three-year period. Three in one week? Impossible.

I turned over the letter and looked at the copy of the envelope underneath. That's when I saw it, and had to remind myself to breathe. The envelope was addressed to Miss Doris Smithfield, c/o Mrs. Walter Schmoulack, 51 Chestnut Street, Iron Valley, Pennsylvania. D. Smith from the Hotel Central? It could be. There was no return address on the envelope. With growing excitement I ran through the rest of the file. Milton Smithfield had been a photographer who held a few patents, none of them of any consequence from what I could see. Mr. Smithfield's business address appeared on several letters in the file. Smithfield's Fine Photography, 220 West 15th Street, New York City.

I decided to look into the Milton Smithfield thing myself. At that point I didn't feel much like confiding in the police, or even Gary.

As if things weren't bad enough, my mother called that evening to tell me Raymond and Noreen were getting a Betamax VCR. To this day, I have only a flimsy notion of what a VCR does, and I'm pretty sure I don't want one, but I told her I'd had one for years and wasn't happy with it.

"Always breaking down, Mom. Can't depend on it for a minute. There you are, a house full of company, and out it goes again. I just wish Raymond had spoken to me first. I would have given them mine. And Mom, by the way, I lost my job today. I was fired." I don't know why I said that. Laid off would have done.

I heard a gasp, then a groan. "Oh, Bonnie. What are you going to do? I thought they liked you. You must have done something."

"I did nothing, Mom. I'm being replaced—by a machine. I'm obsolete." The notion struck me as funny and I started giggling. At the same time, I knew tears were running down my face.

"Bonnie Jean, I don't know what's going to come of you. All those years with dancing, and now there you are in that city, all alone. No job. If only you were married. You need someone to take care of you. But you know, honey, you can always come home. We've still got your room here."

"Mom, I have to go now. My date is at the door." That was for her, not me.

"Well, all right. But think about what I said. And, oh—I want to remind you. Easter dinner at Raymond's on Sunday. With your boyfriend. Noreen wants you to call and give her his name. She's doing those little place cards this year, for the table, so everyone will know where to sit. Don't forget now."

Sorry, Mom, but I had bigger things on my mind than place cards.

For the record, I wasn't really sick. I just called Ely Sneed and told them I was.

"It's that thing that's going around," I moaned to the firm's operator. There's always a "thing" going around. Nobody ever asks, "What thing?" With any luck at all, they'll even provide you with the symptoms.

"You poor baby," she responded. "You do sound awful. My cousin was out with it for a week. The doctor told him to eat bananas, for the potassium."

"Bananas. Yes, I'll do that."

That whole place was bananas. For me, a cup of black coffee, for Moses a whole can of Mixed Grill for Hearty Eaters. We weren't on the breadline yet.

It was what's called in Manhattan "a neighborhood undergoing gentrification." Streets once lined with seedy transit hotels and discount stores were sprouting boutiques and fern bars. I saw a bodega selling twenty-five-pound sacks of rice. Its next door neighbor, newly painted, advertised twenty-five varieties of imported coffee beans. Something for everyone. On West 15th Street the transition was incomplete. Amidst renovated brownstones and those in various stages of construction were old-law, tub-in-the-kitchen tenements, rusted fire escapes crawling up their fronts. Bums stood in doorways in quiet pairs, clutching bottles and watching, impassive, as their world collapsed, brick by brick, around their feet. Ultimately they would go. Some things can't be beautified.

Number 220 was a three-story brownstone, so tastefully remodeled it could have been in the East 70s.

To contemplate an "investigation" is one thing; to begin it, another. For several minutes I stood on the sidewalk and studied the building. There was nothing on it to indicate it was, or ever had been, Smithfield's Fine Photography.

Then I saw a man walking toward me from across the street. On one foot he wore a tennis shoe without laces, on the other a black tassel loafer, its sole flapping with every step. He could have been twenty or sixty. I couldn't understand a word he said, but it undoubtedly involved the fact that the bottle he was swinging at me was empty. I was not in a generous mood and decided to take my chances inside the building.

Fine wrought-iron banisters led up the steps. I felt a little foolish as I opened the carved wooden door and stepped into the tiny polished jewel of an outer foyer. Sneaking around Ely Sneed's dumpy file room was one thing; this was another. There were two mailboxes and two buzzers. The first, for the bottom floor, listed G. Evans and L. Taylor-Evans, tenants. The second gave me hope: SUNSHINE COLOR LABORATORIES.

I pushed the second button. There was no answer. Then I heard a no-nonsense woman's voice: "I'll call the cops if you're not gone in five seconds." All my resolution dissolved. I turned to rush from the foyer. The next moment the street door opened and a stunning black woman carrying about a ton of photographic equipment blocked my way. She stood in the door watching the bum's slow progress down the steps, then turned to me. "I know I should feel sorry for them, but I get so damned tired of these bums."

Could she help me, she asked then. Her questioning stare

froze me. What was I doing, anyway? I should be home, writing a résumé. Or shopping for a gray suit. Or calling my uncle. There was nothing to stop me from quitting this foolish business.

"Well," I said. "Maybe you can. I wondered if there was anyone in the photo lab?"

"Did they send you?" She was looking at me in such a strange way.

I took a chance. "Yes, they did."

"Boy!" She shook her head slowly. "He's not going to like this."

She had corn-rows, slanting brown eyes, and carried herself like an Ethiopian princess. Under her scrutiny I felt like a visitor from Dubuque.

"You're here. I guess you might as well come up."

Unlocking one of the doors, she led me up a steep flight of stairs. There were two doors at the top. When she opened one, I was almost beaten back by a blast of wind and the sound of chaos.

I'll try to describe the scene. Six people were in a big room. From the din they were making, there might have been sixty. The loudest was a thin, obnoxious little woman in a business suit whose function appeared to be screeching criticism at the other five. "You're not getting the right angle, Greg. Look at her hair. She's screwed it up again. Kristi, you'll never work for us again. I promise you that!"

A young man in tight black leather pants was moving gigantic electric fans around and carrying on about working conditions. "I have a union, you know . . ." There was a photographer, the male counterpart to the woman I'd met in the lobby. He had two cameras around his neck and a third one on a tripod. He was dancing around snapping pictures and shouting instructions like a deranged drill sergeant.

The object of all this attention was a bridal party, of sorts. The tallest bride you've ever seen, with her groom towering over her. A bony zombie of a maid-of-honor. They were in continual motion; up, down, smile, serious now. Huge hot lights beat down from every angle. Fans gave out monsoon-force winds, so that their hair and gowns billowed against a backdrop—of children's furniture. I'm not kidding: a set of miniature white Victorian garden furniture—table and chairs set with child-sized tea-party china.

Any remaining conviction I had was gone. Albert Janowski would never have had anything to do with something like this. I was numb, convinced that in a matter of seconds I would be making a thorough fool of myself.

"Enough, Greg," the bride finally shouted over the din. "I'm exhausted. You're trying to kill us." Without apology, or an ounce of grace, she plopped herself down on the bed of fake grass. I noticed a row of clothespins holding her gown in the back. The groom began scratching his head frantically, and the maid-of-honor said, to no one in particular, "Got a joint?"

"Okay. Ten minutes." The photographer unstrapped his cameras and switched off the lights. The fellow in leather extinguished the fans, quelling the gale. Then the black woman, who I later learned was the photographer's wife, walked over to him and whispered something in his ear. For the first time he turned and saw me.

As I've said, I'm not always a delight to look at, but in general I'm at least as good as average. That wasn't good enough for this one. He staggered back a few steps, mouth open, eyes wide.

"They sent you?"

"Well, actually . . ."

"I told them like for Twisted Sister! Ossie Osborne!" He began walking toward me. "Are they crazy? I tell them I need someone for a rock cover—Apocalypse in Concert—and they send me . . ." His hands-out gesture said it all. "I'm sorry." He lowered his voice. "I don't want to hurt your feelings. You're a pretty girl, but you won't do. You're not the right type. Your hair's too short, you're not thin enough, and you're the . . . wrong age."

The guy was a master of tact. I tried to extricate myself from the mess. "If you'd let me explain . . ."

"I know, I know. You need the work. You all need the work, but be realistic. I mean . . . look at you! Maybe when I get some catalog work. . . ."

He stopped for a moment, and looked at me, harder. "Haven't I used you before? There's something familiar. . . ?"

"I'm investigating a murder."

"You're not from the agency?"

"Not really."

"You're from the police?"

"Not exactly. I'm with a law firm." And no need to elaborate on that. "Bonnie Indermill," I said.

"I see." He took my extended hand gingerly. "Greg Evans. Just let me do something with this bunch. Linda," he called across the room, "would you fix these people some coffee or drinks? Give them anything they want. I'll be a few minutes."

"They're from"—he named a high-fashion monthly. "Prima donnas. Think a half-hour is torture. For the money they're getting— You see that girl?" He nodded at the bridesmaid. She was sitting on a ledge by a window, smoking, bored. "She's seventeen, on the outside. Inside, fifty. Won't last another year. Leads a life like you wouldn't believe. One day her face is going to crumble like those buildings across the street. Here. We can use the office to talk." He showed me into a small dim room at the back of the studio. One word from me, "murder," and he'd forgotten all about chasing me out of his place.

The office was a mess. Everywhere you looked were stacks of negatives, slides, and photographs. In boxes, in shopping bags, laid out in checkerboard patterns on the floor and pinned to the walls. I hopscotched through them to a hard modern sofa where Greg Evans cleared a foot-wide spot for me.

"How did you find me, anyway? This is about that lawyer, right? Janowski?"

"Right." Since I didn't know anything, I'd hoped he would

do all the talking. Oh, what I would have given for the power of a police badge, to be able to say, "Now, tell me everything you know," and expect an answer. As an investigator I was a little rough around the edges. I said, in explanation, "Mr. Janowski left some notes. Your name was among them."

"Man, it took such a long time. Two weeks. I thought I was home free." He pulled his fingers back along the side of his face, stretching the skin taut. "I thought by this time no one knew anything about it."

"It took us a while to find his files, with all the other things."

"Well, to tell you the truth, I felt guilty as hell about not stepping forward, after I saw that articl and his picture in the paper. Hey . . ." His eyes narrowed. "That's where I've seen you. I spend my days looking at pictures. You were the guy's girlfriend."

"No!" Was I going to be haunted by that forever? "That was a mistake. The paper printed a retraction. I was Mr. Janowski's . . . associate at his law firm. And I've been in close contact with the police on this case." That, in a manner of speaking, was true. "You owe us some explanation for your . . . actions."

To my surprise he agreed with me.

"You're right. You know, Miss Indermill, I'll be glad to get it off my chest."

For someone I thought was up to his ears in murder, Greg Evans was eager to talk about it. He told me Albert Janowski had come to his studio on the Wednesday before he was killed.

"I was about to close up for lunch. Janowski came barging in looking for the guy who used to own this place. Milton Smithfield. Said he'd known him years back. Said he'd dug up Smithfield's address in an old file. I told him—Janowski—the truth. Smithfield died in '72. I bought the place from the estate for a song. I'd been an apprentice here under Smithfield. Saved up some money, and now I've got a thriving business. A first-class studio."

"I can see that. Tell me about Mr. Janowski. Did he say anything else to you? Ask any questions?"

"He said a lot to me. He said Smithfield and I had caused him a lot of grief. I didn't know what he was talking about. He said I was a liar and he'd have me in front of the authorities where I should have been twenty-five years ago. Fat bastard. I thought he was crazy, or from the IRS. Those guys will do anything. I offered to show him my accounts. I have nothing to hide. No. You know what he wanted to see?"

"What?"

"Smithfield's records. Can you believe that? Twenty-some years old and he acts like I can lay my hands on them just like that. There are some things around, sure, but Janowski's attitude pissed me off. A real pompous asshole. I told him I'd thrown everything out when I bought the business. Then he pulled out a sheet of negatives from his briefcase and started waving them at me."

"What's a sheet of negatives?"

In answer, he fished around through the heap of papers on the table next to him and drew from them a semi-transparent plastic sheet about eight by ten inches, with six or seven horizontal slots through which were inserted rows of photo negatives. I took the sheet in my hand; it folded like an accordion.

"You put your black and white negatives in, sequentially, to protect them and keep them in order. Janowski kept waving them at me and carrying on, saying that I must know something. I took a look. I look at hundreds of those things every week. These I wasn't familiar with. They were pretty good shots, probably professional, but old. Early sixties, maybe, from the clothes and hairstyles. People fooling around at a party. Outside, you know, swimming and playing tennis. I didn't know what to make of it, and I told Janowski that."

"So he left then?"

"Not quite. The final insult. He waved a ten-dollar bill at me and asked me if I'd print them up for him. Right then.

Some big shot. I told him to go to the drugstore and save himself five bucks."

"And then?"

"And then, nothing. That was the last I saw of him, until I opened that newspaper." He closed his eyes and rubbed his temples again. "That kind of trouble I don't need."

"Why is that? If you'd just gone to the police then . . ."

"Because, Miss Indermill, when you're black, you've got to be twice as good as the competition. And when you're black, and in the arts, you've got to be ten times as good and pure as fresh snow. If any hint of crime were to touch me—especially something like Janowski's murder in that hotel, with all the talk about drugs and that hooker he was involved with—my business would be in real trouble. My clients aren't those hang-loose models out there; they're publishers and cosmetics companies, and they're straight. And if I intend to continue growing . . ."

He took a deep breath then, and pushed himself back into the sofa like he was going to force himself to relax. "I shouldn't be lecturing you. You're just doing your job. I'll tell you the truth. I picked up the telephone, five, ten times to call the police, but I couldn't go through with it. I know what it's like to be poor. I grew up poor and there are parts of myself I can't get away from, no matter how far I go."

"Mr. Evans?"

"Greg."

"Greg. And please call me Bonnie. You said you had some of Mr. Smithfield's papers. I know it's an imposition, but if you could dig them out . . ."

"It's no imposition. I already did. When I read about that murder, I panicked and went through this place like a maniac. I wanted to destroy anything that might connect me to Janowski. But there was nothing. Nothing." Greg unbent his long frame and walked over to a file cabinet. He pulled a shoebox-sized container from a drawer.

"This is it." He placed the prize on the sofa between us. My heart beat faster. "All that's left of Smithfield's part of the business. I changed the name, redid the building, got all new equipment."

I lifted the lid slowly, half expecting all the answers to jump out at me. Inside was a stack of yellowing receipts, a few bills of sale, an old deed to the house, and an old rolodex, the same ancient vintage type Ely Sneed used.

"I can save you the trouble of looking through it," Greg said. "The rolodex is the only thing. It has the names and addresses of all Smithfield's clients, along with notes about how they paid. I hung on to it in case any of his old clients came to see me. Sometimes they used to, but most of them were older, ready to retire, and a lot of them . . . they weren't the kind of business I wanted. Smithfield wasn't above . . . entrapment."

"What's that?"

"You know. Catching the husband with the blonde in a motel room. He did some work for private investigators. I remember my first job for him. I was a tough kid out of vocational school in the South Bronx, and what he was doing even scared me. There we were, the two of us, hanging off a roof with a telephoto lens pointed at someone's bedroom window. All that ended when he died. Actually, it ended a few years before. He got crazy. Paranoid. Guilt, I think. At the end he had to be watched all the time. One night he snuck up here and set fire to his file cabinet. I remember carrying him back downstairs. Bet he didn't weigh a hundred pounds. Felt like a bird in my arms. He was crying. I could understand it; his life's work amounted to one file cabinet full of husbands zipping up their pants and wives pulling sheets over their heads."

"Did he have a family?" I asked.

"His wife died a couple years before he did. There were no kids."

There was a soft knock on the office door. Linda Evans poked her head in and beckoned to her husband. "We were behind before we got started this morning, Greg. This is killing us. Let's get these people moving."

"Okay. Set them up. I'll be right there." When she'd closed

the door, he rifled through the rolodex and handed me one of the cards. "This is it. All I came up with. Your firm's name on one of the index cards. They were one of Smithfield's clients. No bills. There's a notation here"—he pointed to a faded pen mark—"Exch. Exchange work. Apparently your firm did some work for Smithfield in exchange for his photographic work."

The studio was cranking up again. As Greg Evans showed me to the door, lights and fans were turning on, the woman in the suit getting louder and louder. To satisfy my own curiosity, I asked Greg about the tiny furniture in the backdrop.

"Perspective," he answered. "Makes it look like there's a distance between the models and background. Look at the June issue of the magazine. You'll see."

"I will. And thanks for your help."

"Glad to get it off my chest. And, Miss Indermill, by the way," he called as I walked down the stairs, "you're a pretty good type. If you're interested, I may be able to get you some catalog work."

It was the nicest thing that had happened to me in ages, and I was hardly out the front door before I was crying again. I stumbled into the drugstore across the street from Evans's studio and bought a double pack of tissues to replenish my supply, then rode a filthy A train home, sniffling and blowing my nose and trying to figure out what all my evidence meant. I'd told Greg Evans he was a big help. From his point of view the interview had probably been a success. He'd been able to exorcize something nasty. But I was still in a muddle, more confused than ever.

Milton Smithfield, semi-pornographer, not above "entrapment." Greg Evans had said no children, but the letter in Smithfield's file was addressed to "My Dear Little Girl." Was his dear little girl the tootsie D. Smith from the Hotel Central? Might he have taken photos of Albert in a compromising situation years before? Or of Stephanie? That was more likely. I had countless possibilities, and no answers.

Before me lay two days of résumé updating—an exercise in

fiction I never enjoyed—and want-ad searching. A deadly combination. The last time I'd been out of the city was for Albert's funeral, and that didn't count for anything. Suddenly, Iron Valley flowered in my imagination. I saw rolling green hills, red barns with painted Amish designs, covered bridges, clean air, clean streets, beloved grandparents, and quiet, obedient children.

There was an eight-forty A.M. bus for Scranton, Saturday morning. I was on it. I had called Gary from the bus station. He was out, but a seductive Englishwoman on his answering machine asked me if I wouldn't like to leave a message at the sound of the beep. I had one minute to make my bus, and said simply, "Gary, I think I've found something."

WELCOME TO BEAUTIFUL IRON VALLEY
HOME OF IRON VALLEY STEEL CORP.
Est. 1924   *Pop. 7,793*

The transmission screamed in agony as the bus wound its way around the blacktop curves. The sign had been erected in what must have been a fit of blind optimism. Valley it was, beautiful, never. It was an ugly pit that had been clawed out of the face of the land.

On the bus, even miles away, I had seen the big gray-red clouds. Fumes from the blast furnace, the driver told me. As we lumbered through the town to the bus station, we passed huge piles, almost mountains, of black slag. They cast shadows over sidewalks and darkened store windows, and all the town—its buildings, the ragged little park at its center, even the people—was gray and in some way gritty.

All bus stations are awful, bleak and redolent with the stench of diesel fuel and exhaustion. The New York Port Authority is one of the worst, but even that squalid horror was better than this one. The Port Authority at least has life. Here there was nothing. No one with an eye on my purse, no obnoxious teenager with a blaring radio, no anxious traveler with crying babies. Just one dumpy, gritty, middle-aged couple and a ticket clerk, all staring out the dirty window at an invisible spot on the horizon. Duane Hanson sculptures of three people in a rural bus station.

The first thing I did was make sure I had a way out of Beautiful Iron Valley.

"How late this afternoon do buses connect to New York City?"

The clerk answered mechanically: "Bus to Scranton every two hours; Scranton to New York every hour on the hour; last bus out of here at eight; first one six in the morning; every two hours after that."

"If I decide to stay the night, where could I find a decent room?"

He had a little monk's fringe of white hair and washed-out blue eyes. They widened at my question. No one ever decided to spend the night. I noticed that the other two zombies had turned my way.

"Well, there's the Royal George. That's pretty nice. Some other places, depending on what you're looking for. . . ." He gave me a pale, knowing wink. I thanked the old buzzard and asked to borrow a local phone book.

There was a D. Smith listed at 102 8th Streeet, and sure enough, a Mrs. W. Schmoulack at 51 Chestnut Street. The second seemed like a surer bet, and after checking my overnight case in a locker, I gave the Chestnut Street address to the lone cabbie outside the station.

There is a kind of housing development that always looks the same, whether it's in Southern California or Long Island or Iron Valley: two ranch styles alternating with one colonial, alternating with one deformed split-level. Trees are ever stringy, grass always parched, and neighborhoods bloom with Maple Lanes, Evergreen Terraces, and Arbor Ways, as if the builder had hoped that words might kindle the experience. Chestnut Street must have been christened before the blight hit the country. There wasn't a chestnut in sight. I suppose it was on the right side of the tracks, but only just. The two well-tended lawns had FOR SALE signs on them; the rest of the homes and lawns were shabby, like the occupants had run out of energy and fertilizer at the same time. At the end of the street I could see one crabgrass jungle. Wouldn't you know it was number 51.

A ranch style, green siding with white shutters, but the white had yellowed and the green had faded to a dull chartreuse until they were a monochrome. One of the front shutters was hanging by a screw. My limited confidence sagged. I asked the cabbie to wait for me.

The broken-up asphalt sidewalk led to a torn screen door. When the doorbell didn't work, I resorted to pounding. No answer. I wasn't about to give up that easily, though. Unable to reach the front windows, I decided to try the rear.

The backyard was guarded by the remains of what had been a white picket fence. I was able to push it aside at a corner and walk through, into a hip-high weed patch. In a far corner of the yard was one of those circular clotheslines, leaning at a forty-five-degree angle. There was a rusted child's swing set in the center, and an ancient, spilled-over sandbox that the neighborhood cats had put to good use.

I climbed the back steps and pressed my face to the door window. Inside, from what I could see, was a mess, with stacks of newspapers and junk lining the walls.

"I got a key if you're interested. They didn't tell me they was sending anybody over, or I'd of met you." I turned around.

She was a worn woman. She could have been twenty or forty. There was a baby in her arms and two toddlers pulling at her skirt. All three were whining. She pushed a couple of pickets away and walked into the yard.

"Well, I guess they didn't have time. I just got here and wanted to see the place right away. . . ." "They," I assumed, were real-estate agents.

She pulled a key from her pocket, inserted it in the back lock, and there I was in the kitchen, with no idea of what I was looking for. Also, for a moment, I felt the most frightening déjà vu, that I had been there before, peeling potatoes over the mustard-colored sink, eyeballing a meat loaf in the all-electric oven. My stomach fluttered and I wanted to run from the place.

". . . copper pipes. Don't build them like this no more."

Thank God. I breathed deep and walked through the kitchen. I don't think I can make you see the amount of clutter—junk, stuff—in that house. Everywhere. The resident, or former resident, must have been mad, I thought. There were newspapers and magazines stacked everywhere, floor to ceiling, and other refuse on top of the papers—pots and lampshades, a tricycle covered with a moth-eaten blanket topped by a rusted toaster. I followed a narrow trail through the dining area.

"Kind of a mess, isn't it?" I was hoping for a clue about the occupant.

"Yeah. It's a nice layout, though. Come on into the living room; you can get a better notion. Your husband at the mine? Most of them are around here."

There was a peculiar odor in the living room, sweet decay and antiseptic. And more junk.

"Quite the collector," I said.

"She didn't go out much. Real old. Scared of lots of things. Just kept herself here with all this stuff. A good neighbor, though. Minded her own business, if you know what I mean. Didn't have no visitors. Was dead in here over a week before anyone missed her. Right there, where you're standing, on that couch."

Was that her outline, pressed into the opaque plastic slip-cover? I backed away from the awful thing.

"There's an old bomb shelter out back. Don't guess you want to see it.."

"No." I was thumbing through a stack of magazines on a bookshelf. "How to Spot the Red Menace," "Global Disasters in the Near Future" (circa 1956), "The Jewish-Wall Street Conspiracy," "The Papish Plot: We Will Smite Them at Armageddon."

"I understand there's a daughter. Doris?" I tried keeping my voice light.

"Doris? She's the old lady's granddaughter. You think that one would have anything to do with the old woman, you got another think coming. She hated her. No way. Doris just came by and picked up a few things she wanted, after the old woman was in the ground. Doris's got other fish to fry. Always did, if you catch my meaning." If I didn't, the snicker in her voice made it clear. "Say, how'd you hear about Doris, anyway?"

"Oh, they just happened to mention that there was a relative living."

"Guess she'll inherit, if anyone ever buys this place. You think you're interested?"

"Possibly. Has anyone else looked at it?"

"Yeah. One colored guy, about a week ago. Imagine that. No colored moving in next to me. I as good as told him that. Bring down the neighborhood; ruin property values. 'Course, you know how it is around here. Nobody much interested in property any more, since the mine's been on half-time."

A crash and a child's cry from one of the back rooms interrupted her inspired pitch. "Where's that brat of mine? Hey, you, Billy. You get out of there or I'm gonna beat your butt!"

I followed her into the bedroom and watched her drag a screaming kid from under a pile of junk.

"Where could I get hold of Doris, if I wanted to talk to her about this place?"

"Why would you want to see Doris? She don't want nothing to do with the sale. Just go back to the agent's office. He's the one you want." She was already counting her commission. "Hey, you got any kids?"

"No, I don't."

"Too bad. I was hoping we might be able to exchange sitting. Be able to get out of the house once in a while."

I couldn't get out of there fast enough.

The cab driver was surprised when I gave him the 8th Street address. "You just up here for the day, you ought to go up to the mountains. Some pretty spots there. You're going to spend your day driving around the slums?"

"Eighth Street's fine."

The wrong side of the tracks. I can't define it, but I know it when I see it. Number 102, 8th Street, was in the center of what must have been the Times Square of Iron Valley. It was a pink stucco (shades of California) apartment building set between a bar—the kind with a neon cocktail glass blinking outside, and a movie theater advertising two adult films. Across the street a nondescript white shingle building announced in red block letters: TOPLESS.

The apartment mailbox showed a D. Smith in 4A. The stairs were on the outside of the building, and Miss Smith's door was clearly visible from the street. I climbed the steps and knocked on the door, first softly, and then louder. I turned to leave, then turned back and tried the knob. The door swung open easily.

Someone lived in 4A. The place looked clean, washed and dusted. The kettle on the stove was warm to my touch.

"Doris?" My voice sounded strange and strained. For all I knew, I was trespassing in the apartment of Albert Janowski's murderer. I called her name again and when no one answered began, in what I thought was fine detective tradition, snooping around. The living room was a French Provincial extravaganza. Everything was white, curly, and striped with gold leaf. The dark brown shopping bag tucked next to the sofa stood out: MACY'S, HERALD SQUARE. That's Manhattan. I took a look at the contents. There were two red-and-white "I Love New York" T-shirts, one medium, one extra large, a little tin Statue of Liberty, and a rolled-up Big Apple poster. Do murderers buy souvenirs, I wondered?

In the bedroom there was a messy vanity—the kind with a million light bulbs around the mirror. Its top held at least one of every lotion and potion imaginable. There were things to remove hair and lines, to darken light spots, to lighten dark spots, there was loose powder, pressed powder, enough lipstick to scrawl your nickname over every subway in New

York. The fuzzy contents of a teacup, which I thought for a second were bugs, proved to be false eyelashes. I looked in the closet. It was crammed with women's clothes of a tacky/exotic type. Zebra stripes, feathers, and lots of red and black things you could see through.

On the bed, folded in fresh, neat little stacks, was someone's laundry. Most of it was the standard stuff: sheets, towels, women's underthings—again, red and black dominated. There was one stack, though, of something else. I couldn't figure out what. I picked one off the top, and the next thing you know I was struggling to refold a pair of jockey shorts that would have spanned Moby Dick's middle.

"You looking for something, lady?"

Honest to God, if the window had been open, I would have jumped out. There, in the bedroom door, completely blocking it with his bulk, holding up his stomach with a rubber basket of laundry, was the fattest man I'd ever seen. He didn't look so jolly, either. He had an unearthly pallor, like he never went out in daylight, and a head of black hair that stood straight up in a tough, greasy butch. He dropped the laundry basket by the door and walked toward the bed. His brown plaid pants were strained to the point of bursting, and his pink nylon shirt gaped between every button. I was a dead woman.

"You just keep quiet there, and hand me your purse."

Jesus! From New York City, and I'm being robbed in Iron Valley, Pennsylvania, where people don't even lock their doors. I did as I was told. You don't argue with Godzilla.

He went through the purse carefully, the wallet, my glasses case, my keys, my Ely Sneed check stub, fingering each item thoughtfully before depositing it in a stack on the bed. It occurred to me that he didn't want to rob me. He was looking for something, like I was, and like me, he didn't know what.

"If you'll tell me what you're looking for, maybe I can help you."

"I'm the one ought to be asking that question. What are you

doing walking around this apartment? Where you come from people just walk in, where they're not invited?"

As a matter of fact, they most certainly do, but I didn't tell him that.

"No. I'm looking for Doris Smith because I think she can help me. A good friend of mine was killed a few weeks ago. . . ."

I clutched at straws, trying to get some reaction from him. He was like a stone Buddha.

"You're from New York? You know anything about that colored boy who was here last weekend? He wanted to help Doris too, he said."

"No. I don't know what you're talking about."

"Well, I'm going to tell you the same thing I told him. Doris left for New York three, four weeks ago on the bus, and she ain't been back. Was going to see someone there. Must of liked what she saw, because she ain't been back. The colored boy, he tried to get tough with me. Pulled a knife . . . He'll be more careful who he pulls a knife on next time." He smiled at me, showing the biggest dimples you've ever seen, and began placing my things back in my bag. His hands were surprisingly graceful.

I decided to drop my ace card. "I'm staying at the Royal George tonight. If Doris should turn up, tell her I was a friend of Albert's, and I may know something about her father's invention—the one that's worth so much—and about the money she's got coming to her." An unadulterated fabrication and a pure shot in the dark. I was waiting for one of his doughy fists to slam me across the room, but he moved his bulk out of the doorway to let me pass.

"Sure, lady. If she should turn up, I'll let her know. Doubt it, though."

After collecting my bag from the bus station, I checked into the Royal George. Given what I'd seen of Iron Valley, I expected another Hotel Central. This one was a delight, really. For a price that in New York City wouldn't get you a decent dinner, I got a little suite, all ruffles and pink-flowered wall-paper.

I dreamed of a moonless, rainy night. I was being chased through a maze by a strange trio: a fat, pale white man, a thin black man with Greg Evans's elegant features, and Stephanie Kellogg. All three were laughing at me. In a half-sleep, half-terrified dream, I felt them catch me. I felt their hands on my skin, soft fingers on my face, a little slap, and then a bigger one. I woke with a horrified start. The fat man was standing over me in the dark. I opened my mouth to scream, and he slapped his hand over it.

"Friend of mine wants to see you. You keep quiet. I'll wait in the other room for you to get dressed." He was a mammoth vision in a purple polyester leisure suit, and I might have laughed if I hadn't been convinced I was in the clutches of Albert's murderers, probably only minutes from death myself.

He hustled me down the deserted back staircase and out into an aged white Cadillac with shark fins at the back and rust spots at the bottom. It leaned and creaked under his bulk. I realized that he controlled my door electronically, from his side.

"How did you get into my room, anyway?" I asked him.

"I got a lot of pull in this town. You ask anybody. Ain't no one in Iron Valley don't know T. C. Crumm, Junior." He maneuvered the big car through the quiet streets. In the distance, rockets of hot gas from the smelter burst through the night sky, turning the Milky Way a dull red. A few turns and we were back on 8th Street. T. C. Crumm, Junior, pulled into the alley next to the TOPLESS place, turned off the ignition, and unlocked my door.

We walked through an unmarked side entrance, past a long makeshift bar and into a cavernous room where a thick cloud of smoke hung from the ceiling and the smell of stale beer was murderous. Through my sleep-starved eyes I saw a dismal scene: scattered around the room were big Formica tables sur-

rounded by mismatched chairs. There hadn't been even a per-
functory attempt at decoration. Not so much as a neon beer
sign. Around some of the tables lifeless men in work clothes
and a few boozy women sat quietly, drinking and smoking,
not speaking. "Your Cheatin' Heart" was howling out of a
couple of cheap speakers.

The fat man showed me to an empty table and left me
there. If I was in the hands of murderers, they were being
pretty casual about me. I could have walked out, or screamed
for help.

A minute later a spotlight fell on a low stage at the far end
of the room, and the fat man stepped through a curtain.

"Now, ladies and gentlemen, here's the gal you've all been
waiting for. Our own little DeeDee Smith."

There are very few people who can take off their clothes in
public without looking ridiculous. Little DeeDee wasn't one of
them. To begin with, she was not little but big, in the raw-
boned way of someone who has dieted strenuously and
whose flesh has shrunken faster than her skin. Put on a faded
housedress and plaster a few whining kids to her legs and she
would have been indistinguishable in type from the woman
who had shown me the Schmoulack house earlier that day.
But, like the lady said, Doris—or DeeDee—had other fish to
fry.

She wore a black semi-transparent blouse, knotted at the
waist, a gold-lamé bikini bottom, red plastic mules, and had
orange hair done up like a pumpkin. When "Your Cheatin'
Heart" was replaced, mid-wail, by a disco song, she artlessly
untied the blouse and threw it into the audience.

The next few minutes was a temporary triumph of tired,
sagging flesh over gravity. Like someone with St. Vitus'
Dance, DeeDee bounced convulsively, sexlessly, taking routine grotesque jabs at the audience with her pelvis. Her
breasts flapped against her washboard rib cage and from
where I sat, even through the haze of smoke, I could see that
her legs were streaked by fat blue veins.

The fat man came back to my table during the show. His

little pig eyes glistened. "I got a real gold mine there." He meant it. His voice rang with pride.

The highlight of DeeDee's performance was something so disgusting I can't even talk about it. You'd have to see it to believe it anyway. It was enough to make one man sitting near the stage leap from his chair, snatch his hardhat from under the table, and back away from the dancer, yelling, "Shit, DeeDee. You're a dirty pig!"

Fatso was convulsed. His tremendous blubber quivered and he pounded his doughy fists on the table while tears ran down his cheeks. His lips puckered like a choirboy's and he made little hootie-wheezie noises through them.

The disco song ended as abruptly as it had begun, there was a smattering of applause, one whistle, someone laughed, and the titillation was all over for a while. DeeDee walked nonchalantly off the stage, pausing to retrieve the black blouse from a waitress.

Fatso made a slow, gasping recovery. "Come on," he finally said. "She can see you now."

DeeDee was sitting in front of a mirror in an office–dressing room combination. The desk in front to her was littered with tubes and jars of makeup.

"Doris, honey, this is the gal I told you about. Says she wants to talk to you. Indermill?"

"Yes. Bonnie." I stuck out my hand and said, "How do you do." She ignored it.

"Take a load off, honey." She pointed to a rumpled daybed. "So, you're a friend of that lawyer Albert's, huh." She had slipped into a leopard-spotted duster. Scooping a big gob of white cream from a jar, she slapped it onto her face and began rubbing furiously, lifting off great smears of color and most of her features as well. "Makeup turns men on. You ever want to turn anybody on, honey, you got to get some more color on you." She shot a quick glance back at me through the mirror. "Don't hurt your complexion none."

Fatso nodded his agreement.

"Thanks. I'll have to try that. Yes, I was Albert Janowski's friend. He told me that if anything happened to him, I should look you up. He showed me a copy of a letter your father sent you. Said you'd fill me in on the details."

They did not look impressed. I tried to add some realism to my story. "I'm the one who identified the body. That hurt."

How bizarre that made me feel. It is one thing to cover yourself with lies. I had been doing a lot of that recently, but now I was starting to act in my own dramas. "I'm hoping you can help me find out who did it. You've got a stake in it, you know, with all that money from the invention. . . ."

Money was the magic word. She snapped to the fat man, "She looks okay, Junior. Get us something to drink. We have a lot of talking to do."

Junior pulled an unlabeled bottle from the desk drawer and poured each of us a glass of something deadly. The fumes from my glass almost did me in. Doris slugged hers down like it was soda and held up her glass. "Hit me again, Junior."

Sometime Around Midnight

"I never met my old man. All I know about him is what my mom told me. He was a big shot from New York. An inventor. Kind of an artistic type, she said." DeeDee/Doris took a long drag on a cigarette, and smoke billowed around her. "See, my mom moved to Pittsburgh in the late thirties. Things was booming out there then. It must have been some good times. At least she had enough sense to get out of this dump."

"You're not doing so bad in this dump, honey." That was Junior, insulted.

"Yeah, but who knows what I could of been if I could of gotten out of here permanently. I just never got the right breaks. Maybe if I get that money . . . You and me, Junior. We'll get a club up in the hills . . ."

Junior nodded from his chair. "Yeah."

"Anyways," she continued. "She met him there—Pittsburgh. He was on a business trip or something. Some big deal. She said he treated her to a real good time. Hit all the night spots, toured the old fort—Fort Pitt—and one of those glassmaking places. Stayed in the best place in town. Here, you look at this. Let me show you. . . ." She reached under the desk for her handbag, fumbled through it, and withdrew a wallet from which she pulled an old snapshot. Mom and Pop sitting at a nightclub table, caught by a harsh flash.

"Good-looking couple, weren't they?"

"They sure were," I agreed. Actually, they were awful. The woman was plump, bleached, and hard-faced, the man much older, a sodden little weasel.

Junior took the old photo from my hand and smiled at it. "That's where my DeeDee got her looks."

"Yeah. I just wish I had gotten their smarts." She retrieved the picture and put it back in the wallet. "Anyways, he was married, and you know how that is. So when Mom found out she was expecting me, she didn't have no choice. Had to come back here to stay with her mother. Changed both our names though, to Smithfield. Told people she was married in Pittsburgh and that her husband died, so I wouldn't have people laughing at me. You know how they make fun. Of course, my grandmother found out. That old bitch. I hope she's burning in hell right now. Made my life miserable. Mom's too. My mom was a fun gal; she liked a good time, like me.

"I remember the fights they'd have whenever Mom went out at night, the old bag screaming that Mom was going to the devil. Mom just couldn't live like that. Nobody would with any smarts. When I was seven she met a nice guy, a salesman. Decided to go out to the coast and find work. She said she'd send for me. Got a few letters. Can show them to you if you want. Then I never heard from her again. I know she loved her little Doris. Something had to have happened to her. And there I was, left with the old witch. Hell of a note that was. Hit me again, Junior."

She was on her third glass of whatever it was we were drinking, and I was afraid she'd pass out before we got to the business with Albert. I tried to steer her away from her mother and onto her father. "What about your father, Doris? Did he ever get in touch with you, other than that one letter?"

"Seems like he did, only I didn't know nothing about it. I remember when my mom was still around, we'd get a check from New York now and then. She'd never give it to the old lady. Always spent it on herself and me. Clothes, restaurants. Caused a big fight every time. After Mom left, I thought the checks stopped. Life was shit for me then. I stayed with the old lady till I was about fifteen, then I met a man from Chicago. Said if I'd come with him, he'd do a lot for me. Get me in the movies. I was a real looker in those days."

"You still are, honey." Junior again.

"I ran away with him. Dirty sonofabitch. He did a lot for me, all right. Got me in a couple of skin flicks, got me pregnant, beat me up, and dumped me. I had a miscarriage. Just as well. After that I kicked around Chicago for a while, doing waitress work, trying to get a break. Finally married an Air Force boy. Met him at the shore there. Lake Michigan. I always was a sucker for a uniform. Filled out his dress grays real nice. But he was no good."

DeeDee's speech was slurring, and her eyes had a faraway look. This was getting out of hand.

"How did you get to know Albert, Doris? What about the letter?"

"Albert? Oh yeah, him. Like I said, I just kicked around for a while. Marriage didn't work out. I wanted to get out to the coast and find my old lady, but I never made it. The . . ." She leaned toward me. "You won't ever tell nobody about this, will you?"

"Never."

"I got caught. Not by the cops. They never got a thing on me. But I was working with this guy. We had a thing going. I'd get some guy, you know, like a tourist or a businessman from out of town. I'd get him to come up to my room. My friend would come in, pretend he was my husband, and the guy would get all shook and pay us something to keep quiet. It was okay. Never hurt nobody. Then we got the wrong guy. One of the boys."

Junior gave his head a doleful shake. "Bad move."

"Pardon me?" I said.

"The boys—the mob. Where you been, honey? They beat

the shit out of my partner. Face looked like a piece of raw meat. That's when I decided to come back here. Been here ever since. Got married one more time. An ironworker. He was no good. Always spoiling for a fight. Took up with Junior here a few years back. That's when I shortened my name to Smith—when I went on the stage. Smithfield sounded like some kind of ham. Junior's the best man I've ever known. Don't get ugly too often." She gave him a woozie, affectionate smile, and held up her glass for another hit.

"I can take care of myself pretty good when I have to," Junior said, refilling her glass.

This was going terribly. I tried to jar her memory. "Doris, that letter. Would you tell me about the letter? You were in New York. With Albert Janowski. Albert got shot."

"Oh, sure. I was getting to all that. I never went to see the old bag. Got a call one day about a month or two ago that she was dead. She laid in that stinking house rotting for a week before anybody found her. Nobody cared about her. After she was buried, I went over there to see if I wanted anything. Place stank all to hell. I was going through some papers and I found this pile of stuff from my old man. Cards to me, mostly. The old bitch. He kept sending money right through the sixties, but you think she ever said a word about it? Just cashed the checks and kept the money. There was only that one letter, the one you saw. Had a bunch of film clipped to it. She had hid it there all that time. Crazy old bag. She was scared everyone was out to get her. No one would of wanted her.

"I took that letter and talked it over with Junior. We couldn't see anything worth any big bucks in that film. Just some people fooling around outdoors. But you can't tell. We decided it could be a break. Guess we should have gotten the film developed first, but who knew. I took the letter and a few bucks and went to New York. Checked into this hotel by the bus station and gave that Lawrence Petit a call. Turns out he'd been dead for years. I didn't know what else to do, so I asked the operator to let me talk to whoever was in charge. That's how I got Janowski."

Junior decided to be sociable and join the conversation. "I was in New York a few years back. On a business deal. I think it stinks. Nothing but spooks and Puerto Ricans. Ought to just blow it up."

Doris nodded her agreement. "Yeah. It stinks. That guy Albert was pretty nice to me, though. I read him the letter over the phone, and told him about those negatives. Felt kind of funny. Like, you know, sounds like my old man was off his rocker when he wrote it. Albert didn't laugh at me. He thought he remembered my dad. That made me feel good, to have family that a big-shot lawyer knew. Anyways, Albert said I shouldn't come to the office. Told me he'd come by the hotel and take a look at those negatives. Got kind of excited when he looked them over. Took me to a swanky place for dinner. Waiters in tuxes. And a wine steward. Can you beat that? Some guy to open your wine for you and pour it out. Stands there while you taste it. I wanted to tell him it was rotten, just for fun, but Albert said it was real good stuff."

"I would of said it," Junior commented.

"Over in Brooklyn, right across the bridge on the river, with a real nice view of New York City. He had a nice car, too. Black Lincoln Continental. Not as nice as Junior's—I always like a Caddie—but nice."

I like to think of that still—that Albert Janowski, staid old dumpy Albert, took this poor, battered floozie to the River Café. I can't imagine what he was thinking, but I'm glad he did it.

Junior had become agitated. He stirred his bulk around. "Just how nice was that Albert? You didn't say nothing about no wine steward."

"Aw, honey, you don't have to worry about that. Albert was a real nice guy, but dull. Just a poor dumb galoot. Sure, he wouldn't of minded fooling around. You can always tell." She smiled at me. I nodded agreement. "You know, he kept helping me on and off with my coat, holding the car door. But I was there on business."

"Yeah?" Junior's voice had a nasty edge. "There's all kinds of business."

I interrupted, not anxious to see Junior get ugly. "What did Albert say about the letter?"

"Oh, he was real interested. Said he wanted to make some copies of it, and get the film developed. Said he found my old man's file and he was going to check out his business. Said as far as he could tell from the file, my old man died . . . intestate."

At that, Junior gave a loud hoot. "That mean he couldn't get it up anymore?"

With no warning and no perceptible change in her mood, Doris splashed the remains of her drink at him. "No, moron. That's what I thought when he first said it, too. Didn't know how you could tell that from a file. But it means he died without a will. Albert said there had been some inventions, but he didn't know nothing about the money. Said he'd check it all out. We had a swell dinner that night, then he drove me back to the hotel. Took the papers and the film. Said I should sit tight and he'd get in touch with me. Called the next day and said he would be by the next afternoon—Thursday. I had a good time by myself. Picked up some souvenirs, even went to a Broadway show. I felt like a society girl. It was all naked. Thought I'd get some ideas for the act. I don't know, though." She shrugged. "Didn't learn anything much. Naked's naked, I guess.

"Albert called Thursday morning and said he'd be by around five. Said another guy knew some of what was going on, and wanted to see the pictures. Albert was going to meet this guy at a coffee shop and show them to him, and then come up to the hotel after that. When Albert got to my room, he told me the drugstore hadn't gotten my pictures developed yet. He gave me back my daddy's letter, and put a copy in his pocket. Says he put another copy in the office file." DeeDee looked at me quizzically. "He was the kind of guy liked to keep things straight, wasn't he?"

"He sure was," I said.

"I could tell. Anyway, he's real nervous. He says when he was talking to this guy, he let it slip that my name's Smith, and he thinks this other guy followed him to the hotel, and maybe we should get out of there. Well, before we can, here's this guy, knocking at the door, calling, 'Albert, I know you're in there.' Well, Albert tells me to get into the bathroom and lock the door while he talks to this guy. I'm thinking it's pretty strange, but what do I know? He was the lawyer. The smart one. He told me he went to college seven years."

"Huh? My lawyer ain't so damned smart," Junior said. "Last time he was out here he got pukin' drunk. Waitress almost quit on me."

Ignoring him, Doris went on. "So here I am, hid in the bathroom. Right away I see there's no lock, but at first it's just funny. I keep thinking about how I could jump out the door and yell 'Surprise.' Then it gets scary, me sitting there on the commode while those guys yell at each other."

"Could you hear what they were saying?"

"Yeah. Couldn't help but hear. Albert was yelling about how it's in the letter, and saying, 'I've got the pictures to prove it,' and the other guy's saying how they're all in it together and Albert's a damned fool if he opens up a can of worms. Then I heard some noise, like they was shoving each other around, and then Albert saying, 'Now you wait a minute. Are you crazy?' and his voice is going all high. By that time I was real scared. I climbed out the bathroom window and hid over by the next room. Then I heard these shots—I could tell what they were—and the next thing I hear someone tearing the bathroom apart, even pulling the top off the commode. I knew it wasn't Albert because he would of said something to me. He would of wondered where I was."

I looked over at Junior. He was snoring softly, his several chins resting on his shirt front.

"Did you ever hear the other guy's name? Did Albert ever use it? Can you remember?"

Doris thought a moment and shook her head. "No."

"Did he tell you which drugstore he'd taken the film to?"

"No. All he said was he had hidden the receipt. I guess my daddy's pictures are gone forever."

"What did you do then?"

"I waited a while, till I couldn't hear nothing, then I climbed back through the window. I was scared, but I couldn't just sit out there, freezing my butt off. You never saw such a mess as that bedroom was in. Torn all to hell. My suitcase dumped all over the place. Some of my stuff turned inside out. I went over to the side of the bed to pick up some things, and that's when I saw the poor sucker Albert. Laid out there dead with his pants pulled down and his feet tied to the bed. Don't know why anybody would want to do a thing like that. Almost shit myself. Said to myself, 'Doris, girl, you get your ass out of here fast.' So I got my stuff together and went out the back way, through this garbage and all. Had to wait over an hour for the bus. I tell you, girl, that was some of the longest two hours I ever spent. I kept looking at the clock, and hiding behind the paper, waiting for some stranger to pull out a gun and plug me like he did poor Albert."

We sat in the smoky quiet for a few moments, both of us contemplative, confused.

"Do you believe in genes?" she asked finally.

"Jeans?"

"Genes. You know, like you get passed down to you, half on your mother's side, half on your dad's? I've been thinking about that, since I saw that letter from my old man. Like I knew my grandmother was nuts. Figure my mom was all right, and always thought my dad was, too. Then I read that letter and got kind of scared, like, you know, another twenty, twenty-five years and I'll be crazy, too. You think there's anything to that?"

I had a lot to think about during the long ride home. Maybe if I'd had some sleep and skipped the "one for the road" from Junior's bottle, I'd have done a better job of it.

I kept trying to work my jigsaw of clues into some order. There is a photographer, not above entrapment work, who in a fit of crazed deathbed remorse sends his illegitimate daughter some negatives, an "investment" he shares with Gary Petit's father. The negatives collect dust for fifteen years, until the daughter finds them and, thinking her break has come, tries to contact Lawrence Petit. She ends up with Albert Janowski by accident. He sees something of value in the negatives. But somehow, someone else finds out about them, and that someone kills Albert.

Had Tony been on the mark about the firm picnic back in 1962? Greg Evans said the negatives showed people in dated clothing. But he hadn't seen anything in the photos to alarm him. Neither had DeeDee and Junior. You can't really tell anything from black and white negatives, though. You need the blown-up positives with their shadings and variations. What if Milton Smithfield had followed Sneed that afternoon and. . . ?

In a rapturous sleep-starved moment I worked out a theory that fit in with my personal bias that Stephanie Kellogg Janowski killed her husband. Stephanie and Ely Sneed, the ladies' man. She wasn't in the greenhouse with the gardner. She was with Sneed. The photographer got some shots of them and started blackmailing her. Christ, maybe she'd even killed Sneed! Had Milton Smithfield been blackmailing Stephanie for killing her lover? With Lawrence Petit's help? Crazy.

I couldn't overlook the possibility of a patent, either. Milton Smithfield invents something, shows it to Lawrence Petit, takes photos of it, or with it, and then both men die before anything is ever done with it. Years later, Emory Hightower, in a routine review of Smithfield's file, comes across it, whatever "it" is, and puts it to his own use. Four-hundred-dollar sports jackets, an overpriced apartment, his expensive car. What, though, could Emory possibly have dug out of that file that could translate so easily into cash?

Maybe the firm was the villain. Had Ely Sneed, Kellogg & Petit reaped the benefits of Smithfield's invention for years? Was there a hidden trust? Was the firm collecting illegal copyright money from Kodak or Xerox that should have gone to the intestate Milton Smithfield? That was so complicated I couldn't go on with it.

And what about that Gregory Evans, anyway? As far as I knew, he was the only black man involved in this thing. What was he doing running around Iron Valley looking at the Schmoulack house? Had that attractive man with his prosperous business, who'd been so nice to me, actually gone at T. C. Crumm, Junior, with a knife? Instinct told me, no. Could I trust my instinct? Probably not, but with all my intellectualizing only making things worse, maybe I was better off sticking to gut reactions.

My detecting was like Gary's *Positions*, going a hundred and one crazy directions at once, limbs sticking out everywhere, supported by vague emotional speculation and personal hopes and no common sense at all. I was a jumble of ands, buts, ifs, and what-ifs.

By the time I trudged down the hill toward my apartment, I was half asleep and long past coherent thought. It was around four in the afternoon. The sun was low and hard over the Hudson. My abused eyes streamed and 191st Street was a curving wet blur. That's when I saw him—a fuzz of gray stepping from under a parked car fifty feet ahead of me, stretching himself awake. I dug through my bag for my glasses, unable to believe my eyes. Moses, whose pristine paws hadn't touched pavement in five years. I ran down the hill to him. He was as glad to see me as I was appalled to see him. Twenty desperate claws pierced my jacket.

The last thing I'd seen Saturday morning when I'd locked my door—and I knew I had locked it—was this fat gray cat sleeping on the sofa. My windows had been closed. I didn't have to speculate this time. I knew I was going to find myself the victim of that New York epidemic, the burglary. Lugging Moses and my suitcase, I ran down the alley to my super's apartment.

Henry was street-wise and laconic, an old-timer who had survived the South Bronx. Claw-foot hammer in hand, me behind him, he tried my doorknob. The door swung in.

"You wait here a minute, Miss. Looks like they're gone, but let me make sure."

He was back in a minute, shaking his head. "They sure did a job in there."

My place was a ruin. The thief, or thieves, had left nothing undisturbed in a violent search for my riches.

The two hulking policemen and the diminutive Puerto Rican locksmith arrived almost simultaneously. I fought with myself, trying to keep down my rising hysteria, while one of the policemen helped me fill out a form.

He was sitting across the kitchen table from me, sweet-faced and blue-eyed. He couldn't have been more than twenty. I don't know what made me do it. Maybe I was desperate to trust someone. I blurted out what was churning around in me.

"This is part of a plot." My eyes were burning with tears. "Someone is after me. It's some kind of conspir . . ."

I saw his face tense the moment I said it. I'd made a mistake. He touched the edge of the table with his palms, ready to jump, and looked around for his partner. He had a live one on his hands. It's probably one of the first things they learn at police academy—how to handle the female neurotic.

"A plot, Miss?"

"I'm kidding. A figure of speech. I've had a rough weekend."

He smiled with relief. "Oh, I get it. Know what you mean."

The trio went at last, leaving in their wake a flurry of aphorisms and many nods of agreement: "Should have had Medeco locks in the first place. Happening everywhere; fingerprints useless. Take it off your insurance; eighty-five dollars for the lock plus twenty-five dollars for Sunday service, Madam. Cash or credit card? We don't take checks." I couldn't wait to see them go.

It was six P.M. I was too tired to think, too tired to worry, even too tired to sleep. I tackled the mess around me. "Probably kids," the patrolmen had said when they saw my place. Okay, vandals, but to go through all that trouble and end up with one gold wedding band and a few pieces of gold-plated junk jewelry? It seemed to me that if you were going to take the time and the effort to ruin a place, risk the tenant's return, risk being overheard, you should have more to show for it.

The thief had missed my old engagement ring, when all he had to do was flip open the little velvet case in my jewelry box. My camera bag had been torn apart, but he hadn't taken the camera. Well, it was an old camera. But my color TV and my stereo unit were still there. And my prize collection of fifties rock-'n'-roll records—they had been shuffled through but none of them was missing. What kind of vandals were these kids, that they didn't want my Bo Didley retrospective, who would pass up Martha and the Vandellas? Buddy Holly? I suddenly felt very old.

I knelt on the floor in front of my desk, trying to make sense of it. The desk had taken a lot of abuse. In the top drawers were my letters, bills, checkbooks. That scared me. Had they torn checks from the center of the books? No. I counted carefully. Everything was intact. In the bottom drawer I kept photographs and some scrapbooks. My robber had looked through my baby pictures.

It came to me slowly as I sat on the floor exhausted, straightening odd bits of paper. I hadn't been robbed. My apartment had been searched. Like the room at the Hotel Central. They, or he or she, my thieves, had systematically turned the place inside out looking for something. My theft, those few pieces of jewelry, was like Albert's wallet. Done to give the search a basis that would be easily spotted and just as easily believed.

I was stacking blankets back in the hall closet when I realized that Emory's four-hundred-dollar hound's-tooth sports jacket was gone. I pushed the hangers aside to be sure. Gone. Stolen. What kind of thief . . . It was a nice enough jacket on a certain type of man, but not on your average sixteen-year-old kid. Could there be a big market for second-hand tweeds? Not likely. Who would leave diamonds and Buddy Holly and make off with a sports jacket? Its peacock owner, who had always admired its cut, and the way it fell?

Energy surged through me. My eyes opened wide without pain, my head cleared. I had a purpose. The thirty thousand dollars was mine. I would summer in Scotland and winter on Mykonos, and Emory Hightower could rot in Attica for killing Albert Janowski.

Emory's apartment key was in my teapot, left for that moment when I recovered my senses. I put my coat back on, locked my new top-of-the-line lock behind me, and headed downtown to confront my tormentor.

When my buzz went unanswered, I just let myself in. If caught in the act, I could always say I'd come to my senses.

It was nothing so pedestrian as your run-of-the-mill apartment building. Emory had a "living space" in an old Soho factory that had been converted into what the real estate section called custom life-style environments. It was the kind of place whose advertisements make much of concept and function.

Emory's life-style had called for a custom environment something like the polar ice cap—all white and shiny, with large stretches of . . . nothing. White rugs, white walls, white modular units shaped into a circular conversation pit, white Formica shelves, white tables topped with glass and jutting from walls at odd angles. Some of the walls even jutted at odd angles. During our affair my shins were always bruised. There was one splash of color—a big abstract smear of reds and yellows hanging over the conversation pit. It was said to represent creative energy.

I began an orderly search for the hound's-tooth jacket. First the closets, the back of the bathroom door, the wardrobe, and the chest of drawers.

The bedroom was a strange thing. A wobbly iron staircase led to an aerial perch where even I, at five feet four inches, had to sit with my back bent. My search there yielded nothing but a crack on the head. I was on my way down the staircase when I heard voices in the outside hall. A man's, unmistakably Emory's, and the softer one of a woman. I barely managed to scuttle through the kitchen and into the little utility closet that abutted it before they opened the front door.

"Here, Princess. Let me hang that up."

Princess again, I thought, wedging myself behind the water heater.

"You shouldn't be so careless with this . . . worth a fortune."

Most of Princess's answer was muffled and inaudible, but I caught "storage next week . . . careless with easy . . . never with you, Hy."

What claptrap. Nobody ever called him Hy. The two must have lunged for each other; there was rustling cloth, gasping, and then some breathless laughter before I heard him walk into the kitchen. He was wearing his cordovan loafers. The right one creaked.

I was painfully conscious of my precarious hiding place. If I could hear his shoe creaking, what about my watch ticking? The power of suggestion became almost more than I could stand; it sounded like Big Ben was in the closet with me. I crushed my wrist under my jacket.

". . . yourself comfortable. I'll open this."

He rummaged around in a drawer and then: "Why hell! What's this? Would you just take a look here?"

My stomach did a flip. Had I left my purse on the counter? No. It was behind me on the floor. The keys! What had I done with them? I didn't dare stoop down and feel through my bag for them. I was sure the next sound would be that of Emory dialing the police.

"I asked that clerk for 'sixty-seven and he gave me 'sixty-nine. Do you remember me saying 'sixty-seven?"

No answer.

"'Sixty-nine was an awful year for these Bordeaux reds. Drought."

The squeak of a corkscrew twisting in a bottle was next. "The cork is dry, too. Oh—now some of it's fallen in the bottle. I'm going to complain. This hasn't been stored on its side."

Princess called from the living room, her voice strident to make herself heard. "That's probably why it was four ninety-nine. We can strain the cork out."

If I hadn't been pinned with the water heater on one side and the wall on the other, I might have collapsed. Princess Stephanie Kellogg Janowski! So that was how she'd known I was going out with Tony. She'd been Emory's date the night we'd run into him at the movies.

Glasses clinked against each other, a faucet ran, and then the wine was poured. "We've got it," he said. "Might as well drink it."

Soft footsteps came into the room. She'd taken off her shoes.

"Glad you liked Newport. Surprised you've never been there before."

"Great place. I'll be glad when we're able to get away more often. See more people. I enjoyed meeting your friends, Stephie. They're so . . ."

"Rich."

"I was going to say interesting." He took a loud slurping sip and it came back to me—how he'd done that and how much it used to annoy me.

"What do you think? Kind of acrid, isn't it?"

"It's all right. How do you think I feel? It's like I've spent my whole life crouching behind windshields. You're right, Hy. It is a little bitter."

"Well," he said with a seductive drawl I recognized, "that's almost behind us now. What about it? Another six weeks or so, and you can surprise your father with one of his ex-associates."

Neither of them said anything, then she gave one of those sighs that always goes with a shaking head. "He probably won't even remember you. He's a mess these days. I feel bad for him. I had no idea he was so attached to Albert." She hesitated, then added, "Six weeks, two months, maybe. I know you think I'm silly about this, but I'd rather let the scandal die down before I hit the papers again."

"Oh? You think I'm a scandal?"

Was that the languid sensuality I'd been so captivated by? That cornpone drawl, those wine-slurping pretensions? As I listened to their mating duet, their verbal singles foreplay, and realized that it was just one more variation on a theme I'd played for twenty years, I thought, with great calm considering where I was, that I didn't care if I never saw another man in my life. I could be content to be alone, with my dancing, Moses, and my $30,000.

". . . didn't mean that, Hy."

Well, they were at it again. I was afraid I was going to have to be an unwilling eavesdropper to some kitchen-floor sexual acrobatics.

"No, not tonight." She was out of breath. "Last night is going to have to be it for a while. Now stop that!" She had an awful giggle. It could have come out of one of those horses she was so fond of.

"Not for too long, I hope. Stephie, do you realize that was the first night we'd been together since Albert was killed? Don't you see . . ."

Heart pounding, I waited on edge for the words that would incriminate good old Stephie and Hy.

". . . dramatic significance. There he is, shot by a hooker while you and I— Princess, there's a play there. I can see it done with a split stage."

"Soap opera. Let me have a little more of that wine. Thanks. Don't get carried away with Albert's murder. I wouldn't want to see it turn up in one of your plots."

"The wife and her lover in a Holiday Inn Motor Lodge off the New Jersey Turnpike, the husband, the hooker . . . a kind of mass orgiastic . . ."

"Please. I can't bear thinking about it."

Whatever he said then was lost on me. His voice was low. Her giggle started that way, bubbled deep in her throat, then climbed to a horse laugh.

"No. No. We don't have time. It's too hot up there anyway, and I always bruise something on the ceiling. I'm going to finish my wine and get out of here."

"All right, Princess. Come on, let's sit where we're more comfortable." Shoe creaking, voices fading, they left the kitchen.

After that, only snatches of conversation were audible. Emory was talking his arty hocus-pocus: "Clarity, wit . . . deviate from orthodox conceptions of theater . . . the nexus is the visual experience . . . germane to my style . . . your mother . . . Board of Directors at Lincoln Center. . . ."

Stephanie's responses were quiet, thoughtful.

Finally, when I was starting to think I'd spend the rest of my life in that closet, the artist offered to drive the widow home. A tedious little tiff followed. She didn't want to be seen with a man; he didn't want to say goodbye. To my eventual relief, they compromised. He would drive her to Grand Central.

I was no more than a minute behind them.

7:30 A.M.

An awful din jerked me from my sleep. Things had bottomed out for me, far beyond or beneath anything Albert Janowski, his corpse, and his kith and kin could have managed. My hand flailed at the wailing alarm clock. Finally, I yanked the cord from the wall, upsetting clock and lamp, and the din quieted.

I was starving. When had I last eaten? I couldn't remember. I dozed in a stranglehold of rumpled sheets, cases half off the pillows. They were gritty. When had they last been changed? When had I last showered? Sunday? No, no time Sunday. Saturday? I couldn't remember.

A genial hoodlum's face, warm nose and silky whiskers, pushed itself into mine.

"Get out of here, alley cat."

The cry that answered was so pitiful I couldn't ignore it. You can forget to feed yourself, but not your cat. Especially a cat who'd spent part of his weekend under a car.

"I'll be late," I told the Ely Sneed operator. "Have to stop by my doctor's office. Another shot." As lame as any excuse I'd ever gotten, but I was past caring.

"All right dear. I'll tell Mr. Decker. He'll be glad to have you back. You should have seen him Friday. By noon he'd let three temps go. And—Bonnie?"

"Yes?"

"Hope you had a nice Easter dinner."

Easter dinner with Raymond and Noreen! I'd forgotten all about it. More ammunition for my mother. Noreen's little place cards were wasted on the likes of me.

There wasn't much to cheer me up that morning. My prime suspects were out of the running. The most Stephanie and Emory could be accused of was fornicating in a Holiday Inn off the Jersey Turnpike. Not that it didn't conjure up an amusing scene, but it wasn't going to solve anything.

A look in the mirror lowered my spirits further. Dark pouches draped my eyes, and fine lines I'd never noticed before creased my forehead. There was an old woman there, the one I would be if I lived long enough.

I took a bubble bath, so long and hot my skin puckered, and then did two loads of laundry and cleaned up the worst of my burglary rubble. It was well past noon when I left for the office. I felt almost human.

On the way out I checked the mail. There were two bills, which would wait, a circular from a local politician telling me that thanks to his tough stand on unemployment, abuses were being eliminated, and an answer to my long-forgotten inquiry to the Connecticut Department of Motor Vehicles. The light blue 1983 Buick Skylark was registered to Mrs. Kathryn Sneed, 2 Cobbs Mill Road, Weston, Connecticut. My spitting grandmother was Ely Sneed's widow.

I stood there in my lobby, the letter hot in my hand, allowing my imagination to lead me stumbling, once again, down a twisted path: an afternoon train from Grand Central to Westport and rent a car there, drive to Weston and . . .

And what? Confront the old lady with nothing? Maybe spy on her, and earn a reputation for myself as a Peeping Tom? I made what I thought was my first sensible decision in weeks: no more mental calisthenics, no more skulking around dusty file rooms and other people's apartments, no more horse rides, no more bus rides, no more frazzled nerves. I would separate myself from all of it, and dump the whole mish-mash of clues and files, pink slips, this new Connecticut letter, and those Albert stories—Greg Evans's, DeeDee's—into Gary's competent hands. He could be trusted to see that if any reward money trickled down because of my sleuthing, I would get it. The first thing Gary would do, of course, was call the police—his experience with them being less painful than mine—and I'd have to face a session with Detective LaMarca. So what! It would not end the way the last one had; of that I was sure.

I was in the office before two, but first Gary was with a client, then he was in another meeting of Ely Sneed's newly activated Management Committee. By the time Miss Peterson rang to say he could see me, it was almost four.

Miss Peterson was away from her desk. Through Gary's open door I saw that he was on one of his phone lines. I was waiting for him to hang up when the other line rang. Picking it up, I gave what I thought was a nice Miss Peterson imitation: "Mr. Petit's office."

"Let me talk to him."

Ha! One of Miss Peterson's boors. "I'm terribly sorry"—in my most officious voice—"but Mr. Petit is on the other line. May I have him return—?"

"Look, Momma. I'm sick of playing this bullshit game with you. You tell that motherfucker to pick up the phone right now, or I'm going to kick your bony ass all the way up Park Avenue!"

Oh my God! Nothing, nothing made sense any more. My tap-dance caller was on the line. I recognized him right away. Not his tone—he didn't whisper or hiss—but the nasty inflections, the language, the threat in his voice. Was I going mad? Had I slipped over the edge into the snakepit?

I was too shocked to move at first. Then, when I could, too confused to draw any conclusions. I put the phone back to my ear, feeling as if this vicious stranger was touching me. "Just a moment please, sir." I mouthed "phone call" to Gary and waved the receiver at him. There was that panic-stricken feeling in my stomach, the kind you get when you think you've forgotten something vital, but when Gary raised his brows in question, I managed a shrug. He motioned me to come in and sit down, then switched to the other line.

He brought it off like a champ. I'll give him that. His end of the conversation was a neat masterpiece of non-information. A few "I understands," one "I told you I'd take care of that," and finally, "No, tomorrow morning would be better for me. Say nine, nine-thirty is fine. Corner of Third and a hundred Twenty-fifth? Fine. I think so, but give it to me again." As he hung up, he jotted a number on one of Ely Sneed's carbonized phone pads.

"Sorry"—without looking up—"impatient client. Needs something yesterday." He tore off the top message and slipped it into his pocket, then looked at me over clenched fists.

"I got your message on my machine Saturday. You said you'd found something? I tried to get you all weekend. What's up?"

I recognized something in the way he was watching me, the eyes waiting for a false move the way Moses watches a roach, right before he springs.

Lying is like tap-dancing or playing the piano, I think. It gets better with practice. My story was already taking vague shape.

"That's right. I went to New Jersey."

"I thought you might have. You wanted to talk to me about something. . . ." He thumbed the pages of his message pad, eyes holding mine. The carbon imprint of the number he'd written flashed before me and then was gone.

"I had an interview. I think I've gotten a job. A position, that is. In New Jersey."

He changed then. The lines in his face slackened, he slumped back in his chair, and after a moment a smile spread across his features. "Congratulations! Through your uncle?

179

Great. About time you took my advice. But what's the matter? You look awful."

I imagine I did. "I had a bad night. My apartment was broken into over the weekend."

"Oh, no. You poor kid. Did they take anything?"

He showed nothing but concern, but by then I was convinced Gary had burglarized my apartment. Our conversation took the usual route. Anyone who has ever lived in New York City knows it—the normal post-robbery, same-thing-happened-to-a-friend-of-mine, terrible-what-this-city-has-come-to talk. I repeated my lines haltingly, like a befuddled actor in an under-rehearsed play. When enough of that had been done, the two of us ended up shaking our heads in disgust.

"Most likely kids, like the police said. But at least you're all right. That's what's important. Now, tell me about your new position."

I was so lost I almost said, "What new position?"

"Oh . . . that. My job. Well, the thing is, I hate to talk about it. Nothing's certain yet. But I'm pretty sure I've gotten it. It's a great job. Lots of opportunity for growth." I remember how my legs and arms kept jerking around in spasms I prayed would pass for enthusiasm. "Of course, I'll have to give up my apartment. Move to Jersey . . ." I proceeded to weave a rapid, improbable fiction of commute times and apartments I'd looked at, ". . . and even a terrace and a dishwasher."

"Well, sounds good to me. Perfect for you. You've never liked living in the city. When will you be starting?"

"It's not definite. The . . . board of directors has to meet on it. I suppose I'll have to get a car. They said something about providing one, but I'm not sure."

"Wow! Sounds like you've grabbed yourself a winner." He looked at his watch. "You know, it's past four now. Why don't we do something to celebrate? What do you say we close up here and go down to the Rose for a drink? There's nothing on my desk that can't wait until tomorrow. How about you? What's all that?" He was looking at my armful of clues.

"Nothing. Just some papers I wanted to file. Sure. I'd love to have a drink." I pushed the papers back into my bag.

Miss Peterson was back at her desk. As we passed her, I seized the poor woman by the arm. She blinked with surprise when I asked her to join us. Then, with "Oh, I'd love to," she grabbed her purse and hurried off to freshen her face. I was glad to wait. I needed a buffer. Gary, always the gentleman, hid his annoyance.

The three of us were in the lobby waiting for an elevator when Wilbur Decker stepped out of the stairwell. He was so involved with his clipboard that he almost ran me over.

"What have we here? My watch must have stopped." He tapped at his wrist in a myopic statement of disbelief, then smirked triumphant. "I hadn't realized it was quitting time."

"It isn't, Wilbur," Gary said, giving the elevator button another impatient push. "I'm taking these ladies down to the Rose for a drink to celebrate Bonnie's new position."

"Really?" Decker's smirk began to fade.

"Yes. She's been offered a nice spot in New Jersey."

"Really." Shades of incomprehension, of disbelief, and, finally, amazement contorted his rat face.

"Please, Gary." I made one last feeble try at giving myself an out. "Nothing is certain yet." Then I turned to Decker, that pompous fool, with his *First Hundred Years* and his dress code and his clipboard and his management professional, and something snapped. "You see, Mr. Decker, the board of directors is meeting on my appointment, and the chairman has asked me to, er, refrain from divulging any of the major details. Then, you know, there will be something . . . in the *Times* Business Section. Perhaps the *Journal*." I smiled shyly at him.

He looked like a man who'd just been told he'd eaten a toad. He recovered himself as the elevator door opened. "Please wait for me. I'd like to buy the first round." He waved the clipboard over his head. "Just let me put this away," and rushed from the lobby.

Let me tell you, the Rose of Killarney has rarely seen such

goings-on, at least not from the normally withdrawn Ely Sneed staff. Decker—"Call me Wilbur"—and Gary fought to hold the door for the ladies. They almost tore my chair in two trying to pull it out for me. Gary won. Decker had to settle for Miss Peterson's. He recouped by taking the seat next to mine.

The Rose is a typical old Irish bar, a little down at the heels, quiet, not too clean. I was always comfortable there. There was a long, L-shaped bar with a worn brass railing at its bottom and lopsided stools around it. These, invariably, were occupied by indistinguishable, one-sized bottoms of the regulars—the slightly overweight men in work clothes who could be seen there at ten in the morning and ten at night. An occasional prostitute wandered in, but I don't think there was much business for them. The regulars' attention was always riveted on the color television set over the bar. At any time, any season, night or day in the metropolitan area, I am convinced a baseball game is being televised. To me, the games, like the men around the bar, were indistinguishable.

Wilbur Decker pulled out his wallet. When I saw him fondle the magic plastic in his hand, I ordered the most expensive Scotch known to man. Miss Peterson, after a coy, "Well, I don't usually," said she'd have the same.

We were on our first drinks when I felt Decker's hand on my arm, and for a delirious instant thought he was going to make a pass. He leaned into my side, pressed his face inches from mine, and said softly, "Fortune 500?"

The old fool with his street hustler's soul. I gave him something to whet his appetite. Cupping my hand over my mouth so only he was privy to this, I said, "Fortune 100."

"What was that?" Gary asked. "Come on, Wilbur, you've got to share her." He bent across the table, smiling at me, and I knew he was planning another big seduction. I gave him a wink, completely forgetting he was my new prime suspect. He must have thought he'd won me over. His smile spread ear to ear and he called for another round.

Something was happening to me. I was like a starving man

who'd just been given a lobster dinner. I really began enjoying myself. This transformation, when I think about it now, was so fast and complete that it's almost frightening. One drink, and I forgot Albert. All my clues were just so much garbage. Once again, I felt Decker's fingers creeping up my arm, onto my shoulder, pulling me toward him.

"My dear . . ." His damp breath was in my ear. "May I ask you this, if you don't mind . . . the, em, remuneration? Just a general area. For a first-class administrative executive like yourself. Nothing specific. A ballpark figure, as they say."

From a has-been, self-taught office manager to a first-class administrative executive. I looked him right in the eye, unflinching, and whispered back, "Eighty."

The man believed me, and if I've failed so far to convince you he was deranged, that should do it. I heard his slight intake of breath, and then he was all over me.

"You know, Miss Indermill . . . Bonnie? Bonnie. With our expanding capabilities here at Ely Sneed—we expect to develop a fine university recruiting program shortly—in a forward-looking firm such as ours, client development is always uppermost. . . ."

University recruiting? Ha!

"Bonnie? Bonnie!" Gary was trying to attract my attention. "Did you say eight-oh?"

I nodded, and he gave a little whistle.

"What did you tell them you did here?"

"It's all in who you know." I turned back to Decker, who was babbling a mile a minute in my ear.

". . . a little secret, too. There's no reason why you shouldn't be privy. We've held preliminary discussions . . . strictly confidential, now," he cautioned, "with Dorey, Jones & Berkholder. I'm sure you're familiar with their reputation in the securities law field. With Ely Sneed's expertise in trademarks, I imagine that we will soon be quite the legal powerhouse."

I sure was familiar with Dorey, Jones's reputation. They specialized in rough-and-tumble corporate takeovers, and their own office manager, a friend I'd met through my Society of Law Administrators meetings, once told me that the managing partners exhibited the self-control of a school of piranhas at dinnertime, and that everyone else in the place worked like a coolie. It was a marriage made in heaven.

Decker paused long enough to take a big swallow, then breathed on me again, and continued, "May I ask, Bonnie, is your new position with a manufacturing concern?"

"A conglomerate. Past emphasis on . . . energy. Oil and synthetics, naturally."

"Oh yes, naturally."

"But now they're diversifying." I lowered my voice. He strained to hear. "Microprocessors, mini-computers. The wave of the future."

I suspect the thought brought Decker as close as he'd ever come to achieving orgasm. His body stiffened, his jaw dropped, and he took in air with a choking sob. I began fueling the fire with some nonsense I'd read about home computers: ". . . newest thing. Thirty-two-bit microprocessors. Revolutionize lives, change the way we live. Within a decade no home will be without one. Does everything. Cost five thousand or so, give or take a thou, depending on things like user memory. Maybe sixty-four-bit by fall."

"Bonnie, no doubt a concern like that . . . a need for experienced trademark counsel." My arm was clutched in his sweaty embrace. "Let me get you another drink. Miss Peterson? Gary?"

We had ordered our third when Old Mr. K walked in, supported on one side by his cane and on the other by Rosalie. Before they got to our table Gary pulled me aside, out of Decker's hearing, and whispered, "Why don't we cut out after this one? There's a place in the East Sixties I'd like to try. Provincial French."

Gary wanted to try more than Provincial French. Sober, without my jumbled perceptions and near hysteria, I would have chosen from one of a dozen ready-made excuses; but "Love it," I said, kittenish and flirtatious.

Rosalie was trying to get the old man into a chair. "We heard you were down here. Mr. K thought we might join you."

"Our pleasure." Gary pushed in a chair and held it until Mr. K was down for good. I saw Rosalie lean over the old man toward Miss Peterson, and whisper something. The two women sat up straight then, looked at me, and at Gary, and smiled knowingly.

Decker, his imagination in a frenzied hallucination of uptown suites and fancy corporate clients, began again, this time on the old man.

"Mr. Kellogg, I don't imagine you've heard about our Bonnie's new position. Of course, she's not at liberty to divulge all the details, but I've confided some of our exciting plans, and she sees, like I do, the possibilities."

"Our Bonnie? What the devil are you talking about?" Mr. K looked over his shoulder at the waiter. "Make mine a double."

"Our Miss Indermill, here." In a gesture so incredibly effusive that I almost burst out laughing, Decker put brotherly arms around our shoulders—mine and the old man's. Mr. K brushed him away like he was a fly.

This may sound nutty, but for a little while there I stopped caring. What had been an interminable cloud of confusion and dread gave way to a transcendental calm. Only the moment mattered. If I was sitting with a murderer, or a gang of them, so deep in my lies that I could hardly keep them straight from one sentence to the next, so what? If I could have been locked up for life for the amount of evidence I was withholding, that was okay too. For the first time in weeks, I was relaxed, happy, and having a grand time. The Rose began to look elegant. Bottles lined up behind the bar reflected off each other like diamonds, the regulars called up and down the bar to each other, and around our table there was a wonderful spirit of friendship: Wilbur Decker shameless, courting my future business; Gary Petit after my body; Miss Peterson, with good reason, finally, for her dramatics. And in a little while I'd be trying that new French place of Gary's. And what the hell. He wasn't that bad. I was sexy, alive . . .

From then on most of our conversation will remain a fuzz to me. One of our associates—somebody Byman, whose bad complexion had shown tremendous improvement since Albert Janowski's death—dropped by the bar with one of our inventors, a wild-looking character with a passionate grip on his instamatic-type camera. He was terribly earnest about it; they always were. I remember bits of his explanation. "You just drop the spool of film in this door. See? Just press this button. Bingo! You've done it!"

What in the world was he talking about?

I had one bad moment. Decker, who hadn't shut up for a minute, whispered something to me, ending with ". . . *The First Hundred Years?*"

My expression must have told him how stupefied I was.

"Our little pet project. I haven't told Mr. K yet. It's going to be a surprise."

I said something very loud. I don't remember what, but Decker shushed me with his finger to his lips. "What is it, Bonnie?"

"Oh, Wilbur. It's gone. Taken by the thieves. I didn't want you to know."

He blinked. "Your housebreaker took *The First Hundred Years?*"

"Almost fifty pages, small type. Wilbur, I'm so upset. I put so much into it. I was up to 1982."

He was very still, then his hands cupped his cheeks. "What do you suppose they mean to do with it? You don't think the robbery was related to our expansion program?"

I saw Gary's repressed laughter, his shaking shoulders. We exchanged grins. Miss Peterson scooted toward me and tittered in my ear, "Rosalie and I have always thought you and Gary made such a darling couple."

And that was the state of things—for my purposes the file on Albert Janowski was closed—when there was an unpleasant reminder from across the table. Someone—it must have been that associate, Byman—said something to Gary. Gary turned and looked at the young man. "No, I can't make it in the morning. Not that early. I have a breakfast meeting. If you can wait until about ten. . . ."

My euphoria vanished. Gary couldn't make an early meeting because he had already scheduled one—with the man who had chased me after my tap class! I stood up as Old Mr. K called for another round.

"Gary, I'm going to run upstairs and get my coat. Could you order a cup of coffee for me?" The room swayed, and I had to put my hand on the chair for balance. Gary said something like, "Are you okay?"

As I walked unsteadily from the Rose, I looked back at our group. Our inventor was standing over Gary and Rosalie, explaining the finer points of his camera, which Gary had pointed at Miss Peterson. That lady was a childlike coquette, coy smile half-hidden by her fingers. Byman, pretending to watch the inventor, was in fact looking down the front of Rosalie's dress, something which did not escape her if you can judge by the way she straightened her shoulders and smiled up at him. Decker was white-faced and grim, lost in his own thoughts. Mr. K, as usual, seemed to be sleeping with his eyes open. All of them were going about their business with the googly-eyed intensity only a bunch of drunks can muster. I wouldn't be missed.

Ely Sneed was deserted. The corridor floor felt like it was rolling under me as I weaved down the hall to Gary's office. I clutched the knob, only to find he'd locked the door. I had to go to my office for a master key. Every step was like a mile on an obstacle course. The liquor and my nerves combined, playing tricks with distances and sounds. Finally, key in hand, it took three tries to get it in the lock. Gary's message pad was on his desk where he'd left it. As I memorized the number he'd written, I recognized that awful churning from the pit of my stomach, and knew that sooner or later I was going to be very sick.

578-1337. An East Harlem exchange.

Back in my office I dialed carefully. My fingers seemed too thick for the holes in the dial. Finally the number rang, one, two, three . . . five times. I was ready to hang up when a sleepy male voice said, "Yeah?"

Sexy would be best, I decided. It came out low and slurred. "Hi, there. A friend of yours said I should give you a call. Said you liked a good time."

"What are you talking about, Momma? What friend? You drunk or something? Hey, you woke me up, bitch."

"Guy named Bill. I met him in a bar near your place. Gave me your number and said you liked a good time and you might want to get together."

"Oh, yeah?" There was a pause. I could hear him stirring around. "What do you have in mind? You want to come up here? I've got nothing going on tonight."

"Sure. I was thinking we might meet for a drink first, but give me your address. . . ."

"Sounds like you already had a drink, Momma. Who's Bill, anyway?" Again, a pause. "You met him down at Hanson's, on the corner a Hundred Twenty-second . . ."

"That's him."

"Momma, you're full of shit. I don't know any Bill, and there's no Hanson's around here. My bitch wife put you on me? You tell her she'll get her money when I get mine. I'm seeing my man in the morning and I'll put her money in the mail after that. Fuckin' paranoid bitch. You tell her Andy Tate's no woman's fool. She keeps checking up on me she's not going to see one nickel. . . ."

I put down the receiver. Andy Tate. He was the messenger Albert had caught in his office and fired, the man who had been at a Ranger game when Albert was killed. So he was my tap-dance caller. But why?

I was sitting in a dense fog, and never heard Gary behind me until his hands were around my throat. I jumped about a foot.

"Bonnie, calm down." He rubbed my backbone between his thumbs. "What's taking you so long? I missed you."

By then my sense of reality was so distorted I was convinced he could read my mind. "Had to make a phone call," I muttered, not looking at him.

Was he watching me too closely, holding himself back? Had he heard any of the phone call?

"Just as well," he said. "I forgot my umbrella. More rain tonight. We've had a lot, haven't we? Look" —he slid my broken side chair over next to me and sat down—"there's something I want to talk to you about. You and I, we've known each other a long time. We have a lot in common, don't you think?"

I could hardly even see him, much less think. I nodded, stupid with drink.

"You must realize that I've always been attracted to you. I never wanted to do anything that would ruin our working relationship, but now that you're leaving Ely Sneed, I feel freer saying that . . . well, maybe it's time to think about us."

"Us?"

He nodded. "I have a good income, Bonnie. Investments, some family money. We—"

I burst into tears.

"What is it?" He reached toward me. Every motion was magnified.

"Gary," I sputtered between sobs. "Can I take a rain check on dinner? I think I'm going to throw up."

"Of course. I understand. What about tomorrow after work? We'll celebrate in style. I'll get some tickets for a show. Have you seen *Little Shop of Horrors*?"

At nine-fifteen A.M. I was on the corner of 125th Street and Third Avenue.

In private-eye fiction, the detective doesn't eat for two days, gets beaten up in an alley at midnight, rises from the dead at five A.M., finishes the bottle of cheap booze in his file cabinet for breakfast, and collars the murderer before noon. Me, I was a mess. My sleep had been an on-off bad dream, my temples pounded, the back of my skull ached, and what was going on in my stomach made mere indigestion seem like a pleasant experience.

My disguise was a pair of sunglasses and a rumpled old raincoat, its hood pulled over my head. For the first time in days, there wasn't a cloud in the sky.

The intersection reminded me of old black and white films I'd seen of war-torn cities. Sheets of steel glared from windows of abandoned tenements, broken bottles and crushed beer cans filled the gutter, and the faint breeze blew paper whirlwinds into deserted doorways.

On the northeast corner was an empty rubble-strewn lot, surrounded by a high chain-link fence. Across Third a bunch of wiry boys played basketball in a graffiti-covered court. La

Charrera Bar-Café, its iron gates padlocked, was on the third corner, and a small Latin American grocery advertising PRO-DUCTOS TROPICALES on the fourth.

The laundromat next to the grocery seemed a good place for me. I walked in, hooded, eyes shaded. The noisy Spanish chatter stopped. It was eerie—the violent clashings of over-worked machines and about forty dark female eyes on me. I made a beeline for the soda machine, hoping for something to calm my stomach, then went over and sat in an orange plastic chair by the front window. No good. My view of the street was half blocked by boxes of garbage from the grocery. I tried kneeling on the chair, stretching to see over the boxes.

"What you doing, lady? You on a stakeout?" She was easily twice my size and about a third my age. An ugly child.

"I'm waiting for a friend."

"Sure. Tell me another."

An older woman barked something at the kid in Spanish and she reluctantly went back to folding clothes. Something I'd heard ran through my mind: They all carry knives.

I continued my partial vigil under the nasty kid's scrutiny. It was stifling hot in my raincoat with all those machines run-ning, but I was afraid to take it off, doubly afraid to stay out on the street. Andy Tate probably wouldn't recognize me—to him I was a pair of legs in tap shorts—but even in my disguise Gary might know me. Then I thought of something—some-thing awful. Why meet on this corner? The bar-café was closed and there were no park benches. What if Tate planned to do his laundry?

I put my shades back on, adjusted the hood over my hair, and walked back into the morning light. A look at myself in the laundromat window was, if depressing, reassuring. I hardly recognized myself. As I started walking toward the grocery I saw the kid watching me from the laundromat door-way.

I was standing in the shade of the store awning, drinking my soda, when a man roughly pushed his way past me and went into the store. My heart jumped. Emory Hightower?

No. Andy Tate, looking like an advertisement in *Esquire* in Emory Hightower's hound's-tooth sports jacket. I lowered my face into a bin of green bananas—"PLÁTANOS, 4 x $1." Tate was back outside a moment later, drinking a carton of orange juice. He looked at his watch.

I was shuffling my way back to the Laundromat when I saw Gary's big metallic car following the line of traffic from downtown. I turned my back to the street and tried watching through the window's reflection. Gary's car pulled past me and stopped at the curb in front of the bar. A minute later I saw Tate cross the street, stop at the driver's window, and then walk around the car and get in the passenger door.

It was a wide avenue—four lanes—and traffic was heavy. In the steamy laundry window it was impossible for me to see anything more than two shadows sitting in a car. I dashed back inside, jumped onto one of the chairs, and used my hand to clear a spot on the glass. I'd become quite a curiosity in there. The kid and two women joined me at the window. "That your friend?" the kid asked.

"I don't need any help," I growled back. "Why aren't you in school, kid?" She skulked off.

From what I could see, the men were arguing. Tate, facing me, waved his hand at Gary. Gary's arm swung up, blocking it. Then without warning, the car slipped into traffic and began moving up Third.

One thing about New York City: if you're trying to follow an automobile on foot, you'll probably be able to go faster than it does. I found myself hanging back. The intersection at 125th was busy, and to make matters worse a big delivery truck, trying to beat the lights, had blocked traffic. I stopped and stared at the kids playing basketball while I waited for Gary's car to move slowly through the jam. From the corner of my eye I saw the girl from the laundromat crossing the street behind me. She walked onto the basketball court at the same time Gary's car started moving again. I heard her say something to the basketball players, ending in "the fuzz."

By then nothing would have surprised me. I half expected

the whole damn bunch—five skinny boys and one fat girl—to take off after me.

". . . full of shit," one boy answered. "She's too old for the fuzz. Some old nut." The others laughed with him. I felt all their eyes on me as I rushed past.

Gary's car turned right onto 127th. My plan involved nothing more than following the two men. If 127th Street entered the fast-moving East Side Highway, it was a lost cause.

The car slowed and then stopped, double-parked in front of an apartment building a half-block ahead. I watched, bent double behind an old Plymouth, until the two men walked into the building. Then, giving my hood another pull, I trotted after them.

The front door was standing open. On one side of it was a buzzer system with a list of tenants. I didn't bother with it. Even in well-kept buildings they're always about ten years out of date. What I needed was the mailboxes. I found them at the side of the lobby. From the look of things, they'd been broken into so often most of the tenants didn't bother locking them any more. Four rows of dented brass doors hung askew. "A. Tate" was listed in apartment 6E, which probably meant that he lived on the sixth floor. His box sported a brand-new lock.

There was an elevator in the lobby and flights of stairs branching up at either side of it. I could hear the elevator clanking way above. Somewhere in the building a radio was playing loud rap music, and somewhere else a man and woman argued. I mounted the left staircase and climbed on rubbery legs to six. A look at a couple of doors and I knew I was on the wrong side of the building. I saw that this was one of those buildings where the apartments make a semicircle around an interior courtyard.

I had worked my way around to the front, past the elevator, around the corner to the right staircase, when I heard gunshots. Two of them, muted but loud enough to make my spine stiffen. They sounded as if they had come from a door just a little ahead of me, on the right. On tiptoes, I moved toward that door until I stood just outside it. It was numbered

6E, Andy Tate's apartment. Suddenly, I heard footsteps in the apartment moving closer.

Across from me, on the inside wall of the building, was a small door with no lock. At the end of the hall was another, similar door. One of them had to lead to an outside stairway. I didn't have time to explore. I pulled open the door nearest me and stepped into a garbage room. It was no more than a box. The floor was caked with brown scum, the walls yellow-streaked. When I pulled the door shut behind me, the light bulb, triggered by the door mechanism, went out. In an instant I was breathless and on the verge of panic. Every fear assaulted me—dark, bugs, rats, small enclosed places—and I wanted nothing more than to shriek at the top of my lungs. My body was shaking uncontrollably when the door to the apartment across the hall where the shots had come from opened. Footsteps passed me by, heading toward the front of the building. Scarcely a second later, they were back. Whoever had come out of Tate's apartment was standing right outside the garbage-room door. I gripped the doorknob with all my strength.

Then there was another sound. Women's voices, soft, distanced, coming from the direction of the front stairs. Not a second later, my fingers almost gave as someone twisted the doorknob from the other side. Gary? Tate? Some tenant trying to empty the garbage? They weren't getting in. Then a voice I recognized as Gary's whispered, "Shit!" His footsteps moved quickly away toward the back of the building. An instant later the small door at the end of the hall slammed shut.

Two women were standing outside Andy Tate's door, knocking tentatively, when I burst out of my hiding place. All three of us started. They must have heard the shots, too. They ran past me toward the front stairwell, one of them shouting, "*Homocidio! Policia!*"

I took their place at the door. "Mr. Tate?"

The knob turned, the door pulled back, inch by inch, and he was standing there, hands clasped on the knob for support. His mouth opened. He mouthed silent words, then stumbled back into the room and fell into a chair. His eyes flickered and closed, and I thought I had just watched someone die. I took a step into the room, and then another. When I was close enough to see his chest moving, I reached out to touch him. He opened his eyes.

"Motherfucking lawyer shot me. I'm gonna burn his ass for that!"

Andy Tate raised his hand from his side. There was a long, vicious-looking knife in it. Then his fingers relaxed and it slid down onto the floor, landing with a harmless thud.

Falling to one knee, I put my hand on Tate's wrist. His skin felt cool and damp, but the pulse was still strong. I got up, found a phone in the kitchen, and dialed the police emergency number.

10:45 A.M.

I sat on Tate's bedspread, propped in the corner, brutally tired, telling my story again and again.

A uniformed policeman leaned on a chest of drawers. Tony LaMarca was sitting in a chair by the window, arms crossed on his knees, looking down at his feet. On the bed in front of me was the clue I'd found while waiting for the police—the stub of a round-trip bus ticket: New York–Iron Valley, Pennsylvania. There was a cassette tape recorder next to it, humming, taking down my statement.

"Miss Indermill—"

Tony looked up at me, impassive. I might have been a total stranger. "I can't understand why it never occurred to you to call us after you talked to that photographer, Evans."

"I was . . . confused. Upset. I'd just lost my job."

Tony spoke to the other policeman. "You want to call Sergeant Scott at the hospital again? Find out what's happening there."

The officer reached for the phone by the bed.

"Use the one in the kitchen."

"Oh. Yeah."

When the policeman left the room, Tony stood up and closed the door. Flipping off the recorder, he sat down on the foot of the bed.

"This isn't the time or the place for us to have a personal talk, Bonnie, but maybe you could give me a hint about what the hell's been going on? I thought we . . . liked each other."

In an exhausted voice, drained at first of anger and pride, I told him about the call from Gary's apartment, about the wife's answer, about the teenage boy asking for his dad, about how I almost saw the woman. I described her. "I just knew." A self-righteous fervor had crept into these last words. I waited for his devious facade to crumble, for "She doesn't understand me," or one of its thousand variations.

"You just knew?"

When I nodded and looked into his face, I thought I saw there a terrible, scarcely controlled violence.

"You're right, Bonnie." He lowered his eyes. "A wife's voice. My sister-in-law's voice." The story he told me was so dull, so unembroidered, that it had to be true. And I wanted to believe him. Tony's brother, his brother's wife, and their two kids had stayed at Tony's place while their own was being replastered and painted.

It's the mundane stuff of life, the trivia, that gets most of us in the end. "I'm sorry," was all I could say. He didn't answer.

I fished into my bag for a tissue. I had been going through them in record numbers. Digging around under my wallet and keys, I found what was left of the double pack I'd bought at the drugstore across from Greg Evans's photo studio. A little light flickered through my mind. Hadn't Evans told Albert Janowski to take the negatives to a drugstore to save himself five dollars?

"Tony, I bet I know where the missing negatives are." He nodded thoughtfully when I told him.

The patrolman pushed a cautious nose around the door. "Tate's conscious. Going to be okay. They haven't gotten anything out of him. He's asking for his lawyer."

"Do you suppose he means Gary?" I'd felt a surge of humor. The men looked at me. Neither of them smiled.

Noon

According to Tony, Gary Petit had emerged as a suspect soon after Albert's murder. Gary's account of his actions on the evening of April 2 never checked out. True, Ely Sneed's receptionist saw him leave the office around three forty-five P.M., and his doorman said he'd entered his apartment building at approximately four-fifteen and left a short time later in casual clothes. But after that . . . If, as Gary claimed, he had driven straight to his beach place, even allowing for traffic (and traffic was light that Thursday afternoon), he would have arrived there by six-thirty, give or take fifteen minutes. However, Gary's nearest neighbors in Southampton, the Cahns, took their Irish Setter for a walk after watching the seven o'clock news. The Setter, an old dog, took his time about his constitutional. At a little past eight, the Cahns were on the path above the beach, walking toward home, when they saw Gary turn into his driveway and carry his weekender case into his house. Exact times couldn't be pinpointed, but no matter how you looked at it, at least an hour was unaccounted for.

Midtown South Precinct was located in a squat, newish building, the kind of building that looks shabby right from the day it is first occupied. Tony's office was a tiny, austere, glass-walled cubicle next to the squad room. As I slumped in a beaten-up green metal chair, I rehearsed the lines I was going to say to Gary over the phone.

The original plan to bring Gary in didn't include me—not directly, anyway. I was simply going to be the bait; but everyone knows what happens to bait.

Gary's gun was the police's greatest concern. A search of the building, the back outside staircase Gary had left the building by, and the street had turned up nothing.

"He generally carry a briefcase?" Tony asked.

I nodded.

"Probably got it on him, or in his desk. Hate to risk walking in there with all those people around."

"We aren't even sure he's at the office." That was Sergeant Scott.

I remembered what I'd overheard at the Rose the night before. "I think he is. He may have had a ten o'clock meeting there, and between that and his lunch plans with me, I doubt if he'd go anywhere."

My fingers shook as I dialed Gary's number. Through the glass wall of Tony's office I could see the policemen in the squad room strapping on bulletproof vests and checking their guns.

Miss Peterson answered on the second ring.

"Hi, Miss Peterson. It's Bonnie. Is Mr. Petit in?"

"He's here all right. Perfectly awful mood. I suppose he drank too much last night. I'll put you through."

"Yes," Gary barked into the phone a moment later. My already shaky confidence sank.

"Good morning, Gary. Sorry I didn't make it in on time. An awful hangover. I feel like I haven't slept."

"I'm feeling a little rough myself," he said.

"Never again," I added, meaning it.

He sighed, a sad sound amplified by the phone. "I must be getting old. I remember when I used to be able to stay out all night."

"Me too. Um—Gary? I was thinking about what you said last night, up in my office."

"Oh?"

"Yes. Why don't we get together for lunch, and talk about—things? It's on me."

He hesitated so long that I was afraid he was going to say no. By the time he said, "You're on," my hands were cold and damp.

"Meet you in front of the building in half an hour," I said, ready to hang up.

"Okay. No, wait. Come up to my office. There's something you've got to see. I've had a couple of design firms draw up proposals for our new offices. Some of these ideas are spectacular."

That was the part the police hadn't counted on.

I washed my face and combed my hair. Lipstick helped a little, but I hoped that in Gary's case, love was blind. Tony, tight-lipped, insisted I wear a bulletproof vest under my raincoat.

He was behind his desk, looking like the wrath of God, going over a big blueprint.

"I'm sorry I didn't make it in this morning, Gary. I felt terrible. Didn't even get out of bed until eleven. Where should we go for lunch?"

"Lunch?" He hesitated. "That's right. Got to eat, don't we? I'm looking forward to it. Something bland," he added. "I was sick as a dog this morning."

Giving the warmest smile I could manage, I walked over to his desk. "Is this what you wanted to show me?" If there was a gun under his jacket, I couldn't see it.

"This is it, Bonnie. This top set of plans is for the floor of a new building. Uptown at Fifty-third and Park. We've taken an option. Have to make up our minds. . . ."

The blue lines swam before my eyes. I couldn't tell north from south, up from down. "Looks terrific." I put a friendly hand on his shoulder. "Why don't you bring them along and we'll look at them over lunch."

As Gary rose from his desk, his hand touched the center of my back. And stayed there a little too long. He felt the shield.

"What the heck's that?"

The door to his office burst open.

"I say, Gary . . ."

"Wilbur."

Yes, Wilbur. Clipboard in hand, red-eyed, oily-faced, and frantic.

"Bonnie, how nice to see you. We'll have to talk later this

week. Lunch, maybe? Right now, Gary, there's something . . ."

Gary was past his desk by then. I tried steering him toward the door.

". . . most peculiar thing I've ever seen. Must have something to do with that riffraff downstairs. That Hollywood bunch. I just happened to open the door to the fire stairs a minute ago, and you wouldn't believe . . ."

I slid my hand through Gary's arm, trying to pull him through the door, pushing Decker out in front of us.

". . . three armed policemen in there. Two of them have rifles. It looked for a moment as if they were coming after me. Frightening. I closed the door and locked it behind me. I'll tell you," he said, shaking his head, "it will be a pleasure to move out of here. The kind of people they're renting to . . ."

The next thing I knew, my arm was twisted behind my back and the cold round barrel of the missing small-caliber automatic pistol was digging into the base of my skull.

"Oh, you stupid damned old idiot," I hissed at Decker. He fell back, mouth gaping, then bolted from the room.

Gary pushed me forward until he could grab the knob to his open door. Miss Peterson's wide-eyed face was the last thing I saw before he closed it and locked us in, together.

I opened my mouth to say something, but it was all I could do to breathe. Gary started pacing then, shoving me in front of him. And talking the whole time, half lucid, half ranting.

"God, I had such plans. Why couldn't you wait, Bonnie? I would have taken care of you. And the firm, too. I was handling everything. You're just so damned impulsive."

Fear had run through me like a shock. Everything else was blotted out. His words meant nothing to me. He was going to shoot me. I waited for the exploding pain I was sure would come, wondering if I'd live, like Tate, or die, like Albert.

"You don't understand a thing I'm talking about, do you, Bonnie? You never listen to me. All you ever worry about is yourself. Here I am with so many people counting on me. I've got a whole cemetery full of high achievers up in Westchester. You want them to see me fall on my face?"

His grip had loosened. Not thinking, I tried jerking my arm free. A searing flare of pain crossed the base of my skull. I couldn't breathe. The room grew fuzzy.

"Albert didn't understand, either. You're like him. You, Albert, my father, Old Man Kellogg. All of you. Cause all this trouble and leave it up to me to get us out of it. You tell me, Bonnie. Is it going to be worth it when you've ruined this firm? A hundred years of hard work? I didn't want to hurt you. I didn't want Tate to hurt you. That jerk! He's another one. Would have blackmailed me forever."

I was starting to pass out. My legs gave way and my body sank toward the floor, hanging on the arm twisted behind me. He never noticed.

"You had to pick and pick. We're right on the edge of turning Ely Sneed around. We have the bankers, financing. We're going to get rid of the dead wood, retire the old man. That old sot. If anyone deserves to die . . ."

He had turned me around so I faced him. I propped myself against the edge of his desk, trying to get the cobwebs out of my brain. One of his hands squeezed my shoulder, the other one, limp at his side now, still held the gun.

"Albert was all for it. Then some damned woman turns up. Supposed to have proof my father killed old Ely Sneed. Crazy Albert! Said he'd always suspected it. He'd waited for proof all these years while he'd lived with the stigma. Stigma! Can you believe that? He was the only one who even remembered his 'stigma.' What the hell did it matter, anyway? Sneed was dead, my father was dead. Nobody but Sneed's wife ever thought Albert did it, anyway. Why did he want to bring it all up again and ruin my father's name? 'To clear his own good name.' That's how Albert put it, Bonnie." Gary shook his head in disbelief. "Albert wasn't even going to tell me about this woman until he had gotten together all his 'evidence.'"

My head had cleared enough to allow me to think. I'd be better off if I could keep him talking. "How did you find out?"

The hand holding the gun waved wildly in front of me. I flinched, but Gary didn't notice.

"Albert was a fool, right to the end. He mentioned something about it to that so-called wife of his. Stephanie called her father and told him Albert had some information that was going to hurt the firm. One thing about Stephanie; she's always known what side her bread was buttered on. The next morning Mr. K called me in to his office and told me everything. I went to Albert and, sure enough, he admitted he had this woman and her 'evidence,' hidden away. He even told me her name—Miss Smith. I thought he was lying about that. I told him that if this 'evidence' was real, we should pay his Miss Smith off and let that be the end of it, but he wouldn't hear of that."

Gary's eyes stared into mine. "You believe me, don't you, Bonnie? I never wanted to hurt anyone. Albert wanted to ruin us. He agreed to meet me at a coffee shop and show me the photos the next day, but then he showed up without them. Don't you see? I had to follow him to that hotel. I had no choice. And you know what?"

I shook my head.

"Damned if he hadn't told the truth. There was a Miss Smith registered. Like I said, a fool right to the end."

A lot of what Gary was saying didn't mean anything to me, but it seemed important to him that I understand. I clung to the hope that something rational remained. In an unnaturally confident voice, I said, "I'm sure if you explain that to the police, they'll understand."

He shook his head angrily. "No, they won't. I've got to get us out of here. All up to me, as usual. We still can make it, Bonnie. There are lots of places. South America. Brazil, maybe."

Brazil! He really was crazy. And he wanted to take me with him. His face was ash gray. He was staring at me, waiting for an answer.

"Sure," I said. "Or Argentina."

"What we have to do now is get a plane. Dial reception, Bonnie."

My reactions were slow. He turned me with his arm. "Tell them we're coming out and we're going to want a car and driver. Tell them I'll have to kill you if they don't do that for us."

I had no doubt he meant it. Tony answered the reception desk phone.

"Mr. Petit and I are going to leave now, Gloria. He'd like you to get a car and driver for us. Right away, please."

"Bonnie, try to stay calm. Play up to him. Be nice. Everything's going to be all right."

"Just a car and driver, please. And hurry, because otherwise Mr. Petit is going to kill me."

Gary pinned my arm behind my back again. "Hang up, Bonnie."

"He's not going to kill you . . ."

My head slammed into the desk top.

"Why didn't you hang up? I'm so damned tired of no one taking me seriously. From now on, things will be different. I'm going to be the boss."

Something sticky was running down into my mouth. Gary pushed me to the door and unlocked it. We made our way up the corridor, stumbling toward the reception room. On both sides of us doors closed. I saw bodies under desks, eyes peering from behind file cabinets. The noise rushing through my head sounded so far away, broken by louder shouts near by. My head hurt terribly.

Tony, Sergeant Scott, and two uniformed policemen were in the lobby. They had their hands by their sides close to their guns. I remember trying to focus on Tony. He seemed to be drifting closer. Talking softly. Was he talking to me, I wondered? My head was clearing.

"Put it down, Petit. We're not going to make a move against you. You can go. Just let us have Miss Indermill. You don't want her to get hurt. Look at her. Her nose is bleeding. Why don't you let someone take care. . . ?"

The gun dug harder into the side of my neck, below my ear. "Just get out of our way." There was a tremor in Gary's voice, but the hand holding the gun was steady.

Something on the side caught my eye. Ely Sneed's staff, most of it, was creeping quietly down the corridor. They were standing back, ready to run for cover, but starved for excitement. One by one the family of happy professionals Decker liked to remind me I was part of slipped from hiding. Decker himself, Rosalie, Miss Peterson, Mrs. Kotch, Old Mr. K. All of them saucer-eyed.

"Sonofabitch!" Byman, the young attorney, took one look and inadvertently started the chain of events that brought the standoff to an end. He ran back down the hall; in seconds he returned, the inventor's camera of the future in his hand. "I'm going to get this."

Tony was shouting at them to get back. Byman shoved past staff and cops alike. He raised the camera and the shutter clicked twice. The glare of the flash blinded me. I heard a scuffle. One of the policemen pushed Byman out of the way. As my eyes cleared, I saw Decker lift his clipboard and jump between the two. "I'll thank you to remember this is still a professional office." He attacked Byman, clipboard swinging. Byman stumbled into the cop, shielding the camera with his forearm. And I realized with a start that my arm was no longer pinned behind me. The fight had distracted Gary. Raising my foot, I slammed it into Gary's instep with such force the heel of my shoe shattered. As I dropped to the floor I saw Tony charge, head down like a football player. A wild shot went off somewhere, and then I was at the bottom of a heap of struggling men.

No one was more surprised than I when Old Mr. K took control that afternoon. I was on the leather sofa in the lobby. Rosalie and Miss Peterson were hovering over me, and Tony and another officer were waiting to take me to headquarters.

Gary was gone, led away with his hands cuffed behind his back.

"Gentlemen."

There was a resonance, a bottomless tone to the old man's voice, perhaps a vestige of the impressive attorney he had once been. Everyone in the room turned to him.

"If you would care to join me in my office, I may be able to throw some light on all this."

The two officers started to follow him from the room.

"Me too!" I had been through it all. I was the one with the bloody nose and the egg-sized lump on the back of my head. If any light was going to be thrown, I wanted to be there.

"We tossed a coin—Lawrence Petit and I—to see which of us would do it."

Old Mr. K lifted his hands and watched their tremor with a mocking smile. His eyes shifted to Tony, then to me.

"You know what I think might hit the spot right now? About two fingers of bourbon. How about you, Miss . . . young lady? You've had quite the afternoon. No? Lieutenant?"

"I'd just as soon you didn't right now, sir."

He ignored Tony. "Looks like I'll have to drink alone." The old man pulled a pint bottle and tumbler from his bottom drawer and splashed the liquor into the glass. "I think I'll take it neat today. Just top it off . . ." The tumbler overflowed and a yellow pool spread across the desk.

"Whoops," he said, holding the glass to the light. "Maybe I should listen to my wife. Every six ounces of this grand stuff supposedly kills so many million brain cells. Or thousand, maybe. Can't recall. In either case, I've had so much over the past twenty years that I must be operating at a deficit."

He paused to drink. The afternoon sun beat through the sad, faded curtains, and as always, the room was warm and musty. I felt curiously comfortable.

"I'm not a strong man." He had shifted his attention back to Tony. "I could have spent the last twenty-five years trying to atone in some way, but instead, I've tried to forget. But you're not here to give penance, are you?"

No one spoke.

"Lawrence lost the toss. He was the one who had to kill Ely. In that way Lawrence was a stronger man than I am. I don't think I could have gone through with it.

"There had been ill-will here for several years. Sneed wasn't happy with the way the firm was being managed. Wanted to give less attention to patent work and strengthen corporate business. 'Get rid of the crackpots,' he said. Our inventor clients. Why, some of them had been with us for years. Too hungry, Sneed was. Grew up poor. That's always a mistake in a lawyer.

"We wouldn't have minded Sneed going. Quite the contrary. He was a devil. But so much of the capital, so many profitable clients, even our best young associates would have gone with him. Lawrence and I worked hard, and a lot longer than Sneed. But Sneed had the name.

"Still, killing your partner is not a decision you reach easily. At first it was only words: 'Maybe his plane will crash,' 'I wish his car would go over the bridge.' But then something else happened that made Sneed's demise even more desirable.

"As I've said, Lawrence and I had become accustomed to doing things our own way here. Occasionally, as the need arose, one or the other of us would . . . I believe the best word here is borrow . . . borrow from various funds we were holding in trust accounts for our clients." He looked across his broad desk, and smiled benignly. "I can see by your faces that you don't approve. I can assure you all that Lawrence and I felt we were operating within the spirit of the law, if not the letter. We never failed to pay back what we borrowed. We treated the trust funds as our personal loan department. That is, until our bookkeeper, Mrs. Kotch, told us she had discovered Sneed nosing around in the books. Mind you, Lawrence and I had been crafty enough to keep Mrs. Kotch from discovering our little game, but we knew that wasn't going to be the case with Sneed. Sure enough, not two days passed before Sneed let us know that he was gathering evidence of financial mismanagement so he could begin disbarment proceedings against the two of us. That we could not have.

"You gentlemen must understand that we lawyers are an arrogant lot. We're educated to believe we are always in the right. We couldn't do the things we do if we weren't. So you bind a group of us together in an unhappy partnership, each one believing the other is wrong, and each of you becomes infallible.

"Sneed couldn't swim. Grew up on a farm in New Hampshire. Helpless in the water. Lawrence and I decided the firm's picnic, out at my place, would be best. Lots of people around, but isolated spots, trails, places where a man could get lost. We worked out our plan right here—that chair you're sitting in, Lieutenant. Lawrence sat right there. The week before the picnic, we went to my place and picked a likely spot. What's the word? Reconnoiter. A place where the woods came right to the water's edge, where there was a sharp drop into the Sound.

"My part was easy, if any part of a murder is easy. I disappeared from the picnic in the late afternoon. Told a couple of people—Albert, for one—that Lawrence and I were going to my study to do some work and that we didn't want to be disturbed. We had our alibi laid out: two glasses, an empty bottle in the wastebasket with his fingerprints on it, a brief drafted in both our hands.

"Lawrence asked Sneed to take a walk with him. Had been dropping hints for a week—a cock-and-bull story that he was starting to see things Sneed's way, that I was the obstacle, the one with his hand in the till. Then, he did what he had to do. Cracked Sneed over the head with a rock and pushed him into the Sound.

"He used the woods as cover. Came back to the house at dusk. I let him in a back garage door nobody ever used. Poor man. Devastated. Looked like a ghost. He couldn't stop shaking. Swore Sneed's eyes had opened and stared up at him through the water. I tried to tell him it was an illusion, but he kept saying, 'He's alive down there. He's alive!'

"It was a bad moment. Lawrence was supposed to have waited to be sure Sneed drowned, but he'd panicked and run. 'Should we go back and be sure?' we asked each other. 'Should we rescue him? What if he's alive right now, hanging onto a branch?' For half an hour we paced that room, unable to focus, unable to think straight. In the end, we did what we'd planned. Went outside at about seven-thirty. There was a beautiful sunset that evening. Some of the staff were on the terrace admiring it. 'Anybody seen Ely?' I said that, bold as you please. Well, someone thought he'd been with me, someone else said he was still on the golf course. Later that night I called the police.

"Damndest thing. Lawrence and I had been so careful, wiping our prints off the back door, making sure there were no footprints out by the water. And who do you suppose suspicion fell on? Albert. He and Sneed had had a bit of a scene earlier that day, and Mrs. Sneed—a terrible woman, that one—pointed her finger at him like some Cassandra right there in front of the entire staff and half the Fairfield County Police Department. Nothing came of it, but, well, you had to know Albert. He could not take something like that lightly.

"Not long after the funeral, Lawrence came to me. Closed the office door, locked it, and without saying a word spread some snapshots on my desk. They'd been taken at the picnic. Perfectly harmless unless you knew what you were looking at. Lawrence and Sneed, walking into the woods together, Lawrence looking down into the water, a shot of the water—you could barely make out Sneed's body. Almost could have been a log in there. And one of me, letting Lawrence in through the back door.

"They'd come in the morning mail in an envelope marked 'To be opened only by Lawrence Petit.' There was a typed note with the pictures. It said that nothing more would come of it if a certain amount of money was sent the first of every month to a post-office box.

"It was quite a shock to us. By then our fears had subsided, and we'd begun to think we were going to get away with it. We were smart men, and smart men didn't get caught. We'd even been smart enough to get a little rumor started around the office that Ely had been caught appropriating clients' funds, and had drowned himself in remorse. Utter nonsense, of course.

"Our blackmailer was smarter. Didn't ask much. Two hundred dollars a month. It was worth more back then, but it wasn't enough to hurt us. Not enough to make us try and find out who owned the box. Don't know what we'd have done if we found him, anyway. Turned him in? Hardly. Or killed him?" The old man shook his head. "No. Lawrence and I realized that murder was not for us.

"Our imaginations ran wild. Suspicions changed continually at first. A sharp word, a smile that seemed a little sly, just a look would get us going. Could have been anyone. Everybody at the picnic had a camera. We had one partner who had been Ely's friend. And there was a professional photographer we'd used. Never liked his look. At one point, Lawrence got so carried away with his fear he suspected me. That's what finally killed him—worry. A heart attack.

"One day—this was while Lawrence was still alive—our monthly check came back from the post office with a note that the box had been closed. We waited, expecting to hear from him with a new address. Never heard another word about it. It should have been a relief to us, like waking from a nightmare. But it was too late. Lawrence died soon after, and I just quit living.

"It will be three weeks tonight. My daughter called me and said that her damned-fool husband Albert had come home talking some rubbish about shaking the skeletons out of Ely Sneed's closets. Well, I only knew of one skeleton around here, and it went back to 1962. The next morning I called Gary Petit in and told him everything, and told him if he wanted this firm to stay in business, he was going to have to handle things because I didn't give a damn anymore.

"Sir? Do you still have your copies of the photographs?" That was Tony.

"No. Destroyed them years ago. Sometimes, when those memories filtered through enough of this"—he drained his glass dry—"sometimes I almost talked myself into believing it hadn't happened at all."

Andy Tate claimed to remember nothing from the time he left the grocery store Tuesday until he regained consciousness in his apartment with me standing over him. He stuck to that story for three days. During that time Gary's gun checked out as the same one Albert Janowski had been killed with. A computer check showed it had been stolen in a burglary in Brooklyn Heights in January.

Tate's memory returned on Friday, April 24, when the fine points of his plea bargaining had been worked out. He made a statement that was such a mess of legal double-talk and mumbo-jumbo that, rather than reproduce it here, I offer my own interpretation.

Tate said that in addition to doing messenger work at the firm, he was asked by his supervisor, Gary Petit, to perform certain "free-lance security" duties on a confidential basis. Tate blew his first assignment. Albert caught him searching his office for the film and fired him. That evening Tate called Gary and explained what had happened. Gary told him not to worry about it. He would find him another job and fix things with his parole officer. Then, in passing, Gary happened to mention that he was looking for a gun, for self-defense, he said. Tate, who claims to have been "shocked" by the notion, nevertheless gave Gary the name of a man in Harlem who was "in the business."

Had Albert died with less fanfare, the Petit-Tate relationship might have died too. But the following Saturday, Tate, like everyone else in New York, saw the full-page newspaper spread. He spoke to his friend in the gun business and found that a tall, nervous white guy had purchased a small-caliber automatic very late Wednesday night. Tate called Gary and offered his further "security" services in exchange for considerable cash.

Tate went on what he referred to as a "retainer" basis with Gary. Gary, apparently refusing to agree to simple blackmail, gave Tate further security jobs. Having discovered the Iron Valley address on the letter he took from Albert's body, Gary sent Tate to Iron Valley on Doris/DeeDee Smith's trail. Tate was to offer Doris cash for the negatives, ostensibly of great sentimental value to his employer. He blew this one too, but had some colorful things to say about his run-in with a "big fat motherfucker."

Tate's second job, to harass me—"Shake her up a little. Make her think about leaving town"—was only partially successful, and his last job for Gary, to search my apartment for the film, also failed. He claimed to have found my door unlocked and said he'd borrowed an old jacket "because it had turned cool outside."

At this point, Gary, no doubt tired at his partner-in-crime's failures, tried to terminate the relationship. Tate, on the other hand, was enjoying his work, and the retainer. Sitting in Gary's car in front of La Charrera Bar-Café on Third Avenue, he upped his price, and you know the rest.

Here a deep thinker could muck around in the similarities—the two cases of blackmail, two unhappy partnerships, the father's and the son's. That sort of thing is too academic for me. My speculations run to what Albert's pants were doing around his ankles. Gary, who for the moment has been found unfit to stand trial, has said nothing about it. I can't for a minute take seriously any of the lewd suggestions I heard around the office the day I went back to help close up the place. I believe DeeDee. Surely, Albert's pants were where they should have been when she ducked into the bathroom to hide. Gary must have pulled them down to make it look like a sex crime, while at the same time feeding me those lies about Albert's wild sex life.

My hunch about where Albert dropped the negatives to be developed was right, and the following weekend Tony and I looked at copies of the pictures together. We spread them on the floor between us, in front of a fireplace in his house in Montauk.

On first glance, three of the incriminating photos looked harmless. You had to know what to look for. Yes, Lawrence Petit and Ely Sneed had walked into the woods sometime in the late afternoon when the sun was moving west. Petit had a brotherly arm around Sneed's shoulders. Lawrence Petit stood at the water's edge, looking down. With daylight almost gone, Mr. Kellogg opened a back door for Petit. In the eight-by-ten police lab blow-up, you could just make out the unhappy lines of their faces. And in the fourth photo, that vague shape in the water, you might have taken it for a log. If only Ely Sneed's eyes hadn't stared up that way.

EPILOGUE

I had a note from Miss Peterson the other day. She sent a newspaper clipping with it:

> Stephanie Kellogg Janowski, daughter of Eleanor and Thurston Kellogg of Fairfield, Connecticut, was married yesterday to the playwright Emory D. Hightower, son of Frank D. Hightower of New Orleans and the Countess Eleanor Abruzzo of Milan and Paris. Mr. and Mrs. Hightower will be making their home in Manhattan.

The playwright? The nicest thing I can say about this is, they deserve each other. I don't imagine Old Mr. K was able to attend. He's in a minimum-security prison in the Berkshires. A sleep-over camp for adults, from what I hear. Gary also missed the happy little occasion. His insanity plea worked, and he is confined to a different type of institution altogether.

According to Miss Peterson, Ely Sneed's attorneys and staff have scattered to the four winds. She's now at one of those big Park Avenue firms. She saw Wilbur Decker in their reception area a few weeks ago, waiting to be interviewed by the partner in charge of hiring. May he suffer the proverbial trials of Job in his job hunt, the old poop.

And, speaking of job hunts—

I wish I could tell you that I invested the reward money wisely, or that I used it to pursue the education that would make me an asset to the business world. I can't. I didn't. I stayed in New York for a few weeks after Ely Sneed's grand finale, long enough to start thinking that for me and Tony, the magic wasn't there. Oh, I still like him, and I guess he's pretty fond of me. He took care of Moses while I was gone, and this is his summer house I'm camped out in. The thing is, I have trouble convincing myself that a pension plan and a three-bedroom house in Queens are what I want from life. Maybe I'm crazy, but in any event, during the past six months I spent the greater part of the $30,000 in air fare to what travel agents call "exotic locales." I enjoyed every penny of it, and I could tell you some stories you wouldn't believe. Not right now, though. Right now I have to think about making another assault on the job market.

Thankfully, the money isn't all gone. I have enough to see me through the next couple months, if I watch it, and enough for one of those gray suits. I've spent some money on clothes lately, but nothing that's going to impress an interviewer.

Maybe I'll run into Decker while I'm pounding the pavement. But I doubt it. I plan to avoid law firms like the plague.

There was an ad in the *Times* this past weekend. It said:

Are you a motivated self-starter with a head for details? Are you trapped in a dead-end job? Become part of the technical revolution. Join our hands-on training program. You will soon be part of the fastest growing sales-leaseback organization on Wall Street.

Sales-leaseback? I don't know what they're talking about. Just reading an ad that energetic makes me tired, but there's something reassuring about the open-ended qualifiers: head for details, motivated self-starter. None of that nonsense about three years' brokerage experience. I should go inside right now and try to work up a new résumé. It will wait, though, until after the sun has set. That's the thing about unpleasant jobs. They'll always be there, waiting.